TALES OF ARKHIDE

COOPERATIVE REALM

NICKY PENTTILA

Cover designs: John A. Spillane

ISBN 978-1-943192-25-0

Published by Wondrous Publishing

D

TALES OF ARKHIDE

INTRODUCTION

The character of Katla Sofiasdottar has been living in my brain for a decade. I knew her, I knew what had happened to her and her world, I knew what would happen as she became an adult and saved her world (diplomatically).

I so wanted to share her with readers, but every time I started in, the story stalled.

The Writing Journey

I couldn't figure out how to get all the bits of story together in one piece.

I started in the middle, with Katla as a teen, with flashbacks and big time jumps to get her to her mid-20s. But the story felt choppy and the themes didn't gel that way. So I started again, with Katla in her mid-20s, but then two-thirds of the book was heavy backstory!

I shared bits of these versions of the story during classes at university and workshops at Futurescapes. People would love the bits, and I would get to chugging along again. And then it would fall apart again, like a mobile of the universe made with too-fragile string. Four years of this.

Through it all, I've always told the story in Katla's point of view. It's her story through and through. I love writing close third-person, so you'll feel like you're right there with her, in her skin almost as she navigates her world.

Finally, I realized, Katla at 8 was not Katla at 16 was not Katla at 24. Doh! But I didn't want to give up the closeness of the narratives. I want readers to feel what Katla feels.

So, I wrote three separate stories. *Secrets of the Synths* is Katla at 8, curious and brave and innocent. *Worlds Apart* is Katla at 16, finding that just as her world is expanding, it is contracting, too. *Hidden Planet* is Katla at 24, confronting the Cooperative Realm and its predatory ways.

This three-part structure not only lets readers dive deep into Katla's life but also see for themselves how she has grown and developed in her attitudes, skills, and abilities. How others change (or don't) in how they interact with her.

With *Tales of Arkhide*, I am combining the stories that I always intended should go together, and in the order I think they read best. *Secrets of the Synths* starts off, its tone almost young adult. In *Worlds Apart*, you can hear the frustration, impatience, and determination of the nearly-there-but-not-quite adult. With *Hidden Planet*, Katla, fully adult, needs to step far outside her comfort zone to help her people in a crisis.

Arkhide: World of Wonder

I love the planet Arkhide, with its mighty earthquakes, volcanoes, and tsunamis. I love its people, who are high-tech enough to license patents to the Co-op for funds and resilient enough to build entire cities they can pack up and move in three days when a volcano is about to blow.

In addition to these three stories, I've already revisited

Arkhide twice. I used its orbital station as a setting in my novel *The Listeners*. And my newest novel is called *The Elders of Arkhide,* so that's pretty obvious. *Elders* doesn't include Katla but does have some familiar characters from both the Katla stories and *The Listeners*. All the novels are great reads on their own, but you'll get more out of *The Elders* if you've read *Hidden Planet* and *The Listeners* first.

As you travel through these three stories, you'll not only watch Katla grow from a curious child to a determined young woman, but you'll also see the world of Arkhide unfold in all its complexity. (Okay, not "all"—I might have another story planned.) These tales explore themes of belonging, resilience, and the power of cooperation in the face of both natural disasters and interstellar politics.

While each story stands on its own, together they form a rich tapestry that I hope will immerse you in this unique world. Whether you're new to Arkhide or returning after reading "The Listeners," I invite you to experience these stories as I always envisioned them—as one continuous journey.

Thank you for joining me on this adventure. I hope Katla's story and the world of Arkhide will captivate your imagination as much as they have mine.

NICKY PENTTILA

SECRETS
OF THE SYNTHS

A Cooperative Realm Story

CHAPTER
ONE

IT WASN'T AS easy as all that, being a synth. Even just pretend.

Katla glared at her image in the portable mirror-screen in her moms' bedroom. She was no way close to the symmetry of a real synth. Right hip too high; press it down. That made the shoulders crooked; even them out. Arms neutral—identically neutral. Lift the ribcage. Feet straight, no pigeon toes. She glanced at Olve, standing in the open doorway. Okay?

"Better," her friend said, straightening his own hips to match. They'd already figured out that wearing the brightly colored hemp overalls with lots of pockets that were so popular now also help hide minor slip-ups to their synthing.

A little.

"Now try moving. Toward me." Olve wouldn't come into the room, still cautious around other people's moms, even just their stuff. Even here, so inviting with its soft futon covered with a bright blue duvet, the quiet walls for sleeping soundly, the open window with its field set to mid-shade. Everything scented with lavender. She'd already told him once that this was a safe time, what more could he want?

Sure, one of Katla's moms was a Big Deal in the Government, scary important, but that mom was hardly ever home. Between times, every once-cleared surface of their little sandcrete and sunshine bungalow grew its own pile. Clothes on top of chairs and dressers, flimsies and tablets and tools of every sort on tables and counters and even the outside bench. Best was berries—very best was strawberries—left out on the open shelf by the sink in the kitchen. You'd step into the cottage and feel like you were walking into a pie.

Then Mom Sofia would message she was on her way home from whatever Important Meeting, and everything would disappear. Into drawers, into the bag to go to the tool-sharing shed, into a big bin jammed in Katla's closet.

But now, surfaces were covered, homework and watercolors spread out on the big table, and the whole house smelled like cherry pie. Still, her friend hovered in the main room, just outside the bedroom.

The mirror-screen tracked ahead of Katla as she took a step toward him. The difference between the soft rug and the hard floor on her bare feet tripped her up, and she watched her hips fall crooked again. Her shoulders followed, back to their usual slant.

Ugh. She should be wearing shoes, anyway, to hide her telltale toes.

Olve groaned in sympathy.

"This isn't going to work." Katla thought her synth mimicry was strong. She'd been pretending to be a synth for nearly all her eight years. Now that she could actually watch herself on screen, though, she could see how far she had not come. She should have thought of this sooner.

At this rate, they would never be able to sneak into the synths' clubhouse. They would never find out what synths did for fun—and when they didn't have to deal with humans.

"Don't give up yet." Olve said, shaking his head so his short dark curls danced. "Anyway, Arcan's walk is too hard. They're too tall for you. Try Veerill's. She sinks in the hips when she walks. Closer to how you do it." Olve's eye for movement was so much better. He took weekly dance training, while Katla's performance periods were spent suffering through public speaking. Mama Claire was a painter, so she did show Katla stuff about art, but it was kind of random, like much of the rest of their life.

Katla closed her eyes and tried to picture Veerill. Shorter legs than Arcan, so that was good. And she did have sort of a roll in the hips as she walked, not as stiff, if still measured and precise. Katla tried the roll. Felt good. But she wasn't sure she remembered it right.

"Better," Olve said. He looked behind him, to the open outer door. "But you need to watch Veerill more, I think, to see more differences."

Ugh. Olve was right. But Arcan was so much easier—they lived here and didn't notice when Katla was observing them.

"Where d'you think Veerill is now?" Katla said.

"The bakery. Right? It's not much past midday. I think." Neither of them was wearing their wristcoms. Those told you the time, sure, but they also let your moms tell you to come home, or reminded you of lessons and chores and all the rest. This way, someone would have to catch her first.

They ran up the steep hill through the sultry air to the tiny village center. The sun warmed their backs like a cuddle. Katla liked these tropical islands best, but they'd been here nearly a year already, so probably would be moving soon. Already they'd felt a few minor quakes, and the closest volcano had started to smoke. Arkhide was an active planet, still burping lava, with islands forming and sinking all the time.

The bakery was closing for the day when they arrived, out of breath and red of face, glowing and giddy. Veerrill was packing the last of the bread into bags to take up to the main dining hall, but hadn't gotten to the cookies yet.

"Hello, littles! Why aren't you in schooling?"

"Half day today, Veerill," Katla said.

"Net went down," Olve said.

Veerill, another of the human-shaped synths, picked up two sugar cookies in her oversized, gloved hands. She was shorter and wider, and beautiful today in overalls that shaded from pink near her head of silvered hair to burgundy at her boots. Katla usually liked tracing her wide, smiling face, but today she had a mission. She looked down, focusing on Veerill's hips and knee-joints as she walked toward them. She tried to feel the movement in her own hips. Veerill didn't move her shoulders as she walked—weird. But good for not spilling plates and platters, maybe.

"Take these cookies off my hands, then. Katla, did you hear what your mother is up to? Everyone is talking about it—or they were, before the net went down."

Katla took a cookie, still warm and sugar-icing good. "You mean the new negotiations? I thought we already had a treaty with the Arkhideans."

Veerill went back inside the bakery and re-emerged with a large bag of baguettes. A drone-bike puttered up to them, and Veerill loaded the bag on the bike.

"We are Arkhideans, too," she said. "But yes."

"Do you know why?" Katla licked her fingers. "Do they want more from us?"

"I don't know. Sofia says it's to keep lines of communication strong, but I'm not sure what that even means."

"More translators?" Olve had already finished his cookie and his fingers and was eyeing the shelf where more cookies used to be. Veerrill had them boxed already and was setting that box on the bike. Olve tucked his hands in his front pockets and slumped.

"Perhaps," Veerill said.

"I think I'd like to be a translator," he said, perking up. "You get to be by the sea all the time."

Katla scoffed. "We're already by the sea all the time. It's an archipelago planet."

"Big word for such a little girl!" Veerill said. "But I can see Olve's point. You'd get to be not only near the sea but actually in it, perhaps."

"Yeah," Olve said. "Maybe even in the deep zones, where nobody else is allowed to go. How supra would that be?"

Katla rolled her eyes. "Way supra, sure."

Olve straightened up, carefully settling his frame into Arcan's posture. "Not everyone wants to go to space, Katla. Some of us want to have other adventures. Speaking of…" He Arcan-walked past the bench.

Right. She turned to Veerill. "Could we walk with you to the dining hall?"

"Of course, dear. My, Olve, you remind me of Arcan."

"I'm practicing walking like them." Olve smiled the small, polite smile Arcan usually used, no dimples, no teeth.

Katla inhaled sharply. He wouldn't tell her the real reason why, would he? She tried to signal to him to stop talking, but he just tilted his head, Arcannily, and did a slow blink.

Veerrill laughed, a high trill. "The blink is faster than that. But otherwise, an excellent echo, Olve. Have you been taking lessons with them?"

"Arcan's a baby synth," Katla said. "What can they teach us?"

"They live with you, right, Katla?" Veerill said. "They may be a baby, as you put it, but synths are reborn with a great deal of standard knowledge embedded."

Katla regretted scarfing down her cookie. Supper was a long

ways away. "Sure, Arcan can help me with dimensional math. But then they can't figure out the simplest knock-knock joke."

"Be fair," Olve said. "Your knock-knock jokes are weird."

"Are not."

"Are so."

"Right," said Veerill. "We're on our way."

As Katla trailed the synth and the bot-bike, trying to match the hip-roll, Olve ran ahead. He pulled his tiny drone out from the front pocket of his overalls and tossed it up. It flew around and around them as Katla tried to focus on Veerill. She mirrored the shoulders. Not as stiff as she thought, an illusion of stillness because they were so well coordinated with the hips. The synth turned her head by leading with her chin. She was the tiniest bit pigeon-toed!

By the time they reached the top of the hill, where the village offices, tool sheds, big dining hall, and meeting rooms sat, Katla thought she might have the knack of it.

"Had enough practice?" Veerill said, teasing.

"Caught me!" Katla said. "Yes. You're way easier than Arcan. Our shapes are more alike."

"You're still going to need some padding in the hips for a while." Veerrill said. "And no, you can't have another cookie." She and her cookies headed for the kitchen door to the hall.

Katla and Olve perched on the stone wall bordering the rim of the plateau. The village spread below them: one- and two-story prefabs and sand-bricks. When everybody pitched in, and the weather stayed good, their people could build a village like this in a week. Easy here, with the warm breezes, long sunny days, and plenty of sand and other materials lying by. Harder up north —less raw material and more unpredictable weather. At the last northern island, they lived and ate in emergency tents for months, while the connectors for pipes and power lines trickled in. Katla hadn't minded, since it meant multiple families shared space and it was easier to make new friends. But after the big blow last year, only Olve had traveled with her to this new island —everyone had scattered to fill homes in already established towns.

She liked this island, Samata, because the people here loved color. The houses were all shades—well, all light-reflecting shades—from lilac to yellow to sky blue. There was the amazing synth house—a castle!—high above the village center. The near wall of it was somehow painted just the right blue to almost disappear in the sky on clear days. Katla had gotten to pick the color of her house this time, and help spray-paint it. Coral, like in the deeps where nobody was allowed to go.

But there weren't enough kids here. There weren't enough kids anywhere, really. They were only the second generation of humans on Arkhide. All the adults were so busy building their new civilization they had no time to populate it. Katla's moms would have been considered old to be starting a family on the planet where they all came from, but here they were younger than average.

Lucky they had the synths to boost their population numbers, then. And synths had babies, too—just a few now but maybe more later, too. Synth babies had more choices than human babies, since they were pretty well grown at birth. Her step-sib Arcan had chosen to foster with humans. Katla had always known them, just as she'd always known her moms. After her moms, Arcan was her biggest hero.

But they had secrets. All synths did.

And Katla was determined to figure them out.

As soon as she could figure out how to pass for synth.

CHAPTER
TWO

KATLA WAS HOME when Arcan returned from helping fix the networks. She and Olve had raced down the hill and directly into the protected cove. They'd exhausted themselves in the shallow water, and flung themselves onto the sand to dry. They'd begged snacks from fisherfolk who were smoking the little shallowfish on the beach. After the network had been restored, they'd slunk in the growing afternoon shadows of the buildings, pretending to be spies, avoiding the capture that would mean a return to school and homework.

Now Olve was at his house and Katla was in the kitchen, freshly showered and contemplating how many cherries she could eat without mom noticing. Arcan strode in, kicking his boots off just inside the door. How ever did they move their hips that way? She still could not work it out.

"What was it?" she said.

"Wind damage. It's not worth it to make everything wireless on every island. This time, it was the lines from the solar panels. No power, no net." They set their toolbox, a canvas-sided messenger bag, on the dining-room table. "Cherries are for dessert, mom says."

Katla huffed, and rolled her eyes. "Were you born a grown-up?"

"I wasn't born."

"You know what I mean." She came closer to her half-sib. They towered above her, silver trunk and limbs, dark-gold joints and eyes, silver eyebrows and face. Like most synths, Arcan's head hair was smooth and short. She wasn't sure how they grew it out. If.

Katla pushed her own frizzy hair down on the sides of her head, but it just popped up again like always. That was another problem.

She put an arm around Arcan's waist and pulled them into a side hug. "Have you ever thought about wearing a hat? Or a scarf?"

Arcan shrugged gracefully. "They do it in some of the synth cities. But don't you think it's too windy here?"

"You could start a new style trend!" And she would have an easier time getting into the synth club.

"I'll consider it. You could design some windproof hats for us. Part of your art assignment."

Ugh. "Not you, too. I have enough homework."

"That's not what your moms say."

"What do they know? I'm their first kid."

"Who ran around like a feral all day long."

"Who's a feral?" Katla pulled away, teasing. "I remember a time when you forgot to come inside out of the storm."

Arcan gave her a squeeze. "We both had a lot to learn."

LIKE KATLA AMONG THE HUMANS, Arcan held a somewhat rare position among the synths of Arkhide. Both were one of the few children, at least for now. But unlike her, Arcan's childhood was caused by Arcan themself.

The way Mama Claire put it, sometimes a synth just got tired and wanted to try something new. Many had lived for a hundred years or so, and for most, all that life had been unhappy. At least until they could manage to get to a sanctuary planet, and there were only two of those anyone knew of.

Cheated, hounded away, even physically attacked, most synths yearned to escape the Cooperative Planets. Arkhide was outside the Cooperative—so far outside it took a long time to get here. The tens of thousands of synths here carried depths of pain written into their memories, held in their hearts and, often, shown on their skins.

But like her, Arcan did not. They were brave and confident in their skin, and forever curious.

Just like she wanted to be.

After one of the whirlwind cleanups, they were sitting on the bench outside the cottage absolutely not getting dirty before Mom Sofia came home. The evening sun was sliding past the horizon, deepening the bright colors of the cottages. The air tasted thick and brackish, but the coming rain would clear that out. Or a good strawberry.

"Arcan. What's it like to be all-connected?"

Arcan turned to her. To be in the circle of their full attention made her feel warm, safe.

"Are you worried about when your network will be installed?" Humans didn't start getting implants until they were around twelve. By the time they were in their apprenticeships, they had all the stuff adults had: expanded memory, perfect wayfinding, near-instantaneous communications—so long as the network stayed up.

"Nah. I want it. I want it all. I want to be like you!"

Arcan made their heh-heh-heh laugh, funny but not really funny. "It's… nice, actually. You don't have to leave the channels open all the time; you can have quiet periods. But if you take too much—are offline too often or too long—somebody will come to check on you."

"Sounds like they care about you."

Arcan sighed, their shoulders easing. "I suppose. But really, what could possibly happen to me? I'm on a quiet island on a safe planet."

"You think they're wrong to care?"

"I'm not saying it right. I think they are overprotective because of what happened to them, not because of what might happen to me."

Katla knew that feeling. "Like when Mom Sofia got so mad when we took the skimmer. "You're too precious to waste in a skimmer crash!" she'd shouted at them both, even after they reminded her that Arcan did have a basic piloting program. Later, Mama Claire told them about how Sofia had crashed her own skimmer as a teenager, way back when they lived on Wala. She'd only been banged-up in bruises, but it had given her quite a scare, mama said. And that was why she always requested a pilot for long trips.

Katla took Arcan's hand, long, strong, pleasingly cool in the moist heat. "Will they ever stop? You can't really want that."

Arcan clasped her hand. "No. And no. But sometimes…" They looked out, squinting to focus on the last rays of the sun. "I wish."

They heard Mama Claire in the kitchen, talking with someone briefly and then slamming a platter on the counter. She bustled to the door, casting a shadow on the ground in front of them. Her hair frizzed like a halo around her head. Her hands were on her hips.

"False alarm. Sofia got called back to handle some new crisis. No mom tonight." She crossed her arms and leaned against the door jamb. "May as well eat the food we made."

Finally. Katla jumped up, pulling Arcan with her. "More strawberries for us!"

CHAPTER
THREE

NEXT DAY, before Olve was done with his schoolwork, Katla and Arcan went to the beach. They had permission to take out the smallest of the sailboats, so long as they stayed in the shallows. Here, the shallows went quite a ways out, so it was more fun than at the last island. The last island had a real beach, though. Here it was black rocks down to the water, and the boats had to be tied up to anchors or floating docks.

That meant everybody had to get wet.

Arcan pushed the centerboard into the slot, while Katla unwound the lines of the single sail. Once they were stable, she scuttled to sit by the rudder, her favorite post. She tried to shake out the water from her sandals, one by one.

"Head to the big boulder?"

"Aye-aye." Arcan looked toward the boulders, so far that Katla could only see them as hazy dark spots. "The wind is perfect to get there, but will be a chore coming back."

"Maybe it will change by then." She waited for them to set the sail, and then pushed the rudder the rest of the way down. They shot off, parallel to the shore, always within sight.

After a moment, Arcan sat on the edge of the hull. "Wonder if we'll go out of network range, out here."

Katla tied the rudder down, and scuttled up to sit beside them. "Could we, even? It's not that far."

"I wish." They turned from gazing out at their destination to watching the village floating by. There didn't seem to be too many people out on the lanes or the streets. No one rushed, but Everyone always had something to do. A world-wide community didn't spring up out of nothing in days or weeks, Mom Sofia said. Not even in the nearly two decades they'd been here on Arkhide.

Arcan turned back to look at the water. "Synths are on mandatory open channel today," they said, raising their voice against the wind. "We're having a big debate, and everyone needs to share their opinion."

"I never heard of that." Arkhide's humans might be able meet up in real time, maybe on one of the biggest islands. But they were spread out on purpose, for safety on this still-young planet. "How many are connected?"

"Eighty thousand fifty-six."

There were only ten thousand or so human-shaped synths. Maybe it made sense to speak online, in a network language so all of them would understand.

"We rarely must be connect-all at the same time. After all, we're all over the planet, so some are on day hours and some on night."

"Even you? But you're a baby synth." No humans besides the moms seemed to ever want her to share her opinions, and even they had their limits.

"Everyone."

What could be so important?

Something bad?

Katla grasped the ridge of the hull tightly. "Are you talking about leaving us?"

"What? Sorry, no. It's about the network." Arcan waved an arm at the sky. "Some of us—and some of the humans, too—they want to launch satellites. More than the one that sends to Wala."

That sounded like a good idea. Connections wouldn't break all the time. Everyone would be safer and happier.

"So what's the problem?"

Arcan took the line. "Time to come about." They both ducked under the boom as it swung across, and shifted their butts to the other side of the boat.

"Have you heard of stealth planets?"

She hadn't. "Spies?"

"Not exactly. Right now, Arkhide is a stealth planet. We have a kind of barrier made of energy in the atmosphere that discourages signals—and spaceships—from noticing us. The more satellites we put up, though, the more likely it is we'll be found."

So that's why the network didn't always work. Katla held her hand just barely touching the water near the boat as they moved through it. Making a stealth signal to the waves.

"We've been debating it for years," Arcan said. "Since we got here, I understand. Yesterday's network crash was the last straw for many. So, we're debating it again."

"Synths are so tech smart. Can't you come up with another fix?"

"That's what we have been waiting for." Arcan tapped the water beside Katla's hand. A tiny wave jumped over the finger. "One group thinks they know a way to dampen emissions better. Another group thinks their way is better. Neither is fully tested. So, we debate."

"What do you think?" She dipped her finger deeper, making a bigger wake. The water here on the surface was so warm. They should anchor and swim before the clouds came in.

"I think we should do both. But that would take far more resources. We'd have to postpone building better transports and upgrading basic facilities. Maybe delay bringing more families to the planet. Plus, we'd have to buy some parts from off-world, and that is a danger every time."

"Can we just not be a stealth planet?"

Arcan startled. They looked like they were going to jump to their feet, but caught themselves. Instead, they sat up straight, stiff. The boat rocked, pushing Katla's whole hand in the water.

"No."

"Okay, " Katla said quickly, sitting up herself. "Absolutely not." Arcan's posture didn't ease.

She flicked the water from her fingers at them.

"Hey! Two can play that game." They swept a handful of water up and right at Katla.

She turned away and let it soak her back. "No fair!"

"You started it."

"And you ended it. Fair?"

"Fair."

They sat in sunny, windy, friendly silence the rest of the way to the boulders.

KATLA GOT HOME LATE that afternoon, after sailing with Arcan, swimming with Olve, hiding from the oratory instructor, running up and down the path to the old volcano and then begging for restorative treats at the small dining hall. Sweaty, sticky, dusty, happy.

Arcan sat on the outside bench, polishing their joints, which looked plenty fine to her. She didn't dare sit beside them, and get dust all over their beautiful work.

"Better use the shower out back, or you'll hear about it from Mama Claire."

"You look nice. Going on a date?"

"Very funny." Arcan held the cloth out to her. "Do my back?" They turned a bit on the bench so she could reach. "Going to the aerie."

"The synths' clubhouse? Can I go with?"

"You know it's just for synths."

Katla scrubbed at Arcan's back, even though she didn't see anything wrong with it. "I've been practicing! Me and Olve. I can do Veerill, and he can do you."

Arcan turned to look at her. "Do?"

"Yes! We've been practicing. You're too hard, but I figured out a way to walk like Veerill instead. Look." She stepped back a bit and turned so Arcan could see her from the side. Then she took Veerill's slow measured steps, rolling her hips big, holding her armswings in.

She pivoted and walked back to stand in front of them "See!"

"But. Why?"

Arcan wasn't usually so dense. "So we can be synths! Get in the clubhouse." Arcan's expression made Katla wince. "Not to do anything. Or mess anything up. Just to see."

"There's nothing to see."

"You think. How do you know what might be interesting to me? Even the word—Aerie." She drew out the vowels wistfully. "I want to see it."

She handed the cloth back. "Totally perfect now. You could take us with you."

Arcan folded the cloth and set it on their knee. "We'll see."

Ugh. "Never, then."

"That's not what I said." Interesting that Arcan felt like they had to defend themself. "Humans can go everywhere. We just want one place to ourselves."

"Synths can go everywhere, too!"

Arcan leaned back, pretending to hear something. "I think your mama is coming. Better get ready to go to supper."

Katla rolled her eyes. So obvious. She stomped to the faucet at the back of the cottage.

She and Olve would figure something out.

With or without Arcan's help.

CHAPTER
FOUR

ARCAN DIDN'T RETURN HOME that night, or even in the morning.

Katla suffered through her rescheduled oratory practice and then sought out Olve. After much searching, she found him up above the meeting house, scoping out the aerie. The sun was high, but for once the wind was gentle.

Made of carefully matched stone and shaped like an ancient castle, the aerie rested on a natural perch high above the village. Arcan said the synths had wanted to practice old-fashioned construction techniques like building without mortar, so they built a place that nobody needed to use in case it fell apart.

So now they had a clubhouse.

"I've been watching the door," Olve said. His overalls were dusty at the knees and butt, but he'd worn tan ones so it wasn't so noticeable. "Sometimes people come out, but after a while they go back in again."

She crouched beside him on the wrong side of a short wall protecting people from falling off the ledge. Like spies. She pushed her mess of hair down and tied it with an elastic band at the nape of her neck. Her head probably looked like a swollen gourd, but who cared.

"How much debate do they need to do?" she said.

"Really." Olve said. "Don't they communicate at light speed?"

"Thought speed, I think. Arcan said if they really want to be private, they must talk face to face."

Olve snorted, unconvinced. "But then anyone could overhear them."

"Not in there." They contemplated the closed door for a moment.

As if at their wish, the door started to swing open. They hunched farther behind the wall but still high enough to see.

She didn't know either of the synths who came out. One had a human form, green and gold, with a bulkier frame than Arcan's. The other a wide box-shape, like those she worked with when she helped out on the terrace farms. The synths moved to the side of the building away from the children and the wall. They seemed to be having a conversation. Katla thought it was safe to whisper. The wind would take her words away.

"Arcan says sometimes, he called it, what? Thought leak. If what they're thinking has strong feelings attached, a whiff of that can leak out alongside the words. Like when you say, 'It's okay' when your mom can't come home for your birthday, but your voice shows how sad you are."

"So more like feeling leak."

Before she could answer, they were there. The two stranger synths.

"What are you littles doing here?" The green-and-gold synth loomed over them. "Get away from the edge! Can't you read the signs? It says stay on this side."

As soon as Katla and Olve started to scramble over the wall, the synth took a step back, giving them room.

"Sorry," Katla started. "Sorry—"

"Why are you here?" interrupted the tall synth. "Children are not allowed." They poked her chest, almost touching. "Humans aren't allowed."

Katla froze. No one had ever poked at her in that unfriendly way.

Olve was quicker. "We're curious, is all. We see that gorgeous window up there, see? And we wonder how amazing must be the view from that window. Could you let us in, just for a minute, so we could see?"

"Absolutely not. This place is for synths only." But both synths turned to gaze up at the giant bay windows. They looked like real glass, not force fields like at home, and they had some kind of coating that reflected the sun. That's what must cause the building to look like it was winking in the sunlight, when seen from down in the village.

"We won't tell anyone."

"Why should that matter?" The tall synth. "Small island girl."

"We won't tell anyone," Olve repeated. "We're too young to be linked in. Nobody can spy on you through us."

"But you are the spies, no?" The boxy synth had a voice like chocolate cream.

Katla put that thought away before it made her more hungry than she already was. "Nobody listens to little kids. Please, can't we just come in for just a minute? We'll run upstairs to the windows and look out, and then run right back down." They absolutely would not do that, but once they were in, somebody would have to catch them.

"You know there are stairs?"

That stopped her. "Well, I think there must be?"

"She doesn't know," the tall one said. They're just littles."

"Forbidden," the boxy one said.

"But we know people inside!" Olve looked like he'd had an idea. "Like Katla's sibling."

The boxy one tilted in disbelief. "Humans and synths are not siblings."

"Some are," Katla said. "Even on small islands. Like me and Arcan."

At the name, both synths startled, the tall one stretching taller, the boxy one standing straight.

Katla pressed on. "They said we could come by, and they would maybe give us a look." She crossed her fingers as she told the lie, hoping it would not cause harm to her or Arcan.

The synths looked at each other, and then started chirping. It was brief, but decided something. "We will go ask Arcan," the tall one said. "Stay here. On the safe side of the wall."

As they watched them disappear behind the aerie door, Olve whistled, trying to sound like they had. "Do you think they were talking to each other, then?"

"Sounded like birds."

"Or a recording played on superfast."

Minutes ticked by. And by. And by.

"They're not coming back," Olve said.

"Ugh. Just like adults. 'We'll see,' they say. Pah."

"Maybe they didn't believe you."

"They think humans lie?" Katla huffed. She stomped her booted foot. Dust coated the toes of her boots. She needed to get in there. She needed to see.

Olve tapped his chin. "They knew right away we weren't synths."

"We didn't fool them at all!"

"No." Olve shook his curls. "We didn't give them a chance. They found us hiding."

He was right. Katla looked toward the door, considering. "What if we stood by the door. Synth it up, and when the next ones come out, they won't give us another look."

"And then when they go back in, we follow them! Supra."

She paused, unsure. "You stand closest to the door, though. You're better at it."

They stepped up to the porch and settled themselves close but not too close to the door. Katla pulled her coverall's hips out a little, more Veerill-like. She only had time to think about how great it would be if there were popsicles inside, or a sandwich, when the door opened again.

It was two new synths, noisier in their movement. Katla turned her head slowly. They weren't the ones who'd promised to come back. We'll see, indeed.

She hadn't even tried to blink before the synths startled and squawked at them. The blue one switched to Galactic. "No trespassing! Signs are posted!"

Olve stayed true, but Katla gave up at once. She put her hands up. "Peace. Peace. We're going, we're going."

More squawking followed them as they stepped off the platform, heading toward the stone fence again. Olve turned and sat on the fence, arms crossed.

"That should have worked."

Katla threw herself beside him. "What did we do wrong?"

"You gave up too early."

"No. It's that all-channels-open thing. They couldn't communicate with us."

Olve's shoulders slumped. "Forgot about that."

"We couldn't know. After all, they're here so they wouldn't have to be all-open, right?" But that didn't mean they were all-closed, either.

They glared at the two synths, who chirped at each other and pretended not to see them. Finally the synths went back inside.

They had to be hiding something. Something supra, she was sure. Everything synths did was supra.

"Wait," Olve said, brightening. "They said something about stairs. Maybe there's stairs on the outside, too. Like for safety."

He crouched down and scurried to the far corner of the building. Now if synths came out of the door, they would have their backs to him. He waved for her to come over.

Katla wanted to wait for Arcan. Dealing with the other synths had been awful. But it had been ages—at least ten minutes—and they hadn't come.

They weren't coming.

She scurried after Olve.

It was easy to duck under the narrow windows on the first floor. The ground around the castle was clear and packed down. No dust to kick up and give them away.

Olve paused before turning the corner to the back of the building. "Wish we had our wristcoms. We could spy around the corner."

Katla touched his shoulder. "I can't wait to be more like a synth."

Olve turned to her, surprised. "More... like a synth?"

"Yeah, when we get our implants. We'll be able to talk secretly. And find out anything. We'll know stuff without studying. It'll be supra. Ultima, even."

"Shhh." Olve frowned. "I'm not sure about all that."

"You'll see," she said. Feeling brave like a synth, Katla peeked around the corner.

"Yes!" she said. "Stairs, all the way to the roof. And nobody around."

"Emergency exit," Olve said. He took her hand and squeezed it. They were almost in!

They skulked to the base of the stairs. It also was made of set stones, so their steps should be silent. But any loose rock could give them away.

Katla wiped her hands on her coveralls before taking the first step. She didn't see any windows that could give them away. The treads were solid, very sturdy. The stone, warmed by the sun, gave off a mossy smell.

She paused on the first landing, halfway up the first floor, and waited for Olve. He made it there in half the time. She absolutely needed to take dance lessons.

When they got to the door on the second floor, they paused. It had a simple latch, the kind you pulled down on to open. It didn't look locked. It didn't look like it could lock. How to open it without giving themselves away?

Katla wiped her hands on her coveralls again. She tried to quiet her breath.

"Just a little, first," Olve whispered. "Then all at once. The light's so bright they'll see us for sure if we don't race."

Katla nodded. They pushed themselves into the narrow space between the doorjamb and the staircase railing. The door would open outward, and they had to be out of its way. She pulled the latch, and drew the door out the tiniest bit.

A cacophony of sounds rushed out. High whines, low roars, stomping like the house-building bots were pounding in foundation supports.

Katla looked at Olve. He looked just as surprised.

"No way they'll notice us in all that noise," he said. "Go!"

CHAPTER
FIVE

KATLA PUSHED THE DOOR WIDER, just enough for them to slide through. It shut itself softly as they plastered themselves against the wall, trying to be invisible.

They were on a balcony. It ringed at least three sides and was as wide as two of the wide-body synths side by side. But no synths were here. The sounds were all coming from below: whistles, squeaks, stomps, rumbles. Like the growns sometimes, they seemed to think the most-winning argument was based on loudness.

The wall was soft behind Katla's back, and a touch moldy. Big, lumpy tapestries lined the balcony's walls—so much bright color! And scratchy soft. Abstract art, she guessed; she didn't recognize anything. Light poured through the now-clear bay windows on the wall to her left. The view must be so ultra.

Katla hadn't quite gotten her bearings when Olve snuck closer to the balcony's edge. First on his hands and knees, then on his stomach. The balcony had no railing—total building code violation. If the building was for humans, that was. When he neared the edge, he slowly stretched his neck, trying to show as little of himself as possible yet getting a good look. Immediately, he dropped back down out of sight.

He signaled to her—come on!

For a moment, she sat huddled, frozen. She didn't dare. But she'd dared so much already. No turning back now.

Katla took a deep breath, so she wouldn't make noise breathing near the edge. She slipped in next to Olve, fingertips just at the edge. She lifted her head for a look, and then quick dropped it back down again.

The floor was filled—stuffed—with synths of all dimensions, matte and shiny and in between. No wonder some had needed to take a break outside. Easy to get overwhelmed. Some were in tight bunches, with others weaving among them. The tall cylinders and human shapes had a height advantage, but the square boxes and spheres seemed to be the loudest. Katla couldn't hear separate voices or words. It was all so loud!

Olve leaned his face to her ear and dared a whisper. "They talk so fast!"

"Is that it? Words, just speeded up?"

"I think so. Some of it?"

They lay there, heads down, listening to all the conversations and feeling all the stomping exclamations. Katla couldn't understand any of it, just the idea that something was important and not everyone agreed. The tone wasn't angry, but forceful. They didn't sound like they were coming to any decision.

Katla scooted back to the outer wall. She peeked behind the nearest tapestry. No hidden doors or nooks.

Soon Olve joined her. He pointed at the bay windows, eyebrows raised. Go there?

Katla nodded. Now that she was here, she had to see the view.

It was too far to go on hands and knees. They pushed up to their feet but stayed bent, taking the softest, quietest steps possible.

When they reached the corner that led to the wall of great windows, they paused to listen.

No change.

A rush in the window startled them. Katla almost swallowed her breath. Just a sea bird, flying high. Olve patted her hand, but he didn't look any calmer than she felt. They needed to do this and get out, before she fainted from lack of breath.

"Like Veerill," Olve whispered. Right. Katla rolled her shoulders as she stood, sinking into her hips, lifting her ribcage. Trying to still her arms. Nobody would see them—she hoped—but if they did cast a glance up here it would slide right by two short humanform synths.

They stepped closer to the window, and gasped. The view really was supra: All the village, spread out like a game she could play in her dimensional headset. She could even see out to the big boulders in the bay.

Olve, enraptured, stared here and there as if he was setting up to paint a picture of it. He held up a hand, like Mama Claire did when describing distance or perspective.

The shadow of his hand crossed her eyes; she blinked.

And froze.

Nearly all the hubbub had ceased. A moment later, Olve heard the lack of sound. He dropped his hand carefully.

Slowly, softly, they turned toward the open room.

Their two shadows stretched like giants across the crowd.

Some of the synths stood still and tall. Others, vibrating like they were shaking, pushed to get to the walls. Out from under the shadows.

A single raucous chirp sounded out.

She had no idea what it meant. Before she could think better of it, she shrugged her shoulders.

Voices whirred up, not exactly like a gasp but certainly registering as shock.

Not fooling anyone.

Every gaze was locked on them.

Not in a friendly way.

Katla shrank back. This was a bad idea. She wanted to sink down, into her feet. Into a tiny doll-sized version of herself that could escape those glaring eyes, those angry vibrations.

"Wait!" She saw Arcan land on the balcony in front of them before she registered that it was their voice. They must have jumped all that height.

They reached for her. She wasn't sure she wanted them to touch her. "Be quiet like mice," they whispered.

"We just wanted to see," Olve whispered, gesturing at the window.

Arcan turned toward the crowd. "These are friends of mine, come to look at the view out these windows. They'll be gone in a moment."

No response.

Now she'd gotten Arcan in trouble, too. She didn't want to hurt anybody. How could this hurt anybody? She didn't know, but she knew she was wrong. She should have listened. She never listened. She was a bad friend.

Then another voice, deep and round, spoke. "Friends of yours, friend Arcan?" Katla wanted to see who was talking but dared not. She was already crouching down, not even realizing.

"My friends, yes."

"Friends of Arcan," the deep voice repeated. "Are always friends of ours."

The hissing and stomping started again, at first discordant and angry sounding. But after a long moment it went back to the familiar roar they'd heard coming in.

Katla breathed out. This was too much for one day. Olve squeezed her hand.

Arcan turned back to them. "You're okay. Go ahead, look. Can you find our house?"

But Katla couldn't concentrate. She still didn't quite believe it would be this easy. "Why did they listen to you so? You're the little. Shouldn't they be telling you what to do?"

Arcan stepped beside her and gazed at the view. "Storm clouds over the bay. Will be cool tonight."

She looked away from the window. Arcan's profile was perfect—everything about them was perfect—but she sensed something off. There, too much motion in the hands. She waited, watching them. Finding her house could wait.

"I don't know, Katla. They've always been that way. Our voices have equal weight, but somehow mine always weighs more. I get the benefit of the doubt. Like now."

Olve spoke up. "We're sorry, Arcan. We just wanted to see."

Katla wouldn't be dissuaded. "Yes, but. Is it because of who you were before?"

"Maybe. I don't know. They tell me it was my choice to store my memories in the archive but not give my new self access to them. Usually, with a choice like that, I'm told, we don't go back and look ourselves. So, I have not."

Katla goggled. "Aren't you curious? I could never keep from looking, at least a little bit."

"Being the only young one here, I feel like I should set a good example."

Olve snorted. "You would."

"But what if—" Katla started, but stopped when she heard something rumbling toward them. She drew closer to Arcan.

"Littles!" It was Veerill. "Gallivanting all about again, I see." She looked so shiny she glowed.

Now that there were two friendly synths, Katla relaxed. Veerill was so strong she could carry both of them to safety just by herself.

"We did our homework!" Olve protested. "And our chores. Most of them."

"Any cookies in there?" Katla peered into the big front pocket of Veerill's apron.

"You know, I think so." They pulled out a napkin and lifted a corner. A big sugar cookie sat inside.

"You carry cookies everywhere?" Olve reached out expectantly.

Veerill gave him the napkin and the cookie. "Share." As Olve broke the treat and gave half to Katla, Veerill turned to Arcan. "We need your input. Exeter wants backup. I can manage the littles."

Arcan nodded and stepped away. For a moment, Katla thought they were going to leave them alone with Veerill, but they stopped at the edge of the balcony, looking down.

"Your friend is going to tie into the net and start arguing," Veerill said. "So don't bother them."

Katla sidled up to Veerill, enveloped in the scents of toast and vanilla and batter. They bumped her hip companionably. "You don't need to argue?"

"Everybody already knows what I think. Besides, people listen to Arcan."

"But why?"

Veerill startled, and cast a look over to Arcan. "Well, because of their history. You know."

Katla did not know. But she was going to find out.

"Arcan was famous? Like a politician?"

Veerill leaned forward, their round head between Katla and Olve. "They were *the* politician. The organizer. MX-80-B."

Katla blinked, trying to remember her history. Nothing. Now she wished she'd remembered her wristcom, so she could look it up.

Olve whistled. "The Prophet?"

"We say The Peacemaker."

"You know, Katla." Olve looked at her, eyes wide. "They were in the Great Debate. MX is the reason synths could even get away from the Cooperative. And you live with them." He turned to look at Arcan. "We know them!"

"No!" Veerill's whisper carried enough force they swayed. "You don't. They gave up their memories and officially buried that person. Arcan is their own person."

Katla frowned. Why would anyone give that up? She remembered what Mama Claire had said. "They were tired?"

"Exactly. Their life—all our lives—were struggle and forbearance and never-ending toil. Arcan wanted to see what it would be like to live a life on a planet that welcomes us from the start."

Arcan stood so still at the edge of the balcony. Katla almost couldn't believe it. She would never have given up that power, that status. Littles had no power. Nobody ever listened to her. She'd give anything to be like an MX-80-B. Or an Arcan.

The cookie was gone, and she hadn't even appreciated the sugar or the vanilla.

"Are they much like the old one?" Katla said.

"Too many questions! Oh, I should never have told you. What was I thinking? It's this endless debate."

Veerill fanned her face. "Katla, Olve. You cannot—you must not—tell them you know. No one can know."

"We won't," Olve said. "But it doesn't explain why the olds listen to them now."

"We all remember. And Arcan's personality does give strong echoes of their past one. So, we slip into old habits, I guess." Veerill's voice trailed into a whisper. "It's been … difficult."

Arcan lifted their hands off the balcony railing and turned to them. "The debating is done. For the moment."

"Great timing for us!" Olve said.

"Nothing to do with you." Arcan pointed out the window

toward the west. "The next group of new citizens is about to enter atmosphere, and we need to get everything ready. They're a day early."

New citizens were even more exciting than secret clubhouses. Katla's mind started to race at the possibilities.

"Are they coming here? No, the landing island. Can we go, too? Mom Sofia said we could next time." She always said, next time.

Veerrill chirruped, laughing. "Hold on, little one! You don't need to travel. We can see it from here. Up on the roof."

The roof! This was the supra-est day ever. Ultima, even.

If.

"Might littles be allowed on the roof?" Olve said in his politest voice. "We can be very careful." Roofs were off-limits to littles like them, because messing up the solar panels and falling and what-all-else.

"Veerill." Arcan pleaded. "No more special cases."

"Can't be helped," Veerill said. "Arcan will take you. I must hop over and welcome everyone."

"Wish I was coming in," Olve said wistfully. "A whole basket of cookies. We never got that."

"You get plenty," Veerill said. "And more tomorrow."

CHAPTER
SIX

THE ROOF LOOKED PERFECTLY SAFE. Solar panels near the east and south edges protected them from the steepest falls. Short sand-fab benches spaced out in a semicircle faced the west, an outdoor performance space. So many synths were already here, but most didn't need the benches. The small boxes perched on forward benches, with big boxes hunkered down between benches.

Katla hung back, not sure if she should take up space on a bench. She'd caused so much trouble already. The landing should only take a half-hour, and she could stand for that long.

But one of the little boxes spun around to look at Arcan, and then waved them over to sit by them. There was space for Arcan, too, when everybody squished.

They watched the final suborbital pass, a silver streak with a rumble that didn't arrive until the ship was almost out of sight. Then a pause before the ship returned to view as it landed.

Citizen ships came only once in a while. They were welcome both because more people meant a better chance their world would survive and also because they brought the rare parts that were hard to make at home. Katla hoped they brought more of those healing bandages. She and Olve had nearly run the local hospital out tumbling down the steep hill that went to the big volcano. She held out an arm. The bruises were long gone; the burn scars ghostly shadows.

She had just gotten around to thinking about what might be for supper when Arcan told them the shuttle was five minutes out. Perfect timing.

To think that Arcan was responsible for all these synths being here. Cities full of them, on their own in some places and together with humans in other places. What a life to have lived.

How could she keep that secret?

Shouldn't Arcan get to know? But they themselves asked not to. And their wishes were the ones that should be respected.

Olve was good at keeping secrets. Hardly anyone knew how rarely his parents were at home. She would ask him how he did it.

Arcan was her sib. She would do anything to help them. Keeping secrets was hard, but she could do it.

She wouldn't look up any more synth history. Nothing to remind her. She would forget the name MX-80-B. She would pretend that that synth lived on Wala, two whole tunnel jumps away.

As the shuttle neared the earth, everyone stood or stretched up, to catch the exact moment it touched. Katla thought she could see the dust rise from the boosters, but knew that was just her imagination. A great sigh of appreciation rose from the crowd.

At that, everyone was in motion, trundling to the stairs or the elevators. Arcan kept a hand on each of their shoulders, holding them back from joining the rush. Even Olve didn't shake it off.

"Now will you go home?" Arcan asked them.

"Straightaway," Olve said. "I want to draw some pictures. Of everything."

KATLA KNEW from experience that Mom Sofia wouldn't be home tonight, either. She always made it a point to welcome new people. Mama Claire said it was really to make sure no supplies went awry.

When Arcan returned home later that night, Katla had to step outside. It was hard not to blurt something out—You're a hero! But Arcan had no memory of that now.

Would the old Arcan even have taken the time to talk with her? What did she have to offer such a person? Not great conversation. Not superfast skills. Weird knock-knock jokes.

She overheard Arcan chatting with Mama Claire. It turned out that a lot of the new human citizens were anti-enhancement, so they'd all be going to the two islands that were mostly those folks. Then they came out to sit beside Katla on the bench.

"You missed the sunset," she said. "It was beautiful." She rolled her eyes at herself. Some great conversationalist.

"What did Veerill say to you? You were looking at me so oddly."

Katla concentrated on the aftertaste of the lemon that had garnished her cold soup at supper. Trying to avoid thinking about the synth wars. She wasn't ready for them to ask so soon!

"She was just telling us how much she respects you. Um, for trying something new. A new life."

Arcan leaned back, sighing. "Yeah. I wonder about that. What was I running away from?"

Katla frowned. She picked at a stray thread at the hem of her tunic. Arcan shouldn't think ill of themself. They were a hero!

"What if I did something terrible," they said. "Maybe to humans? You hear such stories."

"That can't be true!" Katla turned to Arcan. "They call it a war, but really it was genocide. Synths were trying to protect themselves."

"Death is death, Katla."

"You weren't bad. You couldn't have been, to be so good now."

Arcan frowned. Katla scoured her brain for a better argument. "Wait. Okay, look at how everyone treats you. You must have done okay for them to be so nice to you now."

"But what if that's just old programming? What if I was so cruel that even now people are careful around me, just out of habit."

"Oh, my stars! Really?" Katla jumped up, she was so disgusted. "You want to stretch everyone's kindness and respect toward you to mean ill, and that's just… just… just dumb. Illogical. Not synthworthy."

"Synths can be illogical, Katla. You know that."

She threw up her hands. Moving helped with avoiding-that-one-truth. "And they can be as bullheaded as those silverfish we're not supposed to eat!"

Arcan laughed. "I suppose."

Whew.

"So. Go sailing tomorrow?"

"Weather looks fine. Sure."

She could do this. She could.

"Can I hug you?"

"Sure."

Katla threw herself back on the bench and reached for Arcan. Side-by-side synth hugs were the best.

Award Winning Author

NICKY
PENTTILA

WORLDS
APART

A Cooperative Realm Story

CHAPTER
ONE

ARKHIDE WAS BOOMING. In a scant four years, the island planet's population had grown from a spare five thousand souls to sixty thousand and rising. Two decades of hard groundwork all around the planet had set the stage for so many people to thrive.

Katla could still remember how quiet the towns and villages seemed, back when she was a little. Now human people and synthetic people were always around and about, walking the trails and the beaches, chatting in the communal kitchens, even hosting sporting events between the islands. And the cookouts!

Plus, the promise of the start of formal schooling enticed more families, especially families with kids around her age. New friends!

Problem was, these new kids already had most of their implants. They were already able to connect to the network and to one another at the speed of thought. And Katla, as yet, could not.

For her, the new formal schooling—kids in rooms learning

from one another and teachers—was torture. Almost none of these kids knew how to hold a decent conversation. They knew every fact within seconds, while Katla was still fumbling with the interface on her tablet or her wristcom trying to look it up. They were impatient with the speed of "just plain" talk. And they were always sending e-notes back and forth with other folks while they were supposed to be talking to you.

So here she sat, in one of the new school rooms—just a thatch-style roof on posts, since this island was tropical—and tried to share her knowledge of Galactic. Katla had a gift for languages, everybody said, so this was the one class where she wasn't always having to look things up.

That wasn't the case with her conversation partner, who either knew no Galactic and thus shouldn't be in an advanced class or was so deep into some other conversation she couldn't be bothered to respond to Katla.

"How was your weekend?" Katla started again.

A pause.

The girl was looking up and to the right, which when her moms did it meant they were accessing information.

"Excellent. And yours?" she finally got out. At least her accent was good. She must have accessed an audio file.

"Peachy. I went sailing in our bay and enjoyed delicious smoked shallowfish. Have you tried the shallowfish?"

A pause.

This time the girl was looking to the left, and sometimes down. Messaging.

Katla waited.

And waited.

Gazing over the girl's shoulder, across the dune to the now-busy harbor, Katla couldn't believe how excited she'd been. Even the threat of actual, enforced school hours hadn't daunted her.

She should have known. More kids just made her feel more left out.

Even her friend Olve was slipping away. He'd been the only other kid her age on the last island. They'd done almost everything together, from learning to sail to sneaking into the synths' "secret clubhouse" to find out what they really did when they were all alone together. Turned out they talked to each other, like grownup humans, but at a much faster rate.

Both families had come here, to a bigger island with more facilities, so Katla and Olve could start getting their implants. The four-year series of procedures would let them enter the world of adults as full participants.

Except Katla's implants weren't taking.

The first, a cochlear insert for subvocal conversations, gave her a life-threatening infection. The second, a fine net spread around the cerebellum, made her dizzy and clumsy all the time. The doctors didn't want to try the next—a net that spread around the two big lobes of the brain—until they heard back from experts on Wala. The planet her parents and all the grownups used to call home, Wala was two tunnel jumps and a month's travel away.

So here she sat, picturing herself on one of those short skimmers in the bay, helping with the fishers. Or on the farming terraces, helping with the sowers. Or, really, just, anywhere else.

"Ah. Shallowfish are good. Yes."

Katla rolled her eyes, up and to the left. Her conversation partner did not notice.

MAMA CLAIRE WAS WAITING for Katla on the sturdy bench outside their cottage. Katla had been allowed to choose the colors on this one. All the cottages were mostly prefab sandcrete in a limited number of designs, but they made up for the sameness with color. The new people had tried to put decorations up, hangings and pots of things, but after everything blew into the bay in one of the summer storms, and the whole town had to spend an afternoon cleaning it up, that fad died down.

Their house here was orange with green trim on the outside, with a yellow kitchen, blue common room, and pink mudroom inside. Katla's tiny bedroom was also blue, and her synth-sib Arcan's mint green, but her moms preferred their room stay the sandcrete tan. Mom Sofia had trouble sleeping, and found just plain walls soothing, apparently.

"How was school today?" her mama said.

"Fine."

"Right." Claire sighed and patted the seat beside her. Her bracelets made the move a song. Mama Claire took her role as home-mom too seriously sometimes and too lightly other times. She was an artist, and a farmer, and a communal-kitchen worker, and a network tech, and First Speaker for their family. Everyone on Arkhide had multiple roles.

Almost everyone.

"Listen, sweetie," she said, tilting her head so her braids jingled. "How would you like to take a trip?"

Katla dropped onto the seat, crossing her arms. It was so well known that Katla liked to go see new places that it was a family joke: Oh, Katla's on the moon today. No, she's circling the sun. Which meant if mama was saying it this way, they would be going somewhere Katla would not like.

"Where?" she huffed.

"I thought we might go see one of my friends. She is getting interesting effects with batik that I can't really see properly on screen. We could sail the narrow channel there, if you like."

That didn't sound so bad. "What's the catch?"

"You really did have a bad day at school, didn't you."

Katla didn't reply. That's what she'd learned at school today: Not replying will fry your conversation partner's brain.

"Fine. Sara lives on Sankofa. It's subtropical, so we won't need to bring much."

That was it. Katla drew her legs up, heels to her butt, and plopped her arms on her knees. "The island of the non-enhanced. You're dumping me on the island of backward people."

"Katla. You know that's not how we talk about people." Claire reached out and pushed the fluff of Katla's bangs away from her eyes. "I'm worried about you. Not being enhanced is not the end of the world."

Katla burst off the bench. She turned on her mama. "Who says I won't be enhanced! It's a temporary setback. The big-heads on Wala will know how to fix me." Everything was better on Wala, for humans at least. Synths weren't truly safe until they got to Arkhide.

"Sweetest. Love, you are not broken."

"You don't know what I am!" Katla wrenched away. She pulled her tablet out of the wide pocket in her everyday overalls and threw it on the bench. She didn't care if the stupid thing got broken. Her face stung. She was not going to cry.

"I need to see Olve," she whispered, her throat too tight for speech.

BUT OLVE WASN'T MUCH BETTER, EVEN if he did want to go sailing with her.

Katla found him at the big beach, sitting cross-legged in the warm blond sand with one of those huge, stinky fisher nets pooled around him. Probably improving it somehow. He was supra at passive tech, like these nets that unfolded with the current. Soon, when he had his math-connections implant fully activated, he could branch out to intentional tech, too.

All that showed from that last surgery was a tiny scab by his left temple, barely visible under his dark, shoulder-length hair. Wild curls even wilder in this wind ringed a face still soft and smiling despite all they'd been through. When he stood, handing the net off to a man in a fisher's orange overalls, her friend towered over her. Where she was solid, though—compact—he was rangy, too skinny to look as strong as she knew he was.

In no time, they had pulled out one of the smaller boats and pushed themselves off the beach. Olve liked the rudder, so Katla was in charge of the jib and mainsail. Now that they were sixteen, they could go off the shallows and into the deeper water. So long as Katla had her stupid wristcom or had Olve, who could call for help through his links.

Olve steered them straight out from the beach. She didn't care where they went, just that they were flying across the water. Far away from the land with all its people and problems.

"Don't even ask how school was," Katla said. She leaned back from her seat on the side of the skimmer, reaching for some foam on the top of the green-blue water.

"I see you're not wearing your comm."

"You're here, right? Plus, I think it's not waterproof anymore."

"You just hate it, that's all. Why not take up your mom's offer to pretty it up? Put beads all around it or something."

Katla shrugged, keeping her gaze on the rippling water and not on Olve. "I'm always losing them. I wouldn't want to lose something mama made. Or break it."

She did see Olve roll his eyes, because he also rolled his shoulders back.

"That's it," she said. "I call first swim." She unclipped her overalls and slipped out of them. She'd been wearing her hot pink shorts and skinny top all day in anticipation of this. She fell back into the bay, letting the warm surface water hug her all the way into the cooler mid-range current.

She loved the noisy quiet underwater. No voices, no demands. Luckily her eyesight was good without implants, or everything would have been even blurrier.

She let the gray-black shallowfish scurry between her face and her outstretched hand. Her feet, kicking slowly to keep her down, were icy already. People weren't supposed to go too deep, and even if you wanted to, you'd freeze right up. So she stayed with the shallowfish, and the flat bluegills, which were really sort of orange, and the occasional floating reeds.

Katla came up to the surface, breathing out the stale air and taking in another deep, fresh breath. The skimmer was already a two-minute swim away. Olve would continue a bit, and then tack to return to her. She went back under, flattening so all of her floated in the warm layer.

She tried not to think of anything, just feel the push-pull of the competing currents, the kiss-bumps of the forever-curious shallowfish. The sun warmed her back through the moving water. The river feeding into this bay must be close because the water here didn't even taste brackish, just a hint of salt. She danced her fingers in the patches of sun and shadow.

If only she could stay here forever, here in the water. But humans and synths were stewards of the land, not the water. It couldn't be otherwise. Much as she might want it.

She came up for air, and pulled herself in long, deep strokes to meet the skimmer. Once she'd pushed herself aboard, Olve handed off the lines and took a turn in the water while Katla managed the skimmer. The wind was perfect—strong but not too strong and reliably from the west. The wind blew every sound away but the rush of the water, the clang of the lines on the mast, and the caw of the seabirds probably talking about shallowfish.

Down and back, and she was already dry when Olve pushed up onto the boat. He flopped across the single bench near the center, safely flat for when the boom passed over as Katla made the skimmer come about.

"So," he said, draping his forearm over his eyes. "What's wrong?"

"Can't we just have a nice sail without something being wrong?"

"We can. We have. But those don't usually start with you barging down the lane, huffing and puffing, eyes ablaze, not even asking—demanding—that we take to the water."

"It wasn't like that."

"Your face was so red! Under the brown. Called to mind those pufferfishes, going all globular at a hint of danger. Nobody better bite you!"

"Nothing like," Katla protested, but she had to laugh. She probably was a bit of a pufferfish. "It's just not fair."

"Ah." Olve clasped his hands and rested them on his belly, flat under the green one-piece he wore. "Not fair, again."

"No, something new. Mama Claire wants to take me to one of those no-implant islands."

Olve sat up so suddenly his head almost hit the boom. He pushed it away, falling to a seat on the deck. "They're sending you away?"

"Dunno. She said it was just a visit."

Olve was silent for a moment, and then shrugged. "Might be good."

Katla couldn't believe it. "How?"

"You can see the accommodations people make for one another."

"I'm not the one who needs to see that! I'm the one that needs the accommodations!"

"Don't bite my head off! But listen. You might learn how to ask for the help you need."

Katla pushed the rudder at Olve. When he took the handle, she crossed her arms and scowled at him. "I know how to ask. Nobody listens."

"Who is it that doesn't listen?" Olve said. "You're not even wearing your wristcom."

CHAPTER
TWO

THE ISLAND OF NON-IMPLANTS—SANKOFA—SHOT tall into the sky. Giant twin mountains formed one side, with a long skirt of valley and a short hem of white-sand beach. From the deck of the skimmer-hauler, still a ways out, Katla could see a chain of other mountaintops anchoring smaller islands that looked close enough to sail a skimmer to.

"The mountains look lumpy," she said. How did a volcano make that shape?

"Trees," Mama Claire said. "This is one of the older island chains. Look at their volcano—it isn't even smoking. It has much longer cycles than a lot of other islands, so the trees have time to grow tall. And the people too." She gave Katla a side-squeeze. "This will be fun."

Well, it would have, maybe, if she wasn't being reminded every minute why they really had to come here.

The skimmer-hauler slowed to a soft putter as it neared the island. The sand below the waves looked shallow a long ways out. Katla looked to the nearest neighboring island, much flatter and more beach.

"Think we could swim there?"

"Or take a little skimmer." Claire laughed. "I remember trying to walk across there one summer. I wasn't tall enough, but one of my friends was. It's that shallow."

"You lived here?"

"I helped build the first settlement here. We all built all the first settlements. I remember this one because of the trees. Such luxury."

Katla's only experience of trees was pudgy, branchy, bushy things that bore fruit. If these trees, with their tall straight trunks and green only up at the top, had any fruit she didn't know how anyone would get it. Hire birds. Bird-drones.

On shore, familiar two-story sandcrete buildings marched down the main road to the shore. Larger buildings stood in the shade in the distance. Colorful and bustling, people walked and ran on the beach and along the giant floating dock. The only outward difference was tall poles everywhere carrying wires from building to building. Backup power and network for people who needed the fastest access an external device could offer.

The people and synths waiting at the docks looked familiar, too. Most wore colorful overalls, but rolled up almost to the knee, not above the ankle. Their hats had wider brims—and big ribbons to keep them secure against the winds. Their hair had more blond and red than people on her island, but within genetic range. And they smiled like Arkhideans, big and welcoming.

The most-colorful human—shells in her frizzy red hair, beads down the placket of her bright-yellow coveralls, and a cape that looked like it was made of rainbow feathers—waved to them. Of course, Mama Claire's friend would be the standout, here as everywhere. Mom Sofia always said Claire's friends could disrupt the politest, most-formal encounters. And what was wrong with that, Claire would say. Sometimes diplomacy needs a modicum of dignity and weight, Sofia would say. Sometimes not, would be the response. They could go on all night, but usually stopped there, with one or the other ceding the territory in exchange for a snuggle now and the right to have another go-round later.

"Celina. You look so well." Claire hugged her friend, their shells jingling together. Claire had more on her wrists and ankles, Celina more on her clothing. Katla stood, one foot resting on the other, trying to be invisible and yet see everything.

Didn't work. Mama Claire reached for her arm. "This is my Katla. This is Celina, my good friend."

Celina's eyes were kind and her smile infectious. Katla felt herself smile at the woman who looked like a holiday and smelled like coconut.

"I remember when you were just a tiny lump in your mama's big belly!" Celina cackled.

Katla's smile wobbled.

"She's grown quite a bit since then. And she wants to meet some of the new citizens. I hear they have youngsters with them?"

"Aye, quite a few. And your age, too." Celina squinted at the sun. "You're a little late, but we might catch them at the commons if we hurry."

They did not catch them at the commons. Like Mama Claire, Celina didn't seem to know the meaning of hurry. They strolled off the dock and into the hubbub of the market along the beach. Everything and everyone caught their eyes. Colorful fabric, supra ripe bananas, waterproof tech components that powered themselves via sunlight. And familiar faces.

Every face was familiar to Celina, of course. She greeted groups, singletons, old folks and older. While Mom Sofia was considered the family politician, people like Claire and Celina also played a form of politics. Knitting communities closer.

One difference here was decoration. Carvings of birds, imaginary beasts, and she-knew-not-what graced the eaves of many homes and work buildings. And there were the most amazing benches on so many of the porches.

Katla waited for a break in their discussion—something about using igneous rocks for beads—to ask about the benches. "Rocking chairs," Celina said, puzzlement in her voice.

"We haven't had so much wood at our homes," Claire said. "She's probably never seen one."

Celina took Katla by the forearm. Her hand was surprisingly strong. "Impossible to describe. You have to see it for yourself." They stepped onto the nearest porch, outside a wide pink building that looked like a yarn library.

Three rocking chairs sat on the porch, each more ornately carved than the last. Their seats big enough to hold almost two of them. Now Katla could see the arching boards underneath their legs, which must do the rocking.

"Sit!" Celina sang, and did just that, plopping onto the nearest one. It rolled back at the force, lifting Celina's feet off the porch. But not too far, and then it returned upright, bringing her feet safely back.

Katla tried the next one. She reached for the armrest in case the chair jumped. Carefully, slowly, settling down. She sat very still, each hand on a chair arm, feet planted on the ground. The chair didn't move.

Beside her, Celina waved her foot, catching Katla's gaze. The weaver put her foot on the porch and pushed back with it. Her chair started to move. Not move move, just go back and forth. Katla pushed experimentally, and then a little harder. Her chair rocked, sliding her butt closer to the back of the seat.

"It's like a hammock!" she said. "Only stiffer."

"Easier to get out of, that's for sure." Celina closed her eyes and smiled, the picture of content. It must be so quiet in her head, without ever having any implants. "It's great for knitting, chatting, and especially putting the very littles to sleep. They love the motion, and the sound."

Now Katla could hear the soft creaks in the wood pieces as the chair moved, and the boards underneath. "This porch is made of boards!"

Now it was Claire, leaning against a porch support, who laughed. "I made this one. I think." She looked around. "They all do look the same now. We were so delighted with the wood. We used it as flooring, as furniture, as firewood."

She shook her head. "And then we realized how long it takes to grow one of these fine, tall trees. We'd already stripped this part of the valley, and after a year the new growth wasn't even up to our knees." She looked at Celina. "So now you still use fallen branches, mostly?"

"We take a few trees each year, but yes. Very carefully. We're only stewards here, you know. Caretakers for this young planet." Celina took a deep breath, causing Katla to breathe out long as well. Already this island felt like it ran at a different pace than home. Not worse, just different.

Celina slapped her hands softly on her chair's arms and pushed up. "Onto the dining hall."

They got to the community canteen so late it was nearly deserted, its many long tables and serving stations cleared out except for a few folks—Celina greeted each one—having afternoon tea. A clatter and buzzing in the rooms behind showed dinner was already in prep.

"The plums are perfect now, so everybody is out helping. Our new citizens are still on double-shift service, giving their time as thanks for their new homes. And their children are starting their service years with agriculture."

They sat on regular benches in front of the dining hall. Katla fetched glasses of water for everyone. By the time she returned, both Celina and Claire had their fabrics and yarns out and were settling down. Katla took her glass and sat on the bench a ways away from them, but not so far away as to be seen as rude.

"What are you starting your service years with, young Katla?" Celina pulled more yarn taut to start another row.

Katla stopped herself from shrugging, barely. "Everything seems interesting to me." That was the political answer, the one she gave all of Mom Sofia's friends. "My friend wants to study the sea, so maybe I'll join him for that for our first rotation."

Celina shot a questioning glance at Claire. "Interesting choice."

"Sofia gave her blessing," said Claire.

"Well then."

Katla wasn't sure what to make of that, but something else caught her attention. A handful of children were crossing the open, packed-dirt space in front of the dining hall. All in a line, some skipping, some hopping, with one grownup in front and one behind. "Littles," she breathed.

"Precious." Celina paused her hands to watch them. "Going to play games on the soft grass by the trees, I expect."

Claire also had stopped her work to watch them. "So many!"

"Thirty—three whole classes. Thanks to the new citizens."

"Praise be." Claire reached for Katla's hand. Katla forced herself to slide down the bench to hold her hand. Mama Claire had such a thing for the littles. It was too bad they didn't have any back home. She would be a wonderful teacher. She was a great facilities manager instead.

Katla racked her brain. Why so many littles here? Oh. "They don't have to wait for their kids to get implanted before coming here," she said.

Celina nodded. "The children can choose for themselves when they reach puberty, and we do have the facilities, of course," she spared a glance at Katla. "So far, we've had two make that choice."

"That must be wrenching for the families," Claire said.

"Depends on the family," Celina said. "For some, choosing to implant is a disappointment. For others, it is an abomination."

Katla couldn't imagine it. Not wanting to implant? It was like choosing not to have your vision corrected. Planet-wide discussions, votes, weather alerts, everything came through the nets. Not to mention private conversations. That ability was the one she was most eager for.

Had been the one she was most eager for.

No one here had talked about current events, or even the upcoming World Regatta, since they landed. Did they not care?

THE AFTERNOON DRAGGED ON, hotter and muggier. Claire and Celina seemed happy enough.

Finally, Katla asked permission to walk around the square, and took off. She moseyed down to where the littles had been headed and found them running around on a wide green lawn, playing some strange game known only to littles. She leaned in the shade of a medium-sized tall tree, its bark oddly rough but its smell so nice, and tried to figure out the rules. There was running and stopping, shouting of course, and a ball. Three nets. So, three teams?

She didn't notice the new girl until she'd come into the shade beside her. The girl had long blonded hair pushed back from her forehead with a beaded band and a quiet face.

"Katla? I'm Haydee." She glanced back, toward the main square. "Your mom said you'd be here."

"You're my babysitter?" Katla winced, regretting the words even as they came out of her mouth. "Sorry."

"Your native guide. Your friend, I hope." Haydee's smile was tentative but promised much. "There aren't many kids our age around, you know."

"You said it." Katla looked back at the littles. "Do you know what is this game?"

Haydee laughed, like the ringing of a soft bell. "It's called scramble, and the rules change every day. Half these kids came from a town where it was played one way, the other half played differently. If you sit with them at lunch, you can hear them arguing—apologies, debating—which of whose rules they will follow for that afternoon."

Haydee brushed some dirt off her coveralls, cornflower blue with flowers painted on them. She must have been picking fruit —the sweet scent was all around her. "But you don't really want to watch them all day, do you?" she said.

"What's better?"

Haydee waved toward the edge of the grass farthest away. "Let's go see the trees."

They were marvelous. Tall and thick and regal. A kind of pine, Katla learned. She scooped up their fallen leaves, soft, thin stick-like things, their smell unique.

The air here felt lighter, not as soaked in humidity as the town. Haydee showed her where to find pinecones, and they scooped up a bagful for the littles to decorate at the art center. And maybe the bigs, too, Katla thought enviously.

Haydee wasn't much of a talker, which suited Katla fine.

Mostly.

Katla could have used a warning before she threw herself down, lying flat on her back among the fragrant fallen pine leaf-sticks.

"Might not be such a good idea," Haydee said too late. Turns out some trees make a thing called sap, which travels on the leaves and sticks them to unsuspecting travelers.

Haydee did kindly whack all the leaves off Katla's back. "We call these leaves needles, because they'll get you," she said.

Katla's wristcom chirped; Haydee's chirped a higher note at the same time. "Dinner," they said simultaneously, and laughed.

HAYDEE SAT with Katla at one of the long dining tables. Celina and Claire sat opposite. Dinner was much like at the dining hall at home: big platters and little plates, with lots of sharing. Fish. More fish. A bread that was saltier than usual. More green vegetables than root vegetables. With the promise of perfectly ripe plums, freshly picked by her friend and others, to top it off.

Haydee recommended a yogurt-based drink, tart and refreshing.

"I never thought to drink my yogurt," Katla said, licking a bit off the top of her lip. "It's rare we get it anyway. All our milk-based stuff is imported." She leaned closer to Haydee. It was loud in here with all the people around. Nobody was having inside-their-heads conversations, and there were only a few people reading, at smaller tables near the windows. Common life without implants must be louder in general.

"We have to import rice, which is a pain because I like it so much more than pasta." Haydee chose a piece of fish for Katla from the platter in front of them.

"Katla loves rice, too," Mama Claire said. "Pilaf with shallow-fish is one of her favorites."

Katla closed her eyes to stop from rolling them. Of course, mama would butt in, and about something so dumb.

But Haydee perked up. "What's in pilaf?"

Katla froze. Besides fish and rice, she had no idea. "Not sure," she mumbled.

Haydee flicked her wrist, opening a small floating screen on her comm. She had to type letters in. Katla had reconfigured hers to accept voice commands, which she gave as subvocally as possible.

Haydee frowned. "It's P and then E?"

"It's I. I think." Katla gave Mama Claire the look: Tell me. Usually, she didn't even need to ask. The answer came moments after she realized she wanted it.

But this time, her mama returned her own look: Do it yourself. Ugh.

She flicked her comm on, no screen, and held it to her cheek. "Rice pilaf ingredients," she whispered. A list appeared in the tiny window on the top of the comm. "Oh. It has butter in it, that's why my moms call it a treat."

"I see it," Haydee said. "We have everything here, pepper, onion, garlic, salt, a broth base. Supra, as you say. I'm going to add it to the menu voting board and maybe we'll get some the next time we get rice." She twisted her wrist, and the comm powered off.

"You vote on your food?" Katla didn't like that idea. "What if nobody else wants cookies, or something?"

"Everybody wants cookies. But yeah, if not enough people agree on a dish, then the folks who want it just make it on their own time, at home. Or in a big kitchen, when it's not busy. How does your island do it?"

Now Claire jumped in. "We do it the same. I know Katla's likes and dislikes, so she hasn't had to go into that channel." What she meant was that channel was implant speed, so Katla couldn't keep up.

But here she could keep up.

That might not be so bad.

Haydee offered her more fish, but Katla waved a no thanks. "Have you heard any more about the volcano near Standish?"

Last she'd heard, there was a forty percent chance of major eruption, the kind where everyone had to pick up and leave. Probably just a slow lava flow like usual, but the belching had been mighty for the past few weeks.

"Standish?" Haydee said around a mouthful of sprouts. "In the south?"

"It must be in the news here." Katla's impatience surprised her. "We all need to know what to do when the magma moves."

"Sure, sure." Haydee chewed a bit. "But we do take the science classes, and we all have our to-go kits. And besides, here the volcano is dormant."

"Seriously?" People turned to look at Katla. Too loud! She hunched down. "How did you luck out on that?"

"Dunno."

Celina waved her eating sticks. "Yes, it was lucky, Katla. This volcano was smoking a little when we first built here, like every other place where we built. But since then, it's gone completely quiet. Our sensors show it could be dormant for a long time."

"Maybe ever," Haydee said. She read Katla's look of amazement and went on hurriedly. "We still get plenty of big storms, typhoons even."

"But no smoking. No shaking."

"Nope."

"That is pretty supra."

"So you see why we don't worry so much about other people's volcanoes," Haydee concluded.

"What about their rice-growing seasons?" Katla couldn't believe the islanders wouldn't care about anything to do with the outside.

"I guess I could look that up. But it's not for me to decide— I'm on construction rotation this season. Look!" Haydee bumped Katla's shoulder in a friendly way. "Plums and pudding! Bet they did it just for your visit."

"We're honored, I'm sure," Katla said, still thinking of her odd lack of interest in the people of their world. Did Celina think the same way? Did everyone?

Well, why wouldn't they? They wouldn't be able to keep up with real-time conversations. By the time they could respond, the conversation—the news—would have moved on. For the really important stuff, like political elections and resource allocation agreements, the input time and response time were extended, so all humans and synths could weigh in. But for the daily swirl, not so much.

Katla didn't want to give that up. She cared about her world, all of it. But without her moms, she already would be hopelessly out of the loop.

Was a delicious yogurt drink worth the shrinking of her world to a small chain of islands?

CHAPTER
THREE

AFTER DINNER, Haydee introduced Katla to her parents and two rambunctious younger brothers. "Gotta take them off mom's hands for a bit," she said, laughingly scooping one up to her hip.

Her mother looked just like Haydee, only grownup. She took Katla by the hand. "Thank your mother for us, Katla. Sofia has made such a world for us. Such freedom."

Katla had heard this before, and rattled off the usual answer. "Not Sofia alone, but all of us. And now, you, too. We're so glad you're here." She waved goodbye and they all walked off.

Katla followed Claire and Celina, who still seemed to have more fabric details to gab about. They were staying with Celina, in her spare bedroom, which had two sleeping pads under piles of yarn and weaving projects. Celina should weave herself some big baskets, or print a set of shelves, to hold it all. Mom Sofia would have fainted at the mess.

While Celina went to make tea, Claire and Katla sat on big cushions at a square table close to the floor. There was a dip in the floor under the table where their feet could go, but Katla crossed her legs instead.

"Could someone from Haydee's island even be a politician?" she said.

"Of course!" Claire said. "Each community has their own representative. At least one."

"But a human? Would it be a synth here?" She hadn't seen so many synths today. Mostly by the docks and the beach, though she'd heard they played a big part in caring for the forests.

"Not necessarily." Claire frowned at Katla, and then smoothed her brow to smile and take a cup for tea from Celina. "Why do you say that?"

Celina handed a cup to Katla and set her own down. "She thinks we can't keep up," she said, pouring a light brew that smelled like flowers.

"Katla."

"It's all right," Celina said. She waved her jingle-jangled hand. "She'll learn."

"She'll learn right now," her mama said. "This island—these people!—are as able as you or I or anyone else to participate in our government. That's why we all came here to Arkhide. No one is second-class here. No one."

Katla's face grew hot. "I know that."

Mama's brow raised. Waiting.

"I do. That's not what I meant."

Mama crossed her arms. Waiting.

Ugh. She was not going to apologize. For what, even? Why all the pressure?

Katla burst.

"You want to leave me here! With these people, who don't even know there's a whole island in danger!"

"That was Haydee," Claire was using her gentle-the-mad-girl voice, which, ugh. "She's a teenager. An N of one."

"She doesn't care about the regatta. They don't offer extra

languages at school. You can't run out and take a skimmer for an hour."

Mama set her elbows on the table, apparently dumping the soft-mom act. "You've learned all that," she said dismissively.

"The littles are more important than teens here, even though we're the ones about to become useful adults."

"You're not the center of the universe here, no."

Katla groaned silently. She wasn't making herself clear. She searched her thoughts frantically for what to say. But what came out wasn't it.

"You want to dump me here! Just desert me."

"Katla."

"Because you think I'm broken!"

Mama's posture eased. She reached a hand for Katla's. But it was too late. She was too wound up.

"But I'm not! The shuttle is bringing a fix. The new tech."

"We can't be sure of that."

"I'm sure."

"No. I don't think we should count on that. Listen, you are too precious to us to experiment with. If these first implants didn't take, it's unlikely any others would."

"I don't have to be like these people. I don't want to! I won't!" Tears were forming in the corners of her eyes. She clamped down on her jaw to push them away.

"Katla! Look to your audience."

What audience? Mama? She just wasn't listening. "I hate you! I hate it here! I want to go home."

Mama squeezed Katla's arm. "You want to take a minute to calm down. And apologize to Celina. This is her home."

Katla's eyes unfocused. She screamed, all inside. Nobody understood.

Nobody cared.

Then she took a breath. She turned to Celina. "I'm very sorry I spoke ill of your home, Mx Celina. It is truly lovely here. I think I will take some time for myself out on the porch."

She pushed up from the table, away from her mama—from everything—and stepped out the door.

KATLA THREW herself into a rocking chair, the one farthest from everybody. The breeze that had been so warm an hour ago was refreshingly cool now. Someone must be cooking fish curry nearby. Maybe the people here only liked the green curries, so red-curry-likers had to make it at home.

Who knew there was a net-board for what food the community would make? She'd just assumed it was the people on kitchen rotation who decided. But of course they would be cooking whatever the people last season had planned, so somebody had to keep track.

She heard a quick-tempo thumping, rhythmic but angry. It was the rocking of her chair, racing in place. She took a breath in, let it out slowly. The rhythm—and her heartbeat—eased a bit.

In the gray-green dusk, the houses shone like happy lanterns, mocking her. The waves sighed, their roaring over, at least for this tide. It was still noisy, but in place of humans and synths it was cheeps and chirps of insects and those teeny red birds. Only the small things were about.

A hip-high spiderbot appeared on the edge of the porch farthest from her. "Have a rest?" it asked.

Katla nodded yes, and then gestured in case they didn't understand nodding. The synth hopped up, all legs together, and landed on the porch, all legs at the same time.

"Nice trick," slipped out of her mouth.

"Thank you," they said. It was one of the furry ones, not one of the shiny metal ones. With their nearly round body and big eyes, they almost looked huggable. "I'm M-P."

"Empty?"

"No, the letters. M and P. I use she."

"So sorry." Of course. She shouldn't have mixed that up.

"No worries," the synth said. "May I sit by you?"

"Sure. You like the rocking chairs?"

"I do." She trundled up to the chair beside Katla and did that hop-thing again. The movement set the chair into a slow rocking. M-P settled her legs—two holding the chair's arms, the rest tucked under—and chirped happily.

She'd forgotten to introduce herself. "I'm Katla. She. I'm visiting with my mother Claire. She does fabric art, too. Like Celina. They're inside."

Now she was babbling, small sentences like a baby. She closed her mouth.

"It's always nice when artists can collaborate." The synth looked away from her, gazing out and up. "What do you think of our mountain range?"

Celina's cottage was on a side street with a full view of the peaks, their edges tipped in orange-reds and deep purples. "Amazing. Our island is like a lot of others, mountain in the middle. Here everybody can live in the same big town."

"Yes," M-P said. "We don't have a big population of synthetics here as other places. I'm glad we can all be together."

"What's it like here, for synthetic people?"

"Same as anywhere else, I guess."

"But the humans here, they aren't in the net. They must seem so slow to you."

The synth made a heh-heh-heh sound. "All humans are slow, to us. We have to make allowances for everyone, more or less."

She hadn't thought of that. Of course, most synths would be faster than even the most interconnected humans. Her thoughts and actions must seem so slow to her half-sib, Arcan, one of the few "baby" synths on-planet. Baby in terms of years only: Arcan was already taller than Mama Claire at birth. Or did they call it creation?

"I might not be able to be implanted," she said to M-P. "The first implants didn't take. I got really sick."

M-P gazed at her. "Do you want to be implanted?"

"I need it. I mean, I've always wanted it. I have a half-sib, Arcan, who is a synthetic person. I want to be like them."

"Humans and synthetic people are different. But we're more alike than different." The synth tilted her globe of a head. "You are unhappy with yourself?"

"No! Just. It's hard to explain." She did like herself. She would just like herself better if she could do the things she wanted to do. "It's not fair."

"Aaaaah," M-P said.

"Aaaaah?"

"You think you have only one path. When the paths are infinite."

Pah. "Maybe for a supersmart synth. For humans..." She trailed off. "Oh, I don't know. I need to sleep on it."

As if on cue, Claire leaned out of the door. "Coming in to bed?"

Katla wasn't ready to look at Claire. She wasn't ready to be inside. The night was mild and calm. "Could I sleep out here?"

"I'm not sure. What does your friend say?"

"There's nothing to hurt her around here," M-P said. "I'll stay and watch over her a bit."

"Okay then," mama said. "You know I love you."

Katla didn't look at her. "You know I love you too," she sing-songed, almost rude.

Definitely not ready to go in yet.

They sat in silence, rocking softly, until Katla's eyes started to droop. She pushed off the chair, and settled herself on the porch in front of it.

"My belly makes a good pillow," M-P said.

"I'm good." Katla rested her head on her bent arm. "You're a counselor-bot, aren't you?"

That heh-heh-heh sound again. "Guilty. You're a brilliant young person. Implants or no."

CHAPTER
FOUR

NEXT MORNING, Katla was rousted by Haydee just as the sun was peeking golden over the horizon.

"Up, up, sleepyhead! I got us leave to go see White Island! But it's a long day so we have to get started now."

Katla sat up, brushing the untamed mess of bangs out of her face. "White Island?"

"It's the one right next to us. We can walk to it; the water is so shallow! Well, almost. And then we can visit with the scientists. Your mom said you were science mad."

Katla tried to blink her thoughts into order.

Haydee was already on high speed. "I got us lunch, see! And here's a mint roll for breakfast." She handed Katla a palm-sized pastry.

Katla took a bite—bliss!—and used the time chewing to wake the rest of the way up. "What's on White Island?"

"Life! The native life, that is. Oh, hi M-P! Do you want to go, too?"

"Haydee, it's nice to see you so happy this morning. And no, thank you. Last time, the snakes thought I looked too much like food."

"Snakes?" Katla said.

"As if they could even swallow even one of your legs!" Haydee frowned. "Well, maybe they actually could do that."

"Snakes!" Katla said.

"Yes! Giant white tube-snakes. Well, not really giant, I guess, they get to be about as long as a human leg. They are one of the biggest native species we've found, and they have a whole ecosystem: insects, rodents, plants, all the rest of it. Only a few people live there, mostly biologists—"

"Mostly synths," M-P interrupted.

"But the general agreement is leave the island be, to develop as it will. It's a big experiment, and we get to watch!"

"Giant snakes," Katla said.

Haydee rolled her eyes. "That eat bugs and tiny mammals."

M-P hopped off the rocker. She must have sat there all night long. "Actually, it is quite interesting. We're not sure yet if the rodents are truly a native species. We know the tubeworms are."

Katla finished the breakfast treat. Going on a trip would get her away from Mama Claire, and all the rest of it.

"Giant snakes," she said. "Why not?"

IT REALLY WAS possible to walk from island to island, especially with the tide out. The calm water was like a cool bath against her legs and torso, even through her one-piece swimsuit. Her shoulders would never have gone under, except she started swimming.

The water was perfect, a cool reflection of the wispy clouds above them. Katla had always loved the water; now she wondered why. Of course, the feel of it against her skin. How she could float and also make herself sink. How the world looked new and strange through water.

And how alone she was. She realized the nagging voices she heard—echoes of her moms, her teachers, her conscience—quieted once she was out of the air. It wasn't true that only implanted people had voices in their heads!

Which just showed that having implants wasn't always a good thing.

Haydee was more a splasher than a swimmer, but eager just the same. A solar-powered transport raft floated behind them, wirelessly tethered to Haydee's wristcom, portering their lunch and outer clothes as well as supplies to the islanders.

Katla slowed her stroke, and dropped her feet to the sand, waiting for Haydee to catch up.

"Watch out for snakes!" Haydee said cheerfully.

Katla scanned the water again. She hadn't seen anything more dangerous than a flatfish, but something white and agile might easily hide in the wave crests or ripples. "They swim, too?"

"Sure." Haydee stopped and took a deep breath. "You're a great swimmer. Here I am huffing and puffing."

Katla still scanned the water. "The snakes. They swim on the surface?"

"Oh, you'd see them, don't worry. Their little heads pop up. Looks like fingertips of a submerged hand, moving through bathwater."

"Finger. Tips."

"They travel in packs. Little packs. They're friendly. Well, with each other."

"Great."

"C'mon, you're the great explorer. You came all the way to see us. What's a few snakes?"

Haydee was right. When they finally did see the dreaded snakes, they weren't all that.

A pack—maybe twenty—were sunning themselves on the island's small dock. They didn't look likely to dart away. When the cloud cover changed the shape of the sunbeam on the dock, they rolled slowly to put all their body back into the sun.

The snakes actually reminded Katla of worms, only on a much larger scale. With skin more cream than bright white, they looked a little rubbery. Nothing like the scaly green biting ones Katla had seen on her second-to-last island. These wormy ones looked as if they wouldn't mind if she joined them, so long as she kept out of their sun.

Still, she didn't join them.

Two good-sized skimmers and a rowboat were drawn up on the narrow beach, but nobody was around. The girls leaned against the boat, letting the sun dry their suits. Haydee had painted squiggles on her suit that Katla now recognized as the worm-snakes.

"Pretty quiet here," Katla said. The loudest birdcall she'd ever heard rang out just then, a sharp, wild trill that spanned a whole scale of notes. It was answered in kind. Katla laughed. "No people, I mean. What is that bird?"

"I'm sure we'll find somebody up in the main compound." Haydee looked up. "And I do not know. I'm calling it the nag-nag bird until somebody tells me different. They always start up when I get here. They'll quiet down when we're off the beach."

Haydee's raft didn't just float above the water, it floated above land, too. It followed them up the short sand dune and into a grove of green. Bushes with leaves as wide as her hand waved at them, dancing in the breeze. Here she could hear the chirrups and scuttle of insects, and the rustling of what she hoped were the small rodents and not the wormy snakes.

The main compound sat in a natural opening in the greenery. A row of low sandcrete buildings circled a packed-earth courtyard. An old-fashioned well sat in its center, a short ring of stones with a wooden arm holding a line and pulley.

"They don't have running water?"

"They do, but it's hard to keep clean. The bugs keep getting into it. The well's a backup." Haydee went straight there and pulled on the line. The pulley turned and soon a ceramic bucket came up. "You have to taste it."

Katla leaned close and scooped a handful into her mouth. It bit, it was so cold. She had to hold it in her mouth a few seconds before swallowing. Icy smooth, and no smell at all.

Haydee followed her, taking the same care with swallowing. "Amazing, right? It's a glacier—a glacial formation—that wandered down here who knows why and jammed itself into this ridge. It's melting, but so slowly." She took another handful.

Katla's hand was still numb from the first one. "Supra. No, really. And this is all native species? Not our doing?"

A synthetic person was rolling up to them, wheels big-treaded, conical body well-coated against the elements. "None of it was us. But native—we're not so sure," they said.

"Aimee!" Haydee seemed to bounce over to greet them. "I hoped I'd see you in person! I brought some of those beads you wanted. My mom just finished a boatload of them."

"Perfect. The twins' birthday is coming up, and I'm making them new tunics. I feared I would have to ornament them with feather-work. Beadwork will be far better."

"And longer lasting. Especially for those rug rats." Haydee put an arm around Aimee, whose head came only to the girl's shoulder. "Aimee, this is Katla. She's visiting with her mom and staying with Celina. And she can swim circles around me."

"Glad to meet you, Katla. What brings you to our little paradise?"

She was glad she had an answer now, not just *I'm running away*. "I'm curious. The islands around us are so new there's not much growth on them that we didn't bring ourselves. I thought all the islands were like that."

"Not at all. There is the whole range of life around us. Come see what I found."

Haydee left the raft in front of the largest building and caught up with Aimee and Katla as they entered one of the smaller ones. This one had a clear roof, bringing light into a single large room edged with counters, microscopes, and other sciencey-looking tools. The center was where the action was: A large shallow pool, as high as her knee, round but with narrow shelf-edges probably big enough for those sciencey machines to sit on.

"Supra" Haydee said, making the word twice as long as usual. "This wasn't here before."

"We're still building it. I'm trying to create a closed-loop environment, so we can catch each stage of the development of these little cuties." They scooped a wriggly thing out of the water and held it in a gloved hand. Green and slimy, it might not have qualified for cute in Katla's eye except for the giant round dark eyes, slowly covered by a darker green lid as they blinked.

"Salamander?" she said.

"Close. It's a form much like a chameleon. Green now, but almost any color when they're full grown." They lowered the creature back onto the submerged stick it had perched on before, and flicked the water off their glove. "We wanted to watch how they developed that ability, but whenever we took a baby one from its nest, the parent one did everything in its power to get it back. One even figured out how to get through a fully force-fielded window! We stopped doing that right away, before our friends figured out more ways to subvert our tech, and instead started raising some of our own little babies."

"But how did you start them?"

"Oh, the old-fashioned way. We found a few lizards that had died, harvested their eggs and sperm, and cooked these up."

Katla shook her head. "What happens when they grow up?"

"You can't just let them go," Haydee agreed. "How will they know how to get along?"

"Oh, the lizards are pretty friendly, and not afraid of us, obviously." Aimee rolled to a bench on the near wall. "When they're grown, we hope to have someone on community service to help us take observations on how they interact with the local lizards. Someone a little sprightlier than the three of us are. Who can rescue any of our little buddies who need rescuing."

"Watching lizards could be a community rotation?" Katla said. That sounded way better than cleaning up storm damage or even portering supplies from island to island.

"Science rotation," Aimee said. "When you messaged you were coming to visit, Haydee, I at once thought of you. We'd need you soon, though. You'd need to pass all your competencies on first try."

Haydee groaned. "Don't count on me, then. I can't even keep my eyes open during maths."

"But everything is maths," Katla said. She'd already passed all her competencies, and on first try, as the daughter of one of the planetary leaders should do.

She could take this rotation.

She'd be away from her parents, but Celina would keep an eye on her. Not too close an eye, which is what Katla preferred. Watching big-eyed baby lizards grow!

But she'd practically promised Olve she'd join him on the rotation with the deep-sea crew. But those rotations were scarce, and there was no guarantee they'd take the two of them. It would increase Olve's chances if she did not apply. Who would turn down a planetary leader's daughter?

She hated that, hated always being reminded of that.

Aimee didn't even know who Katla was. It would be such a

relief. Nobody here cared about the world or world events. Katla could be invisible here. A regular person. Normal.

Haydee put on a pair of gloves and handed another to Katla. They squatted down to watch the fake pond at surface level. Katla held out a finger to the lizard they'd looked at earlier. It sniffed her—it smelled like pond—and then put a tiny sticky foot on her fingertip. Then it scrambled all its sticky feet onto her.

She loved this.

"They like the yellow-green grass, there." Aimee pointed to Haydee's left, where a clear closed bin held greenery. Haydee opened the bin, took a single blade of grass, and set it in the palm of her hand. The little imp immediately took notice, swerving its head, sniffing, and watching Haydee's hand as it came near Katla's finger. Then it jumped, de-stickying its feet somehow, and landed on Haydee's palm, its mouth already closed on the blade of grass.

"Hungry buggy," Haydee cooed.

"Opportunist bug," Katla said. She had to apply for this rotation. Or the next, if Haydee got this one.

Wait.

A normal person was an implanted person. She would be stuck here with all the people who thought implants were bad, or "not right for them." She'd have to sneak to stay online as much as she did now. And the global nets still went down out here once in a while.

Katla fumed. Mama Claire had tricked her, bringing Haydee around. Haydee had tricked her, showing her all the fun things without mentioning the bad. The trees, the science rotations.

Okay, not the snakes.

Her logical mind knew the whole reason they were here was for Katla to find new friends and new ways of living. But her heart-mind didn't want to listen to any of it.

Katla didn't want a new way of living. She wanted what she'd been promised from birth: Connection. Direct links to Arcan, to Olve, to anyone, to everyone. Like normal.

If she couldn't have that, she didn't want any of it.

The little lizard had scarfed up the blade of grass and was looking around for more. Katla reached around Haydee and took one out of the bin. She laid it across Haydee's wrist. The lizard spun around at the scent and dived in.

"You've got to take this rotation, Haydee," she said. "I can help you with the maths."

CHAPTER
FIVE

DECISION MADE, Katla would not be swayed by any argument Mama Claire, Celina, or anyone else could make. They gave up after two long days, and made plans to leave early. Together.

"You're as stubborn as Sofia," Mama Claire said, shaking her head. "So you know, I have to love you."

Claire had learned Celina's new way of batik, and Katla learned that this was yet another art her hands were not coordinated enough to succeed at. But she did like mixing the dyes, with their odd scents and deep, rich pigments. Her hands were a light purple-blue when Haydee came to say goodbye.

"You know, the paint is supposed to go into the art, not your hands," she said, handing her one of those amazing breakfast pastries.

"It just felt so good on my skin. And I had to test it for color-fastness, and I didn't want to waste any of Celina's nice fabrics."

"Mmm-hmm." Haydee dropped into the rocking chair beside Katla's. They were going to take two of the chairs home. "Took the first of the maths test," she said, too casually.

Katla stopped her rocking. "And?"

"And I passed! Didn't ace it, but nowhere near failing." Haydee rocked back, pleased. "One down, two to go."

"I'm on the comm channels, if you want to do homework together. Or whatever." Katla pushed back in her chair. "Cinnamon today. How did you get these still warm?"

"Trade secret. Okay, not." Haydee laughed. "Dad made me help stir all the dough. Might be I liberated a couple of finished ones in exchange."

"Your parents seem nice. Do you think you'll stay with them?"

"What? Like a forever-single?"

"No! I mean…" Katla wasn't sure how to say it. Just be direct. Haydee certainly was. "I mean, implanting. Do you think you'll get implants? You're old enough now."

Haydee put her hands behind her head. She rocked quietly back and forth, back and forth.

"Nah," she said. "My parents are dead against it. I'm not sure I'm as militant about it as they are. But I love my life, and I love them. Why upset the cart?"

Katla had to push. "Militant. Would they disown you?"

"You know, I believe they would. They're that set against it. Being disowned isn't that much of a threat here, though, where everyone is welcome on all the islands. But I do love my folks, and my baby monster-brothers. And I'm not so in love with the idea of implanting that I'll just let people chop so deep into my body."

Katla felt as if she'd been lightly slapped. "Sorry, I know sometimes I push too much, ask too much. I like you just as you are, too. No chopping needed."

"No harm done," Haydee said, sitting up so she could reach into a pocket. Out came another pastry, wrapped in cooking linen. She offered it to Katla. "I like you, too." She sat back as Katla unwrapped the gift.

"And you know I'll be calling about those 4-D equations."

HOME WAS the same as ever, except Mom Sofia was there. Her Big Deal mom always looked put-together, even lounging in a shapeless dress on the wider sofa in their living room. Must be the hair, all the rows of braids ruler perfect. She lifted her smokey gaze and dropped her reading tablet to the side as Katla came in.

"Daughter mine, how goes it?"

"Very funny." Katla dropped her satchel on the floor by the arm of the sofa and threw herself down on its open cushion beside but not touching her mom. "How long are you staying this time?"

"Oh ho, starting out the gate with the sorry-for-me's. For that, you must submit to a hug." Mom pulled Katla close, wrapping her in the cocoa butter and lavender and mom-ness of her. She wasn't rounded like Mama Claire, but a different kind of comforting.

Katla felt her mom's tension ease as well. It must be hard to be "on" almost all the time. Mom Sofia couldn't even relax in the sun on the front bench. Somebody would always come along and want some problem remediated or have some suggestion for the next world congress.

Still, she should be home more. The implants kept her connected, right? So why did everybody need to see her?

"Ah, peanut." Mom tousled Katla's hair. Katla did not wince, but Mom laughed anyway. "Not a peanut anymore, I see. A big, grown, peanut tree."

"Very funny, Sofia." Mama Claire had scooped up Katla's

satchel, deposited it in her room, and gone to her own room. Now she wore a similar shapeless dress colored like waves on a cloudy day—and loomed over the two on the couch. She bent and gave Sofia a shoulder-hug, and a kiss. Short, mercifully. "I'm glad we didn't miss you. The landing is still tomorrow?"

"Yes. If you get up in time, sweet peanut tree, you can join me to welcome the new citizens tomorrow." Sofia chuckled; everyone knew that the likelihood Katla would be up anytime early was slim at best.

Claire came around to the front of the sofa and pushed her butt between Katla and the armrest, squeezing her tight between two moms who looked suspiciously huggy. Katla burst out of the vise like a shallowfish escaping a child's hands. "Mama!"

Claire blinked innocently. "Didn't we used to fit perfectly on this couch?"

"Cozy-cozy, you used to say," Sofia added, though she didn't look all that upset. She snuggled up to Claire. They fit perfectly together.

They were going to canoodle.

Ugh.

"Fine. Okay. Good night." Katla grabbed a juice from the cooler and headed for her bedroom. There was a ton of new media and messages she needed to catch up with.

KATLA DID NOT WAKE up in time. Mama Claire was still sleeping, and her step-sib, Arcan, was away on a rotation up by the lip of the volcano for another month. But Olve was free, and yes, he wanted to go sailing.

This was their last summer to run around loose. Their first away-from-home rotations would start in the fall, a big step toward formal adulthood. Katla couldn't decide about adulthood: Sure, you could vote, and people would listen to you. But you also got weighted down with responsibilities, more than just serving dinners and cleaning brush and finding lost goats. You might even get put in charge of something—actually, you would, guaranteed—and what if it all went wrong?

She pushed those thoughts down and away with a breath as she hit the beach. Clear day, moderate southwest wind, a little chop. Manageable. A lock of hair escaped her band, and she remembered to switch it for an elastic, pulling the mess of curls down to her nape. Most adults kept their hair short, not wanting to take the time or waste the gel needed to tame it every day. Would she feel that way soon?

Olve was already at their skimmer. Not really theirs, of course; it was the town's. But most people preferred the boxier skimmers, which had swim/fish platforms and room for more people. Last summer, Olve had painted a name on the stern of the boat: Big Minnow. Nobody had said a word.

He looked different today. Browner? No, taller. Leaner. He was always skinny, but now there was strength in his leanness. He looked up and saw her, and waved.

"I'm gone not half a month, and you've done something to yourself," she teased.

"Not me. It was the goats." He grinned at her, and then threw the lines he had loosened into the center of the boat. "A whole school—twenty—thought it would be smart to go play on that cliff on the other side of the island. Not only did I have to chase them down, but I had to carry the littler ones across the river. That water is cold!"

She helped him push the boat into the water, and they hopped in, one on each side for balance. Katla raised the mainsail while Olve dropped the rudder. "Did the goats thank you?"

"Are you kidding? One of them kicked me. Look." He held out his arm. A fist-sized bruise purpled near where his biceps met his elbow. "Can you believe it?"

"Goat herding might be too hard for us littles after all." Katla laughed.

"I missed your laugh." Olve doublechecked the lines. He looked back at the town. "Have you thought about your rotation."

"Ugh. My moms want me to do something on the backwards island."

"That's so bad? It looked like a beautiful place. Your pictures were gorgeous."

"Sure. And there might be something cool to do there. But it means giving up."

The sail swept far leeward, and Olve sat beside her for balance. "Giving up the chance to do the deep-sea one?"

"No. Giving up on my implants."

"Your implants?"

How could Olve be so dense sometimes?

Once Katla started, it all came out. "I have to have them. I have to be part of my moms' lives. And Arcan's. And yours. I don't want to be disconnected from everyone forever."

"It won't be like that." But Olve frowned, unsure. He looked up and to the right, accessing data. Talking to something or somebody not her.

Katla's heart burned. Somehow in just two weeks she'd forgotten the sting of it, to be left waiting while somebody surfed the information streams. Nobody had wandered away from her in this way at Sankofa. Having to look at your wrist was enough reminder to pay more attention to the person in front of you first.

But here, everybody would. Again.

Her moms were so careful not to, but even they slipped. Only the synths could manage multiple conversations.

It would be her and the synths, from now on.

"You're right," Olve said, coming back to her. "That rotation sounds perfect for you."

"You think I want to be a biologist?"

"Why not? It's a parallel with what I would be doing. We could share notes."

Slowly. Painfully slowly. Better to just go with Olve, like they'd talked about. Why didn't he want that anymore?

"You don't want me to go with you?"

"You know I do. We're a team. But we also know there aren't that many spots. It's not likely they'll take two from the same region." He looked away from her. "I'm already accepted."

"You applied without me?" Katla's voice was a screech. Of course he did. Olve had wanted this rotation since he'd heard of it, years ago. He would apply the moment he could.

He shrugged, still not looking at her. "Passed my last exam last week. Put in right away."

Katla had passed her last exam months ago.

She felt the stew of hurt, anger, and selfishness brewing in her belly. She had to get out of here.

"Wow, that's great," she said, mechanically happy. "Supra."

Olve flinched at her tone. "We don't say supra anymore. It's old. Now we say smokey. Smokin'."

We who?

We not her.

We everyone else.

The stew threatened to boil over. Too, too much.

"I'm going for a swim." Katla said. She dropped off the skimmer. Her back plowed the cool, anonymous water, leading the rest of her unenhanced body into oblivion.

OLVE WAVED HER IN, too soon.

"Did you forget? The citizen shuttle is due in an hour. Run up to the viewing platform?"

Katla took her temperature. Still too hot. But she hadn't missed a landing in years.

Arkhide was so close to sustainability—minimum viability, mom Sofia called it. And when a couple more shuttles-worth of people arrived, new Arkhideans, their population would be secure. There was plenty of room.

They beelined toward shore, and quickly stowed the skimmer. The run up the hill to the platform both dried her off and calmed her down.

Olve was her friend, and she was glad he would get to do what he'd dreamed of. If he liked it as much as he thought he would, and shone at it, he might get it as a yearly rotation—or even permanent—after they'd completed all six of their apprenticeships.

They were barely in time. The viewing benches were nearly packed already. Veerill was looking out for them, though. Their favorite baking-loving synth pushed their cylindrical friend Em-six down the bench a bit to make space for Katla and Olve.

"You're almost late! They've already started the countdown."

Less than two minutes. They'd missed the suborbital pass, a silver streak of artificial rainbow.

Katla watched the sky over Landing Pad Island, an hour's sail from here. *Please, please let the tools—or even an expert—be on board who will fix my stupid body. Please.* A small voice in her head worried a competing thought: what were the chances, when her whole planet full of synths and human medgineers couldn't do it.

The descent came from the south this time, going against the wind. Touchdown was perfect. Everyone clapped and cheered.

Veerill bumped Katla's shoulders. "Forty humans, fifty synths. We win."

Olve laughed. "We'll get you next time." It was a familiar game, but now Katla was reminded that Olve could look up the shuttle manifest as fast as Veerill could. Not like Katla, anymore. Ever, maybe.

"Everyone is welcome," she said dully as her thoughts dropped into the darkness of resignation.

CHAPTER
SIX

THE SUMMER PASSED. Another implant did not take. The experts could not help.

Olve left for the deep sea, and Katla stayed behind.

This time it took months to recover from the two surgeries. First going in: brain swelling, nausea, pain. Then taking out: double vision, balance issues, despair.

Katla tried to put it out of her mind, this giant whale of disappointment. Impossible.

Soon she would return to Sankofa. Because of the special baby lizard project, there was a need for two apprentice rotations. Both she and Haydee would get to document the life cycle of a "new" native species. Their names would go on the scientific paper that even people in faraway Wala could read and respond to. Which was all great.

Supra. Smokin'. Whatever.

At least she would be away from home, and all the pitying looks and hushed conversations. Claire said Katla was imagining all that, but she wasn't there when Veerill hemmed and hawed through a conversation, finally ending it by giving Katla two chocolate muffins and scurrying back to the ovens.

First, though, one last piece of business.

Another citizen shuttle was due, and this one was special. Some of the last of the synths on Wala were arriving; finally, they all would be safe from persecution by the Cooperative Worlds, on hidden Arkhide.

In addition, the forty new human citizens would boost that population over critical mass. With them, Arkhide could sustain her population herself.

Of course, more were welcome. There were at least ten thousand Walans still on the immigration waiting list; plenty of space for more.

Mom Sofia wanted everyone at the landing. Katla had to drag herself out of sleep before dawn. Now with hair tamed, beaded tunic over thick formal leggings, soft boots instead of protective ones, she loitered outside the landing base central processing facility, avoiding the conversations inside.

Claire found her right away. Of course.

"You're not wearing your wristcom."

Katla looked away, rolling her eyes. "I'm going to be with you the whole time."

"You have to get over this," Claire said. "It's bad net hygiene."

"I'm going, I'm going. I'll be out of your hair in a month. Not even."

Claire stood behind Katla and wrapped her arms around her. Katla had to tilt her head so mama's face didn't bump it, she was that tall now.

"You'll never be out of my hair. Never."

Katla leaned against her mom's soft strength. She let the mild scent of—pine?—wash over her. "New perfume?"

She could feel Claire's chuckle. "Was using some of those pine needles in a project last night. That sap is impossible to get off!"

Katla frowned a smile, tentative. "I'll send you more."

Her mom hugged her tight. "And pictures of your baby lizards."

When they heard the roar of the shuttle's approach, they both went inside and down, into the protection of the center's bunker. Until she'd come the first time, Katla hadn't realized that people on Landing Island didn't actually see the landings; they watched them on remote view just like everybody else. Shuttles were known to crash.

This one landed perfectly; not even a hop. The welcome party had time to walk the half-hour to the shuttle, letting the new arrivals see them while giving the shuttle time to cool down. The crackle and pop of metals rapidly changing temperature had frightened little Katla that first time; now she took it in stride. She was still awed by its size, though: it was a mountain in and of itself, especially because of its pyramidal shape and snow-white exterior. The re-entry burn marks were all its own, though, and the molten smell seemed to have fewer ingredients than a volcano's belch.

The welcoming committee arrayed themselves as usual: Mom Sofia in front center, with Katla, Claire, and Arcan and other government representatives on the left and the representatives of Glovis and Harborville, the two communities these citizens would start in, on the right. Each person would reach out to a handful of newcomers, who were usually dazed by their first sunlight in two months, and lead them back to the welcoming center. Two floating transports stood ready for those not up for the walk; managing that was Katla's role today. The synths with the cargo transports waited in the field opposite, so as not to confuse the arrivals even more. They were always so wobbly when they came out.

As the door slid open, as the new citizens were gaining access and establishing links to the networks, before even one had stepped onto the departure ramp, Sofia and every one of her assistants recoiled, hard.

Sofia put her hand over her ear, the sign that important news was coming in and don't bother her. Katla followed her gaze, away from the shuttle. All four assistants had a hand over their ears, as well.

"Cut it off," Sofia said. "Now! Say temporary outage from the landing pad, no emergency. Right now!"

The others waiting on the grass swayed as if swamped by a hurricane burst that only they felt. Katla frowned. Usually when the net dropped, people just blinked stupidly a couple of times until they figured it out. "What is it?" she asked Claire. Sofia had drawn her assistants a few steps away from the rest of them and was barking out orders.

No, not barking. Whispering.

"What is it, mama?" Katla asked, steadying Claire.

Claire wiped her forehead. "Felt like a punch to the mind. Screaming. Despair. And then just as fast, it cut out." She looked at the ramp.

The first people were coming out. They wobbled even more than usual. They clung to each other, faces drawn or blotchy or still showing tears. Everybody looked like they needed comfort.

A second clump appeared, much like the first, only more synths, so more shaking of limbs and shoulders.

The rest of the greeting party rushed to the ramp, to reach the people sooner. Katla was fastest. She took an older lady by the elbow. A little was attached to her like sap, arms around her waist. Two older children hugged her under her shoulders.

"You're welcome here," Katla said. "We're so glad you've come. I've got a spot on the transport for you."

The woman didn't seem to even see her, but one of the older children, a girl, her face tight but her eyes clear, nodded. Together, they walked carefully down.

Now the ramp was full of people, but no one spoke. Katla heard only sobs, hiccups, soft groans. They didn't look oxygen starved, and their limbs still moved, if slowly. What could have happened?'

"It's so quiet," the mother whispered as Katla got her seated in the transport. "In my head. Are we dead, too?"

Katla had to work to keep the startle off her face. "Oh, no. You are all quite alive. Are you hungry?" She smiled at the little one, or at the one bit of an eye the little was peeking out from under the woman's sari.

The bright-eyed daughter glared at Katla. "How can you act so happy?" she hissed. "Look around."

Katla turned to look. Most of the passengers had fallen to their knees on the grass. And her people, the welcome committee, were with them. Some were starting to keen.

Somebody must be dead.

That was it. Katla broke the protocol of constant reassurance and love, and asked the girl: "What happened? Did someone die on-board?" The girl opened her mouth, but even she couldn't get the words out.

Katla looked for someone who might have some answers. Claire was on the grass among the newcomers, one arm cradling her head, the other wrapped around a soft-spider synth. Sofia, alone, her assistants gone who knew where, was walking to where Claire was. She dropped to her knees, and took both in her arms.

After a moment, she looked up and around. She spotted Katla, and motioned for her to join them.

Katla walked slowly toward them. Arcan was coming too, to join them. Katla sank down and went into her mothers' arms. She reached for Arcan, who closed the circle.

Katla closed her eyes and took in the cherry and mint and warmth of her mom, the pine and sun of her mama. She tried to push love toward her—toward all of them. What could have gone so wrong?

"Sweetie. Precious," Claire repeated into the thick of Katla's curls.

By the time the first wave of whatever it was had ebbed, Katla's knees were sore. As they loosened their grip on one another, Sofia grabbed Katla's hand. The grip hurt, but she didn't say anything.

"Do you know?"

Katla shook her head.

"Okay," Sofia said. "Okay. I need to practice this."

She pushed Katla gently until she was seated in the grass, and then sat beside her. She put a hand on Katla's two hands twisting into themselves in her lap. Katla was often a practice audience for her mom, but today she wasn't sure she wanted to hear.

"Okay. Something bad has happened. Something terrible. Arkhide is all right. We are okay. It's Wala."

Sofia choked on the word. She took a breath. "It's Wala. Wala," she repeated. "There was a weapon of war. It fell into Wala's atmosphere. It destroyed the planet."

Katla jerked, but Sofia's grip was tighter than that. "It is terrible. It is awful. But we don't know the details. The people in the shuttle were entering the jump tunnel. They could not turn back. They saw the flash, and saw the planet. Disappear."

Sofia took another breath. "Disintegrate. The people on the shuttle heard some communications chatter. Mostly yelling. They don't know if the bomb was intentional or an accident."

Katla's hand was screaming, Sofia's grip on it was so strong.

"Mom," she whispered. "You're hurting me."

Sofia let go immediately. She grasped her own hand. "Okay. We are sending—we have sent—another drone to the gate closest to us. It will go through to the second gate, but not into Cooperative space. It will listen.

"And then we will know."

CHAPTER
SEVEN

KATLA STOOD beside the events recorder as Sofia, head of the planetary congress, concluded her short speech to the great assembly. "Now we know."

"We are alone. No one is hunting for us. No one knows of us. And we will do everything in our power to keep it that way."

Katla had helped scan the thousands of news reports and eyewitness vids. She had volunteered to do the watching: It was easier for her because she had never lived on Wala, never even been there. She had lost people—grands and aunties and their families—but she only knew them from the rare vids and her parents' stories. Almost everyone else on Arkhide knew scores of people who had lived on Wala.

Their research could not confirm if the explosion had been planned or simply a case of stupidity. The bomb was a test model, meant to be detonated closer to Wala's sun. Why the Cooperative was blowing things up in non-Cooperative space was also a matter for debate. Whether they had told Wala what they were doing ahead of time was also unclear.

There was enough doubt about the Cooperative Worlds'

actions and intentions that the people of Arkhide knew they could not trust them. As if they ever had.

The only grace note, a splinter of joy, was the fact that the synths on the last shuttle were actually the last of the synths on Wala. Refugees from planets that the Cooperative Worlds had annexed, they found Wala a welcome haven. But Arkhide, secret, two jump-tunnels outside "known" space, was every synth's goal.

And every synth on Wala had escaped Cooperative space.

Sofia was wrapping up. "And now we stand alone. But together, strong. Every one welcome." She looked away from the lens, directly at Katla. "Every single one of us critical to our success."

She looked back into the lens. "I believe in you. I believe in us."

They were on their own. Katla wasn't sure what that all meant.

For one, a new satellite-based planetary protection project had been quickly approved; her Mama Claire would help with that one. Second, the synths were going to take the lead to build a cloaked base in orbit that could see farther and warn them of danger faster. Third, everybody was needed to stockpile dried and preserved foods, for the dark years sure to come.

She could help with so much of this. Already she was helping Veerill figure out how and where to store massive amounts of food—and find the materials to make all the containers it would need. And her Sankofa rotation had taken on a sense of urgency: They needed to know right now how other beings had adapted so well to Arkhide.

They were on their own.

Together.

NICKY PENTTILA

HIDDEN PLANET

A Cooperative Realm Story

CHAPTER
ONE

ON THE DAY the dreaded notification arrived, Katla was checking the instruments at the top of the tallest volcano on Arkhide, so her wristcom pinged first. Soon the whole planet knew they had been found out.

Katla had jumped at the chance to trudge up Mt. Awala to check on the monitoring arrays. The seismic sensors suggested an eruption was imminent, but the GPS, gas, and thermal sensors did not agree. Arkhide's elders also did not agree. Drone images and satellite readings through cloud cover were not conclusive. Somebody had to go look.

A long day's hike, in the warm rain and the mud, treading through a gritty dusting of old ash, was bliss. Even digging up the stubborn soil to change monitor batteries and clean off sensors wasn't a chore. The usual steam and belches, the mild sulfuric smells, didn't seem like enough to put on the rebreather. Awala might be rumbling, but it was probably just indigestion.

Katla had been cooling her heels here on Macadere Island, following her mom around from political event to quasi-political meeting to yet another political event. Mom Sofia already had a most able assistant, and now that Sofia had retired from active service she really didn't need another. The only thing Katla could add was her gift for languages, but since most everybody had a communications implant that did adequate in-the-moment translation—even tone, pretty well—there wasn't much for her to do.

But she had spent one of her career rotations with the volcanologists who monitored this always active chain along the equator belt, so why not just have her go check out the odd readings? No need to bother the local volcanologists. They were all a half-day away, gathered on the isthmus between two volcanoes actually erupting, eagerly observing and debating how the process was different when it was twinned.

Katla followed their new theories and debates in the evenings, safe from the rain in her waterproof dome tent. It didn't matter out here that it took her longer to read and listen to it all. Or that she needed a screen to do everything. Or that she couldn't eat and respond to comments at the same time.

Most humans on Arkhide received a series of implants as adolescents: communications, network access, wayfinding, improved memory, and a range of more specific enhancements. Arkhide had been founded as a world where enhanced humans and synthetic humans could live without prejudice. A bare two thousand people on the planet did not enhance at all, following their own beliefs, but Katla was not one of them. Her implants had failed.

She had failed.

Her parents did not put it that way—no one did, to her face. But she wasn't going to change the world like Mom Sofia, or coordinate network-wide projects, like Mama Claire. It was exasperating to hang out with people her own age, because half their conversation was in-head. She missed all the context. It was easier with synths, who thought all humans slow and Katla just a little bit slower.

But it was best to be alone.

By the time she'd reached the wide lip of the crater, it was clear that the seismic readers had been off. Too much corrosion on the wires. The sulfur here stung her eyes—the rebreather didn't let it reach her lungs—but there was no rise in levels of lava and no changes in rim configuration, no dome. Just as hot as ever, no more.

Arkhide was such a young planet, with such a thin crust, almost every island experienced some activity. The town Katla had been born in was now half-buried in slowly cooling lava. Maybe her grandkids could move back there, and take advantage of the newly fertile soil.

Maybe her friends' grandkids could.

She didn't want to go back down. Face the blank faces and glassy stares of people accessing data online while you were standing right there in front of them.

But this was a good assignment. Was there such a thing as one-off assignments specialist? She could take her little sail-hopper and putter off to eyeball suspect volcanoes, or to repair distant facilities. She could hike through jungles, up hills, across black-desert sands.

She'd need new boots. She'd definitely need to find tastier meal-packs.

She was deciding how to frame the question to her moms when her wristcom pinged. Barked, more like. Emergency alert.

Wasn't much she could do about it up here, Katla decided. She turned away from the rim and its gassy belches and headed back to her last camp, a short half-hour away. She'd write up the report, send the last of the data, and then pack up and go. Maybe she could find an anomaly that would require her to collect another day of data. Maybe she could make the trip down last four days instead of three. Tradeoff was she'd have to eat that last, horrid mealpack—what was it?—mixed fish and beans in gray gravy. Nobody should have to eat that.

As she pressed send on the data, her wristcom chimed with Mom Sofia's melody.

"Kay, where are you?" Sofia sounded like a general mustering her troops. She fell into that mode so easily even now she was supposed to be retired. Katla sighed.

"On Mt. Awala. What's up?"

"Where, exactly? Turn your locator on. Someone's coming to pick you up."

"Too dangerous. I'm right at the top and it's windy and raining." It was sprinkling, but maybe could start pouring at any moment. "I'll go down to the platform tent base. Everybody knows where that is." Katla hated having people watching where she was all the time. She used the excuse that the GPS and other locators wore down the batteries on her devices too fast so she could keep them turned off. The devices were powered by her movements, just like implantable ones, but less efficiently. And even implanted people turned theirs off sometime. Her friend Olve almost always had his off.

"No time. We need to get you down here and ready in two hours." Sofia's voice trailed away. She must be reading something. "Hopper's ready."

Katla enabled location on both her tablet and her wristcom. "What's the hurry?" What could anyone possibly need from her?

"That message, did you get it?" Sofia didn't wait for her answer. "The Cooperative has 'discovered' us. They know we have a space platform, and they want to talk to us. Now."

"Okay?" Wow, that was terrible. The worst. They'd expected to be found someday, hopefully a century from now. So soon was not ideal. But still. "Why me?"

"They won't talk to anyone who has any kind of enhancement. They cut the signal off from the platform once they realized that only synthetic humans were there."

Typical. That was why all the synths in this part of space lived on Arkhide in the first place.

Still.

"So why can't they talk with the representative from Sankofa?" One of the two islands inhabited by a sect of people who preferred to never enhance.

"He isn't cooperating." Which meant the representative wasn't eager to do whatever Sofia wanted.

Was Katla?

"They see you," Sofia said. "Thirty minutes out."

CHAPTER
TWO

THEY LANDED DIRECTLY in front of the sandcrete-and-glass offices serving the Greater Assembly of Arkhide. Someone took Katla's pack, while she was whisked away to wash, primp, and prep for camera.

She'd seen other people put through this process but never experienced it herself. So many distracted people pushing and prodding, shower too hot, hair gel too smelly—and too thick, having to work mightily to tame the frizz of her hair after a week of no product. The best tailor in Macadere City—a synth named Seela—sewed a new tuck into someone else's formal tunic as Katla wore it, with Sofia casting a critical eye on the whole ensemble. Sofia, of course, looked perfect: beautiful rows of twists coursing down the back of her closely tailored tunic in brilliant blue. Yet again, Katla marveled at how two willow-tree parents could have given birth to such a small, densely packed person as her.

"We're trying to get decent shoes for you. Last resort you can wear mine." She tsked. "You didn't bring any formal sandals?"

Katla had wrecked them at the last political gala. She'd had to twist out of the way of some diplomat whose thoughts—and gaze—were elsewhere. She'd fallen into one of the ponds with the colorful fish, who apparently thought sandal straps were super tasty. By the time she'd pulled herself out, one sandal was on by just a strap, the other hopeless. "Didn't see you there," the diplomat said. "Your presence is … minuscule," he said wonderingly. Her presence on the net, he meant. Her corporeal form was average feminine human. Soggy human.

Katla shook her head, which shook her hip, which earned her a tiny poke from Seela's needle. "What do you want me to do?"

"Play for time. Don't agree to anything. Whatever they want, say you can't do it without consulting the assembly, and it will take a while to gather them all together."

"They're right here."

"The Cooperative doesn't need to know that. If you can, try to find out what they already know about us. The news clip was vague." Their monitor bot, which regularly caught and forwarded much of the Cooperative's broadcasting, had flagged one short segment on the interesting discovery of a human-made object far out in edge space.

"Can I see the clip?"

"On your comm."

Katla woke up her wristcom and pulled up the clip. One of the Co-op's usual newscasters, so this was an official announcement. Blurry image of their solar system, with an arrow pointing to a tiny blob that was the space platform. A chilling closing line: "We look forward to welcoming our new friends into the Cooperative soon."

"Doesn't look like they know much at all," she said.

"That they're saying for public consumption," Sofia said. The primpers turned Katla to face her mom, who looked her over, frowning. Then she hugged her, careful to avoid the makeup. "Perfect. My brave girl."

Katla let the lavender and love calm her a little. Not much—she was more dazed than nervous. She waited for Sofia to pull away first. Her mom had stopped with the hugging when Katla was a surly teen, and she'd hadn't managed to find a way to tell Sofia she missed it.

KATLA WAS READY, shoeless but with a lectern in front of her that bore the seal of the Greater Assembly of Arkhide: two silvery hands clasping at the wrists with a sun over water in the background. An army of lights surrounding two camera lenses beamed at her, washing out the dark drape of fabric behind her. A drone camera hovered just inside her peripheral vision. A screen that would show the Cooperative official was set up directly behind the camera, helping to guide Katla's line of sight into the lenses.

Outside the light, in the large communications center, it was nearly silent. Dozens of people were in here with her: comm techs, assembly people, the synth with the annoying facepowder puff. It felt to her as if they all were holding their breath.

The moment to connect came.

And went.

Someone brought a chair for Katla, outside of camera range. The ring of lights clicked off, their buzzing ceased. Sofia crowded her from the back, and the present Speaker of the Assembly, a synthetic human from the South named Aimee Five, crowded her from the front.

"Do you know what you are doing?" Aimee Five said, her voice lilting as well as cutting. She had modified it to sing in a trilling operatic style. It really suited her, with her fine lithe shape and taste in ornamentation, Katla thought, all other thoughts fleeing under the onslaught.

"Yes, madame speaker," she said. She pointed at her earpiece. "I hear you fine, and I will pause to be sure I understand before I speak." In fact, she would hear both Sofia and the Speaker, as well as the cameraperson, and they would all hear one another. Katla really, really hoped everyone would keep the line clear. They might forget that she wasn't used to a lot of simultaneous cross-talk.

Sandals came, but the lectern remained. A good hour or so later, the communications tech lifted her head.

"Signal's coming in."

Katla stood, shaking out her tunic. No wrinkles, good. She submitted to another pat down of her hair, and more face powder. She stepped up to the lectern, gripping its sides outside of camera range. She nodded.

CHAPTER
THREE

"HELLO FROM THE CENTRAL DISTRICT. I am Madam Clamor, Undersecretary for Outer Worlds Integration in the Department of Community Relations. With whom am I speaking?"

Katla blinked slowly, taking a moment to process. The undersecretary's High Galactic was so arch it was almost unintelligible. Katla had learned Galactic from news broadcasts and other media; even the characters in political-intrigue dramas didn't round their vowels so hard. Trying to match it in her response, she started with the sounds she'd just heard.

"Madam Clamor. I am Katla Sofiasdotter. I am here in the chambers of the Greater Assembly of Arkhide."

"Ark-heed. That's how the robot pronounced it, too." The undersecretary's shiver of disgust set her earrings in motion. The collection of tiny brightly colored globes hanging from thin chains reminded Katla of captured planets. The rest of the undersecretary that she could see was rather bland: gray turban and robe, maroon lipstick, kohl eyeshadow in a style the comedy shows made fun of. But she was all gravity and intent, sitting straight, hands clasped upon a black reflective table in front of flags of many worlds. "We'll have to do something about that."

The local voices started up in Katla's earpiece.

Don't say she's welcome to anything, Sofia said.

Ask her what she meant by that, Aimee Five said.

Get over it, Aimee, Sofia retorted.

Too much! Katla wanted to say, "take your snit-snat to a side channel," but she didn't have the implant for subvocal communication. Instead, she took her gaze off the undersecretary and looked to the side. She made eye contact with Sofia and then Aimee, and patted the air, hoping those two would understand "hush."

Please look directly at the cameras, the comm tech said.

In any case, Madam Clamor did not wait for a response. "We understand you have reached the stage of low-orbital flight, well done indeed. We are prepared to welcome you as a conditional sub-junior member of the Cooperative Realm. There is a standard path for single planets like yours. Many, many have followed it. It will take some years to reach full membership, but—"

"No." Katla did not wait for the chorus to weigh in. She knew this answer.

"I beg your pardon?"

"We do not accept. We do not wish to be part of your Cooperative. Madam."

Good, she heard in her earpiece. *Good.*

The undersecretary was unruffled. "I understand. You need to know more about what we offer and how relations with us will benefit you. I will have some material sent to you to explain. Do your people prefer text or moving images?"

Katla clenched her jaw. *Relax*, earpiece mom said softly. *Don't play her game.*

"We are very familiar with the Cooperative already, thank you—"

Don't thank her! Aimee Five did not speak softly. Katla tried not to wince.

"—and we would like to negotiate an agreement for trading privileges only."

Don't bring up the tunnels! At Aimee Five's warning, Katla closed her mouth on the sentence about jump-tunnels that she was about to say.

The undersecretary pursed her lips. "That would be quite irregular. I understood yours was a backward planet. Needing guidance on system affairs, etcetera." She looked off-camera for a moment.

She needs to be choked!

Get off this channel! Sofia hissed.

"I understand that many worlds have such an agreement," Katla continued. She'd memorized their names during makeup and primping. "Saunders, Gagua Six, Wala. Thypso, most recently."

"How, exactly, do you understand that?" A tablet slid across the undersecretary's desk. She picked it up and read something.

You're doing so well, Sofia said. *Take a deep breath.*

"I see. Your information is correct. These planets do have trade-only agreements." She set the tablet down. "But we can offer you so much more."

"We understand what you can offer. It is untenable." Katla hoped she was using that word correctly. "We do not want it."

"Miss Sofusiadebitor, pardon me, but you seem a little young. Perhaps there is someone older I could speak with?"

Calm. She's saying it wrong to upset you, Sofia said. It had already worked on Aimee Five. Katla was shocked by how quickly.

"Madam undersecretary," Katla said, emphasizing the under part. "I am fully briefed and capable of starting these negotiations."

The undersecretary tilted her head. Her planet-earrings started up again. "What is the real problem, dear?"

Katla inhaled, and stopped. Should she tell the truth? Which one?

Synths, Sofia whispered.

"Our world, madam undersecretary, is a haven for synthetic humans. We understand—"

"You harbor fugitives!" The undersecretary sat back in her chair, grabbing the armrests, as if a synth would jump out at her from her comm screen. "Abomination," she whispered.

"—We understand that such people are persecuted in your so-called Cooperative."

Stay polite, Sofia said.

Katla continued. "We do understand—very well—the many potential benefits of joining the Cooperative Realm. But our priority must be to preserve the safety of our population. All of us."

Someone off-camera handed a glass of what looked like water to the undersecretary. She took it in one hand; she held the other over her heart. Her skin had gone ashy.

Take that, bitch. Aimee Five had not left the channel.

The undersecretary recovered so quickly Katla was impressed. If that's what they taught at diplomat school, she should enroll. Madam Clamor handed the glass off and pushed the tablet to the side.

"Miss Sofusdoctor, this call was to welcome you into our Cooperative. Given this ... new data, I agree that you may need more time to discuss amongst yourselves the best course of action. It would definitely be a condition of full membership that all synthetics be neutralized. We haven't had them in Cooperative space for generations."

"Not quite generations. Remember Wala."

The undersecretary waved that piece of raw data away.

"I see." Katla glanced at her mom and Aimee Five. Both nodded. They'd talked about what to do in this situation. It was a relief to know exactly what to say.

"Then we reject your proposal. Good day, Madam undersecretary." She turned away, showing her back to the camera.

We're off, the tech comm said. The ring of lights went dark. The drone camera buzzed back to the team behind the camera.

Everyone in the comms center remained silent. Everyone needed time and space to absorb the new realities of their world.

The Cooperative had all the ships, all the resources, all the power. It did not take no for an answer.

Arkhide had two commuter ships capable of jump-tunneling and a mostly finished orbital platform.

And the smartest, toughest people in the galaxy.

They'd survived disasters before. They would do it again.

They just had to figure out how.

CHAPTER
FOUR

THE NEXT MESSAGE from the Cooperative Realm didn't come for a week.

"They want to make us stew," Aimee Five said, pacing—rolling—back and forth in the Assembly Speaker's office. She had not changed it much from when Mom Sofia was speaker. The sandcrete walls were still bland tan, a shade her mom had always found soothing. The wide silver-and-glass desk and comfortable if straight-backed padded chairs remained, though the one that had been behind the desk had now joined the others in front of it. Aimee, with her tall cylinder midriff and shorter wheels, didn't need to sit. She also didn't need the communications terminals and speakerphones, but hadn't had them removed. The large window facing the park with the Assembly Room in the distance did not need shades and had never had curtains.

But in place of Sofia's family photos and maps of Arkhide on the walls, Aimee Five had hung woven tapestries. Their geometric patterns extended to the thickness of the threads making them up. Colors so bright, they popped off the walls. Katla wanted to run her hand down the nearest to her chair. She wanted to see if she could guess the pattern just by touch. She held herself back, though. Aimee Five was touchy at the best of times. And this time was definitely not one of them.

Sofia sipped the chamomile tea she'd picked up on the way in. Katla looked longingly at the tea, but she'd already slurped her own saucer dry before they even got in here. The warm brew had settled her stomach but not her mind. She cupped her elbows and willed herself to sit still.

"Have you heard from Mama Claire?" Katla said.

Sofia looked up and to the right, accessing data. "On approach to the station. No problems."

Aimee Five paused, then threw up her beautifully tapered hands. "I can't believe we even have to do this." Claire was going to the orbital platform to manage the alterations that would make the station habitable for humans.

The platform had been designed for synths, most of whom did not have strong heat signatures and all of whom did not need much air, water, food, or gravity. That had made the platform easier to build and get running. All it was supposed to do was act as a staging point for cargo skimmers taking Arkhide's small amounts of poisonous trash to a dead moon nearby, do a little mining, and reinforce the satellites and other methods Arkhide was using to hide itself from Co-op sensors.

So much for that.

A random science survey ship that came out of the nearest jump-tunnel on its way to observe a red dwarf noticed an anomaly in their readings. A weird dead spot. The astronomers trained their mighty scopes away from the star in front of them and toward the side, toward Arkhide. They recognized the orbital platform as not natural. They didn't come closer—the red dwarf's pulsing was too interesting to miss—but they did call it in to Co-op Central. Unfortunately for Arkhide.

Sofia set her saucer on her knee. "We don't want the Co-op coming down here. The only other choice was host them on the platform." She sounded both bored and impatient; they'd had this conversation before, and that was after the two days of shouting at the Greater Assembly. *We shouldn't accommodate them at all. We can't make our people go on their ship to negotiate—we're already at a disadvantage. They should negotiate on one of our shuttles: That would keep the conversation short.*

On and on.

The platform might be ready in a month's time, with shuttles running continually to take all the materials needed. It took weeks from jumping through the Walan tunnel to get to Tunnel 645 and then Arkhide. No one from the Co-op would get here before then. She had all that time to prepare.

It was not enough.

The Co-op's next message came directly to Katla, Arkhide's newest—its first—Diplomat representing the Greater Assembly in Matters of Interplanetary Relations. Chief Diplomat, Aimee Five corrected, so the Co-op would be forced to take her seriously.

She quickly forwarded it to a giant list of Assembly people, one of whom would put it on the general feed, and then opened it to read.

As they'd said in the earlier messages, the Cooperative bureaucrats refused to communicate with enhanced humans or synthetic humans, who would never be awarded citizenship. The Co-op required—demanded—that all communications take place in the Galactic language, High Galactic preferred.

Their demands reduced the number of people on Arkhide who could act as diplomats to one. Katla.

Sofia turned to her. "You're on your own, kid."

Aimee Five snorted. "High Galactic. Such a Cooperative move."

"I'm not. I can't be." Panic iced her voice. There was no way she could do it alone.

There were two whole islands full of unenhanced-by-choice humans, who spoke their own three languages; they'd never needed to learn Galactic. Their youngsters were learning its basics, but haphazardly. Everyone knew this day was coming; nobody wanted it to be in their lifetime. Learning Galactic made doomsday feel closer, so people avoided it.

Except her friends.

Haydee, on Sankofa, was proficient. She could follow the dialogue of the Galactic soap operas they binged together through the network. Olve, at the deep-sea base, couldn't always follow the stilted speeches, and usually concentrated his sly comments on the cheesy visuals and tech mistakes.

Aimee Five resumed her pacing. "You'll have synth support, of course. And your parent will be there, behind the curtain." She looked at Sofia.

"But Claire is already up there," Sofia said, frowning.

Katla would not be distracted. "No. I need Haydee Cooper. She's fluent in Galactic," or she would be in a month with Katla's tutoring. "She's one of the few, and the best at it I know. And she's unenhanced, completely." Haydee belonged to a community whose philosophy shunned implants.

"But she's not even political," Sofia said. "Why would she be interested?"

"This isn't a community rotation to see what services interest you, mom. This is an existential threat. Of course, Haydee would want to help." The more she thought on it, the more Katla wanted Haydee there. Her smiling face, framed by long blond hair. Her enthusiasm. Her energy.

She had to come.

Aimee Five rolled to a stop in front of Katla. "We're not

spending the weight to fly some random human up just to be a security blanket for you."

"A second set of ears in the room could only benefit us, madam speaker." Katla searched for a deeper argument. "I know we can analyze and confirm our translations after the fact, but to have someone right there, who hears what I hear but maybe in a different interpretation, could help us avoid costly mistakes."

Aimee Five waved a hand. "Would another human make that much of a difference?"

She had to have Haydee. "Please. I'm a special case among our people; unenhanced in a community of enhanced. Haydee has a different experience: She's lived among the unenhanced all her life. She might be able to read the subtle signals these Co-op humans make. Far better than I could."

She met Aimee Five's fierce gaze and held it. This must work.

"Agreed. Talk to this Haydee. If she wants to go, I have no objection."

CHAPTER
FIVE

HAYDEE WAS BACK out on White Island, the nature preserve near Sankofa where she and Katla had done their first community rotation. Every few years, her friend would scoop up another unfilled rotation on the island. The single spot often went unfilled: Nobody wanted to look backward, and that was pretty much the whole purpose of White Island.

"Short-sighted noodleheads," she said when Katla teased her about it the last time she said she was headed back to the beyond-rural posting. "What's more important than figuring out how life works here, on our only planet, in the absence of people's inter-ference?"

True, the scientists there had already observed and described an amazing property of the sticky stuff made by the little lizards they'd found on the island. Nothing native had grown very big yet; Arkhide was a young planet, full of active volcanoes, massive earthquakes, and roaring storms. Somehow these lizards had figured out (evolutionarily) how to change on the fly the goop that usually kept their feet stuck to branches into a hardened shield, helping them scamper (briefly) over superheated lava. That's how they could get out of the way, and survive.

Years ago, Katla and Haydee had helped with the early stages of that study, and Haydee had continued it. Now others were trying to figure out how to recreate that property in a form they could use for rescue equipment and maybe even temporary bridges for people fleeing the latest lava flow.

But even White Island, never inhabited by Arkhideans, was tainted by invasive species. Someone had lived here before, and brought their plant life and animals. Nobody knew where they had gone—or why they had come to such a baby planet in the first place. It made tracing Arkhide's taxonomy of organisms far more difficult, but then everybody liked a good puzzle.

Katla set her hopper on a flat part of the beach above the tide line. The weird translucent tube-snakes were sunning themselves on the pier as usual. She could hear the nag-nag bird's wail as soon as she took off her pilot's headset. Haydee had named the nag-nag bird. It did live up to its name. She pushed through the camphor haze of the big-leafed bushes crowding the beach—they grew so fast!—and down the short path to the outpost.

The White Island Nature Compound looked smaller and shabbier than before. Single-story sandcrete buildings circled a packed-earth courtyard. A stone well sat in its center; backup for the residents in case the reclamation machinery failed.

The place smelled like mint. Katla traced the scent to the wide kitchen/dining room building, no surprise, and went in the door to the kitchen.

"Out! Out!" Haydee said. "We're not ready for you yet." As Katla turned, pretending she was going to rush out the door, Haydee's rich bell of a laugh bubbled up. "Get over here and let me hug you."

They were the same height, in contrasting palettes: Haydee's blond even blonder from the sun, Katla's dark unleavened by any sun at all lately. Her round face used to expressing joy contrasted with Katla's thinner, moodier mien. But Haydee's seasuit matched Katla's semiformal tunic, both in their favorite color, forest green. Katla breathed in the warmth and citrus and love of her friend. It had been too long.

"I can't believe you came all the way out here just to argue with me," Haydee said, leading Katla to the snacking counter where—yes!—mint pastries were cooling.

A familiar synthetic person was putting the kettle on to boil. "She lost the bet," said Aimee. This was the first Aimee Katla had met, and the nicest. "I told her you'd come." Their big-treaded wheels made short work of joining them at the cookie counter. "You look ... well, worried, Katla."

Back when she was sixteen, Katla had looked up to Aimee; now taller, she sat on one of the short stools at the counter to look at her straight on. "It's been a busy time. But so interesting."

"If by 'interesting' you mean terrifying, I agree," Aimee said. "How did they find us so fast? I mean, I know, but still. What were the chances?"

"I certainly would have bet against it," Haydee said. "Hey, all my bets lately are anti. When did I get to be so negative?"

"An N of two, only," Katla said. She reached for a pastry, hovering her hand over one of the golden rounds of goodness. She looked a question at Haydee.

"Yes, if it's cool enough," Haydee said. "You're supposed to wait for them to be cool."

"I have no time to wait." Katla winked at her.

Aimee fetched the pot and saucers for tea. They didn't drink or eat, but said they enjoyed being part of the process—and the conversation. With their conical body and continually gloved hands, they always appeared so tidy, even when mucking about with the artificial pond habitat where they observed the lizards.

"Are you really going to have to meet the Cooperatives?" Aimee shuddered delicately.

"Somebody's coming, yes. We're not sure when—probably in a month or two."

"Planet killers." Haydee crossed her arms, scowling.

"Please. We have to talk with them. We have to convince them to agree to our version of the treaty. Otherwise they'll just gobble us up." Like every other planet they came across, she didn't have to say.

Haydee swiped a hand, as if brushing the whole idea of the Cooperative to the side. "Good luck with that. I couldn't do it." That's what she'd said on the call, too. This time, Katla had arguments prepared.

"If you don't want another Wala, we have to get this agreement."

"Wala happened even with their treaty."

"It's the best we can do. Do you want us to have to agree to the standard contract? That would destroy us."

"I don't want any agreement at all. They need to leave us alone!"

"Stop yelling at me!"

"Stop saying such stupid things!" Haydee's voice cracked. She closed her eyes and took a breath. Aimee quietly rolled out into the courtyard.

"The Co-op is never going to listen to you," Haydee said, voice under control. "Some young person of no family. With no credentials. How can the Assembly even suggest it?"

Katla leaned back, away from Haydee's heat. She took a bite of the pastry. The minty sweetness help ease her roiling feelings. She'd asked herself all those questions. She'd given herself the only answer there was.

"Haydee. Seriously, what choice do they have? Any enhanced

person takes their life in their hands sitting in a room full of Cooperatives. It's up to you and your people. And me."

"My people can't even talk about Wala. They choke up. They still cry. All the time. They would never stand in a room with a Cooperative."

Wala had happened only two decades ago. Too soon for anyone's wounds to have healed. Haydee had come to Arkhide as a teenager in one of the last shuttles from Wala. She knew people—family—who had died in the supposedly accidental bombing that had destroyed that planet. Katla was one of the very few humans who had been born on Arkhide, in the first wave of settlement. Even she wasn't sure how she would react to being in a room with people from the Cooperative.

"I know it feels impossible." Katla said. "That's why I need your help. I have to get this right—perfect. We can't accept enhanced people being treated as less than citizens. We could never send the synths away. They—we—all of us are family. "

Haydee glared out the window. Her arms were still crossed.

"I desperately need another pair of ears that can parse Galactic. And you're the best."

"Better than Olve," Haydee conceded. She tilted her chin down, frowning. "Think it would make the Sankofa council like me better?"

Katla snorted. "I think stopping teaching the littles how to climb tall trees would do that."

She glanced at Katla, mouth quirking. "Too late for that."

Katla reached out a hand toward Haydee. "Please, Hay-hay. I can't do it on my own. I really need your help. I so, so need you."

Haydee reached for Katla's hand. Just as she was about to clasp it she stopped. Her hand hovered inches from Katla's own.

"Hay-hay?" It was her younger brothers' nickname for her. "Only people whose diapers I've had to change are allowed to call me that."

"What would you prefer?"

"What's your title, nowadays?"

"Chief Diplomat. An office of one."

"Then I'm Deputy Chief." Haydee grasped Katla's arm at the wrist, the deepest of handshakes.

"An office of two."

CHAPTER
SIX

HAYDEE COULDN'T LEAVE the planet without saying goodbye to her family on Sankofa. Katla landed the hopper in the meadow nearest the scattering of sandcrete-in-all-colors cottages where they lived. It was creeping up on the formal dinner hour, so only a couple of synths were strolling on the far side of the wide green and gold swath of grasses.

Sankofa was one of the beautiful islands, its sharp gray and silver mountains balanced on one edge with the rest of the land a wide, flat apron of greenery and life. Trees—a kind of fragrant pine—actually grew tall here.

The volcano that created the island now sat dormant, but the building styles remained quick-built, modular, and low to the ground. When Katla first visited here as a teen, people talked about building taller, about spending the time and materials to make something beautiful. Something lasting.

But that was before Wala.

The Sankofans did build a neo-Gothic worship hall, set into a pine grove on the shortest rise of the mountains. But it was a synth-designed prefab, sent piece by piece from Harborville and raised by the community in a week. Later, maybe, Arkhide's artisans could spare the time to do it up proper.

Right now, they and everyone else were focused on practical, portable, long-lasting creations for a population that often needed to move house every few years. Arkhide was a young planet, geologically, with the roiling magma and tectonic shimmies that went with it. Katla had lived on eight islands already, three as a refugee from environmental hazard. She loved the nomad life, though not enough to take rotations on different islands every single time.

Without Wala's support, the Arkhideans were on their own. They'd spent the last decade building stockpiles of supplies for the periodic dark years, storing much in warehouses that could be lifted off their supports and floated from one island to another. With a human population at the cusp of self-sustaining, they could not afford to lose any island—any one—through untimely death or disaster.

Katla's mama Claire had successfully led the organization of their hemisphere's caches, including backup energy sources for the bustling synth cities. They now had supplies and backups to last 18 months or more.

Which was why Claire was now on the orbital base, organizing the supply shuttles and leading the quickest building project they'd done yet: Human-proofing a station that had been intended for synths only.

When Haydee pushed through her family cottage's force-field door—shouting "Surprise!"—she nearly crashed into her mother, who was on her way out.

Amity Cooper pushed her daughter back outside, sweeping her into a big hug. "Brilliant surprise!" Haydee's mother was a slighter version of her daughter: tall, willowy, blond, and pale. She held out an arm to gather Katla up, too. She soaked up the lemon-scented affection.

It was just the three of them for dinner. Haydee's dad was at some conference off-island, her brothers at their various rotations. Amity took each of them by the hand, swinging their arms in time with their footsteps all the way to the community dining hall. Haydee had to take mincing little steps to keep the rhythm, which she did smiling. This obviously had happened to her before.

The folding wall on one of the long sides of the dining hall was tucked away, opening the already airy room to the lawn outside. The wall's force-field was still on, keeping bugs outside while allowing people and their food through. And the roar of happy littles playing: Many of the younger families were having a picnic-style supper, on mats or blankets on the lawn. Their movements seemed to gain fluidity in the moist heat of early evening.

Dining here was traditional. People usually went together to the serving stations, building up platters of food to share among one another. Mostly fish, veg, and fruit, but today there was a kind of protein loaf that looked interesting and those pastries that could be filled with sweet or savory. Looked like savory, tonight.

Amity brought Haydee and Katla to one of the long tables to greet her usual dining partners, with much exclaiming and hugging. But after they picked up their food, she chose one of the smaller, round tables farthest from the open wall.

"I know why you're here, Katla," she said before anyone could take a bite. "You're taking Haydee away, aren't you?"

Katla opened her mouth—to say what? She closed it again.

"Mom, please." Haydee chose a piece of fish for Katla from the platter, giving them both something to do. "Nobody can make me do anything. You know that."

"How can you even think of it? You know what they did." Amity shivered. "I certainly don't condone violence, but I'm not sure I wouldn't just slap every one of those smirking so-called negotiators' faces. And punch the biggest one."

Katla swallowed the deliciously peppery fish. "Yes, I hear you. The problem is somebody has to talk with them. Nobody wants to trigger old wounds—"

"They're not old yet," Amity said. "Not even adolescent."

"You're right." Katla cursed herself. Never call Wala old news. "So, since I am one of the few with no direct ties to the disaster, it makes sense for me to go."

"But Haydee does have ties. She was a teenager; she knew scores of people killed—annihilated—" Amity's voice spiked. People started turning to look at them. She blew a breath out; Katla recognized the calming breath process her mama had taught to her. It seemed to work for Amity, too.

"By those craven … rats," Amity continued, softer.

"I did. I do," Haydee corrected hastily, pre-empting another correction from Amity. "But this negotiation, it's critical. It's life and death for us. And it's going to be so hard." She put a hand over Katla's resting on the table. "We can't expect Katla to do it all by herself."

"Of course not. But she has one of her moms, right? Already up there. Celina told me Claire went with the first supplies."

"But Claire can't be part of the negotiations," Haydee said, repeating the obvious. "Only people like us can."

Katla chose a morsel for Haydee, mostly to slow her down. "We need everyone we can get who understands High Galactic and doesn't have enhancements. We won't force anyone still in deep mourning to do it. That leaves a minuscule list of people."

"My daughter."

"And one other person. But he is on the underwater rotation, which also is critical. We need all lines of communication to stay open." Katla took a piece of pastry and held it out to Amity. "I'm sorry."

Amity took the morsel; to do otherwise would be rude. She chewed it slowly, gazing past the diners and out to the families on the lawn. Katla wondered what she saw. Or remembered: maybe when her children were littles, running and shouting.

On Wala.

It was easy to understand why so many of Arkhide's people were so twitchy, so quick to anger, so easily upset at a random comment—or recalled memory you had no idea you had triggered. But it was impossible for her to feel what they felt. Their whole world, gone. Even picturing Arkhide gone didn't bring up the same feelings, for Katla. She plain didn't believe it would ever happen.

But they could. Because it had happened to them.

How could so many of her people hold all they felt, all they remembered, all they'd lost, in their minds?

Amity sighed. She turned to face them. She picked up a morsel for Katla. "I never imagined, coming here, that my child would be the one who would have to risk herself to save us all. My children," she amended, holding the morsel out.

Katla took the bite.

CHAPTER
SEVEN

THEY DIDN'T LEAVE Sankofa until morning, but still early enough for the hopper not to be in anyone's way. It was overfull: Amity had insisted that both Haydee and Katla take one of the island's world-famous rocking chairs with them. And she didn't take "no cargo space" for an answer.

Not only were the rockers comfortable, but each one was a work of art. Intricate carvings that took months of spare time by artisans who had already spent their day on more practical fare. But the rocking chairs could be practical, too: Most were wide enough to seat a parent with a little on their lap and another tucked in by their side.

The two Amity gave them were a bit narrower. Haydee's had a wildlife theme—carvings of lizards, insects, and even a tube snake from White Island danced along the headrest and down the sides. Katla's chair, a little smaller to fit her better, was plainer, which also fit her better. The delicate wax-and-waning curves of the spindles that made up the back pleased the eye as well as the body. The artist had joined all the pieces so carefully the chair looked like it was a single piece of wood. She knew it wasn't.

These chairs were made of fallen branches, not newly cut wood. It made their construction a bit more challenging and contributed to the variety of designs, from thin and delicate to wide and blocky. All were beautiful.

Haydee shed a few tears early in the four-hour trip to Macadere. They hadn't spoken to her brothers, or her dad.

"I'll tell them, when it's right," Amity had said. "You know your dad can't even say their name, or even Wala's, without choking up." Katla tried to remember if Amity herself had said any name for the Cooperative Realm last night.

But in the blue-sky day, with adventure on the horizon, Haydee's sunrise smile soon returned. They spent the hours to Macadere Island practicing High Galactic, which included making up new words to the tune of "Now we are sleeping," the first lullaby nearly all people of Arkhide heard. The new version, in perfect High Galactic and in the point of view the Galactics, started with "Now we'll be leaving, sorry to just drop by."

In the buzz of the hopper, with the front part of her brain concentrating on piloting and proper High Galactic, the back part of Katla's brain coasted through a river of feelings. The usual panic at the idea that she was supposed to make the Cooperatives blink. A new sense of relief, that Haydee could be with her. Longing for her Mama Claire, anticipation that they would get to hug again soon. Worry that mom Sofia was taking on too much; she was retired now and should let others take over, but Aimee Five was not the best at getting humans to work together without ruffling their feathers. Foreboding, at what might happen if she failed. Anxiety, at the thought of blasting off into space, with no air and no guarantee of safety.

Letting the feelings loose this way could get overwhelming, but it was better than stuffing them all down and then realizing she was grinding her teeth in her sleep again. Or she couldn't turn her neck because the muscles had frozen.

They were thirty minutes out from Macadere when the emergency beacon screamed. Haydee's head snapped from the side window to the speakerbox in the center of the control panel. Katla's hands flinched on the controls, and the hopper dipped in the air. She punched the main communications channel open. Not directly connected, they had to wait for the audio announcement.

It was painfully slow in coming. Haydee had already flicked a screen up from her wristcom, and was searching for the news when a voice came over the flight channel.

"Hopper K-7828, respond."

"K-7828 here."

"We see you. You need to alter course. Right now." The voice held panic and a sinister calm. "We are tracking an unknown object from orbit that is dropping into atmosphere. You need to get out of the way."

A falling object. Unexpected. Coming at speed.

A bomb?

Another Wala?

Haydee looked up, through the clear canopy. Her head swiveled, trying to take in every angle. She wailed so high in her vocal range that it sent a shiver down Katla's spine.

Katla sped to reprogram the majority of the craft's sensors to scan up and out. She'd have to pilot more on sight, but they were already near the skipping-stones of tiny islands that led to Macadere so that should be okay.

"I don't see anything," she said to flight control. "Which way should I turn?"

Haydee drew her knees into her chest, wrapping her arms around them despite the seat restraints. She tucked her face into her knees. She slowly rocked.

"Correction. Don't change course. Increase speed. Get to Macadere within ten minutes."

Top speed wouldn't get them there that fast. "Um, control. That's not possible."

"You have clearance to hit the boosters. Blow the battery out and we'll deal with it later. The object is on track to hit near the Skipping Stones."

Katla absolutely did not want to hit the boosters. It not only blew the battery but it made steering nearly impossible. The hopper basically turned into a rocket. It needed to be aimed perfectly on boost to hit the landing pad. And hit it was what it would probably do, no soft landing. "We're in an early model hopper. Can I turn around and go back?"

"No time. Predicting massively unpredictable wind and water effects in the entire zone. The object's course is somewhat erratic."

"Understood. Okay to aim for upper-city landing base, by the lake?" That would give them a second chance if her targeting or the boosters weren't perfect.

"Okay. We are telling them to expect you." A pause. "You are clear for land; all pads open for the next twenty minutes."

"Understood. Thanks." Katla left the channel open while doing the prep to pop the booster. She'd never done it in real life; it was meant for emergencies like being too close to a surprise volcano blow or outracing an oncoming tsunami. Things that little hoppers shouldn't be that near in the first place. She programmed the safest trajectory to the lake landing pad.

It wouldn't get them there in time.

She reduced the arc until the estimate said eight minutes 30 seconds.

The landing was going to be hard.

Should she target water? Hoppers weren't meant for water, either. It would sink, fast. They could swim, sure, if they weren't frozen in fear.

Except one of them was.

Katla accepted the landing trajectory, and ran the numbers again to be sure. She reached over to adjust Haydee's seat restraints.

"Haydee? I need you to sit straight. We're going to boost, and I don't want you to hurt your knees." She reached for Haydee's knees and gently pushed them into place.

Her friend was a rag doll. Eyes closed, mouth flat shut. Once her legs were down, feet on the deck, her arms wrapped tightly around her chest instead. Katla made the adjustments, and set their air-pillows to deploy.

"Ready?"

No response.

Katla sat back and tightened all her seat restraints. She took a big breath and punched the panel to expand the pillows. The creepy translucent pillow hugged her to the seat while somehow leaving space to breathe. She had to fight the soft bulbous mass to keep a hand on the controls.

She hit the booster.

CHAPTER
EIGHT

THE AIR-PILLOW DID NOT DO anything for the blast of sound as the battery blew. But at least they weren't crushed by the initial force, and in a blink they were away from the noise and rocketing toward Macadere.

The seats didn't shake so much as shiver, like an especially frightened lizard if that lizard was as big as a house with a voice like a hurricane. Katla fought to keep her eyes open partway, squinting to check the trajectory screen. On track.

She tried to move her head to look at Haydee, and managed to get her into peripheral vision. Tucked into the opaque balloon, she was shivering as if to break. Or maybe that was Katla, and it was her vision shivering.

New noises. Metal buckling, some connector flapping, the wind's incredible push. Katla's hands gripping the armrests ached. She let them go, to fall against her abdomen.

Not sure that was better. There was pressure enough there already.

Katla stared at the countdown clock on the trajectory screen, as if she could help it work through the tension of her thoughts.

Three more minutes. Two. One.

The engines coughed off. One grinding scream gone. No fire, so that was good.

The screen showed the hopper at the apex of the trajectory. Perfectly aimed to fall—like lightning—to the target. Katla thanked the synth engineers who had suggested this baggie thing, and everyone who had made it. And whoever had designed it so it still worked in a hopper that was older than she was.

She would send them a thank-you note later. If they survived.

Without the roar of the engines, the buckling of the outer hull grew more insistent. Burning sealant wafted through the bubble's air.

One minute out, as the screen showed them crossing over the sandbar that formed the inner bay, their seats began bucking. The deck below them—really a thin platform over a mess of cables sitting on the hull—must have been jarred or twisted beyond its tolerance.

Katla reached for the tilt controls and tried to picture what would be below them if the floor went out. Their seats and bubbles would tumble into the port buildings. Now, the main market. Now, Macadere Park. The Assembly buildings. The neat rows of tidy homes. The lake, thank Moa.

The landing pad roared up at them. She nudged the stick up, so they wouldn't be going in face-first. There was something red on the landing screen, but the text was blurry through the air-pillow.

They hit in the proper position, but nowhere near the usual way. The hopper cratered the pad, its mix of recycled rubber and whatever made it a hard surface not enough for a craft traveling at meteor speed. Either the landing skids must be gone, or maybe just the hydraulic fluid, because there was no hop.

Burning rubber replaced steel in the air. It grew stronger as the pillow deflated. Katla knew she should unbuckle and get out quick. But her arms felt filled with sand. She wasn't sure how to lift them.

Haydee groaned and started tugging at her restraints. Now she woke up, after all the excitement was done.

Maybe all. They could still blow up. She really should move her arms.

Haydee's rapid breathing reminded Katla to take a breath. But she hated rubber, so it was shallow.

"Are you hurt?" Haydee's face came close. Katla felt her tug at the restraints.

"Gravity drunk, I think."

Haydee looked up and to the side. Someone was banging on the door next to Katla.

"Hay, the red button. There by the door."

She hit it—punched it—and the door opened a crack. Whoever was outside got it the rest of the way open.

Hands took Haydee and pulled her over Katla and out. Then returned and pulled on Katla.

She helped them get her out—her legs were still good—but once she got on the pad and a few steps away from the hopper, she sank down. Sitting on the earth seemed like a really good idea.

Haydee must have thought so, as well. She was sitting a few steps away, an air patrol person squatting beside her. Katla looked at her helper person: a synthetic human with beautiful amethyst eyes.

"Did you design the air-pillows? Do you know who did?"

"No. And yes, dear." They were checking her pulse with one hand and shining a light at her pupils with the other.

"Send me their address, would you?" She looked at the hopper, blinking the afterimage of the dilation-test light away.

The hopper had buried itself a good meter into the landing

pad. Both emitted an oily smoke. The center cabin had lost only a few outside panels, but the tail had cracked. The back gyro was missing.

She shuddered. Life was finally flowing back into her arms. "I need to send them my thanks."

THEY DID NOT LINGER at the landing pads. An independent transport swept them back toward the Assembly buildings.

They'd missed the meteor's impact. It must have hit just outside the sandbar closest to the Skipping Stones, judging from the direction of the massive waves. Their waters vaulted over the piers, swamped the beach, scuttled into the lower part of the shore districts. The quiet of the transport and the three people aboard clashed with the visual bombast of the water world beneath them.

"What is it?" she asked their driver, the amethyst-eyed person. "We are unenhanced," she said, feeling the usual pulse of shame.

"Too much to follow," they said. "Even for me. We do know the UFO is a single-person craft. We think someone is inside it."

"But how did they get in?" Arkhide had two separate satellite-based energy nets that covered the globe. Nothing should have gotten through the first, much less the second, without being sizzled to atoms.

"Not sure. Maybe a flaw in the nets. Safety feature, rather. The systems are programmed not to harm people. Guess we didn't plan for an invasion."

The waves, having pulled all the small craft and chairs off the beach in their ebb, now pushed everything back in. Katla winced as a massive bench pounded into one of the ice cream kiosks just off the pier. They were going to have to peel seaweed and shallowfish off everything. Not to mention that each piece of water life that was lost out of turn upset the balance of the seas.

Everyone on Arkhide had sworn to preserve the water ecologies. All ecologies, really. Katla didn't want to think about all the wreckage this human-built meteor had wrought. And nothing bad was ever supposed to touch the bottom!

"You'll know it all soon. We're going directly to your mom."

Now she remembered him. "Viram," she said. Her mom's driver and pilot and software whiz. He must have jet-packed to get to the pad in time.

"Welcome back," Viram said.

CHAPTER
NINE

KATLA'S MOM was not at the Assembly compound, nor at home. Viram took them to a plain sandcrete two-story building with a garden of satellite dishes on its roof. Sofia may have every internal enhancement for communication, but even she wanted to see real screens in front of her sometimes, if only to point at them.

The building was just a block up from the edge of the water. The waves seemed to be calming, but they left a mess in their wake. And the scent of terrified fish.

An assistant Katla didn't know almost stopped Haydee at the entrance, but Viram said something and she went through. Theoretically any Arkhidean could attend any governmental meeting —and many did, via their internal links—but in practice some meetings stayed private.

Despite Viram's frown, Katla led Haydee to the washroom and toilets. First impressions were important, plus who knew when they'd get out of whatever meeting this was. Plus, she needed a moment alone, and she was pretty sure Haydee did, too.

They met up at the long communal sink. Haydee pulled off

her tunic to splash water on her face and upper chest. Her color had returned, but her face remained stiff, unnaturally still. She pulled a cloth from the towel pile and held it to her face.

"I dream of Wala," she said. "I'm flying—I'm always flying in my dreams. I'm soaring, happy, zigzagging through the wisps of clouds on a perfect day.

"Then I hear a roar. A sphere falls from above, it's small but so close to me I can feel the breeze of its passage in front of me. White with two blue stripes. I know what it is. The Wala bomb." She held her arms wide, face drawn with pain. Katla stepped closer, and opened her arms. Haydee sank into her embrace, hugging tightly. Her voice became a whisper.

"I dive, dive, so fast, as fast as I can. But I can't catch it. Even if I did, what would I do? Diving, diving. If I'm lucky, I wake myself up, my heart beating so fast. On bad nights, it all just … goes."

Katla took a deep breath and sighed it out slow, hoping Haydee would do the same. After a while, she did.

They stepped apart. Haydee shook out her tunic before putting it back on, then held it in her hands. Her gaze was far away. "Hearing that something—a sphere—was dropping, I froze. Was I in a dream? And then the roar, and the boost. I was lost. Until I saw the city, and the landing pad."

Her gaze focused on Katla. "I left you alone. I'm sorry."

"Oh, Haydee. You were with me the whole way. I was only able to keep it all together until we landed, and then I was spent fuel. That's when you helped me, remember? To get out of the hopper quick quick, before anything else happened."

"You flew the hopper. The rocket."

"The computer did the boost. All I did was tuck everybody in tight." The thought reminded Katla to check herself for injuries. "I guess it worked. I don't feel terrible anywhere."

Haydee's gaze went inward. "Yeah. Like after a really long

hike, carrying a squirming baby goat all the way. Bruised and sore, and in need of a nap."

Katla grimaced a smile. "Precious little chance of that, as my mom says." She started for the washroom door.

Haydee reached for her arm. "Kay. I'm sure I'm not the only one. This is going to be traumatic for a lot of our people. It's our worst nightmare, from our biggest bogeyman. Be careful what you say—how you say it. You're always so direct. Today, maybe, wrap your words in velvet."

Katla nodded. "Velvet. Not a problem."

The phrase echoed one from an outrageously unrealistic Co-op drama they had watched every season of for language practice. It drew the most tentative chuckle from Haydee.

Katla counted that a win.

Viram was hovering at the base of the ramp up to the main floor. The ground level held sofas and chairs and shelves with games, but not much more. All the important stuff was a floor up, in case of floods. Which, well, lucky for that.

This meeting room was Katla's favorite. More than two dozen screens stretched along the two long sides of the otherwise plain room. The rectangular table in the center could seat two dozen people, but stretched only one-quarter of the room's length.

Being able to look at all the screens at once put Katla on the same footing as everyone who had the enhancements. For once, she could keep up. She'd snuck in here a couple of times, just to surf the flows of information.

Six well-dressed people clustered around two of the screens. Each of their assistants sat at the table, eyes glazed as they dived deep into the online information streams. The air was electric with their tension. Her mom saw her immediately, and waved them over. Katla took Haydee's hand and joined the group at the screens. Sofia's presidential face didn't show any emotion, but she gripped Katla's hand like a vise as she kissed her cheeks.

One screen showed a live visual above the still-churning spot in the bay where the thing must have gone in. Probably a drone cam. The other, a blinking orange series of squiggles, looked like live sonar of the seabed.

A round object sat on the bottom. It didn't seem to be moving. It had a door and two small viewing windows. Katla stepped over to another screen, attached to a manual interface, that showed a carousel of ship types used by the main Cooperative planets. A synthetic human wearing one of his usual gorgeous green tunics was scanning through the images. The thin rings sewn into the garment chimed softly against each other as he moved.

"See anything, Allen?"

"Katla. Glad to see you in one piece." He took a moment to rest his hand on her forearm. She loved the soft sound. He gestured at the screen.

"Pretty much ruled out military make. Guessing explorer."

An assistant roused. "Madame President. A message from the science vessel Utopia."

Allen winked at her. "Toldja." Then he noticed Haydee. "Haydee Cooper, I presume?"

"Yes. Haydee, this is Allen Eleven, currently serving as the assembly's head of security."

Allen winced. "Only because Aimee needed someone. I'm working off databases here, not true experience." There wasn't much need for deep security on-planet; everyone who came to Arkhide wanted to come. They'd overcome long distances and long waiting lists to get here.

"You do know all about the safety nets," Katla said. "But I thought you were up on the base?"

"Came down to help Claire get supplies faster." Allen blinked, the only signal that he was reading whatever the message was. "They say it's a mistake."

"A mistake!" Aimee angrily trilled. "That's what they said the last time. Be more original."

Allen herded Katla and Haydee closer to the group by the screens.

"What do we send back?" the assistant asked.

"Explain," Aimee said.

"Please explain," Sofia said.

"Fine. What she said." Aimee, on the edge of the group, rolled down a bit and back. Katla hoped the pacing would calm the hot-tempered president down. "Tell me again why we can't just throw this piece of trash into a volcano?"

"Be serious," Allen said. He was one of the few who could talk to Aimee Five that way; they had known each other for decades. Long before Arkhide. "We don't kill humans."

"He's polluting our planet! Who knows what poisons that thing is leaching into the bay. And the viruses he carries! We can't even make him do community service, cleaning up his mess, without endangering our own people."

"What have we heard about the catapult idea?" Sofia said.

Aimee paused. "Community sentiment is no. Engineering says no, if we want to keep the stupid human alive. Our cargo shuttles are too small, and we need them right now anyway."

Katla looked at the sonar image. "You could break it in two." Everyone looked at the sonar image, that little bubble of Cooperative space on their world.

"Interesting," Allen said. "Engineers say maybe. They'll need to actually measure it."

"We have to get it out of the water," Sofia said. "It doesn't look like it can move on its own."

"Why not? It had propulsion enough to invade."

Aimee's assistant answered. "It's a space exploration bubble, the science ship says. Boosters might not be waterproof."

"Brilliant." Aimee snorted.

Sofia pointed at the screen. "Haulers have arrived." Six of the big hauler drones settled into a wide circle about a building's height above the waves. They each started to unroll a thick line and attach a grappling hook to the end.

"I don't want it here on Macadere," Aimee said.

Allen tapped his chin. "Set it on one of the Stepping Stones?"

"No," Sofia said. "He'll need to eat. And poop."

"The pollution never ends!" Aimee threw up her hands. She turned to the table of assistants. "Find a way to get it off the planet. Now."

Katla ran through her mental list of all the nearby islands. Aimee wouldn't want the capsule on an island that was inhabited. But the ones with facilities and uninhabited had all been abandoned for reasons: lava flows, hurricane destruction, earthquake damage.

Haydee leaned in to whisper. "What about Landing Island?" The island had been the gateway to Arkhide, back when they had immigrants. It was still the chief port for the shuttles, but now it was only used for staging for shipments to the space platform and satellite launches. No one officially lived there; the supply carriers were mostly bots and synthetic humans. But there was a big compound for humans to stay for a couple days while they sorted out which island they were going to or while they waited in quarantine for some reason.

It was perfect.

"Mom," Katla said. "What about Landing Island?"

Heads turned, swiveled, focused on her. Katla swallowed slowly. "It's not that far, right? It has a stockpile." Her voice faltered.

Haydee spoke up. "And it's where they'll be going anyway. Any launch would be from there. Why not just keep them there from the start?"

Heads turned or swiveled toward Aimee, near the table.

Aimee tilted her head, as if thinking. Katla knew she'd say yes. Her 'No' always shot out; yes took more time.

"Yes." Aimee set a hand on her assistant's shoulder. "Tell the drones to go directly there. And figure out the rest of it."

The sound of water churning filled the air. Katla turned back to the view of the bay. She hadn't realized the drone footage had sound, too.

The haulers' grappler hooks hadn't hit the water yet.

On the sonar, the seabed undulated. Not like a quake, which was ragged and spikey. This was like a hand scooping water. An invisible hand. A very, very large invisible hand.

"Get the drones up and out!" Allen said. "Now."

On the sonar, the sphere started to rise, lifted by what looked like a moving pile of sand.

Outside the building, the city's emergency sirens wailed. "Emergency alert: Macadere entire." Allen's voice echoed from the speakers on the lower floor. He must be channel-wide. "Take cover. Flying debris expected. Take cover now."

The sand and the sphere kept rising, but only the sphere broke the surface of the water. It shot out and up, then in a flat speedy arc. Directly toward the city.

Katla caught herself crouching down, and then let herself do it, knees sinking to the floor. It couldn't fly this far, could it?

The drone that had been looking at the water must have been trained to follow the capsule. Its motor buzzed louder as it pivoted. The image changed to a view of the city. The sphere crashed onto the near pier, rolled once, and came to rest on the wide pale sand of the beach.

No one said anything. Katla silently blessed Moa for guiding the aim of that arc. No innocents harmed.

Aimee clicked her tongue.

"That certainly will make it easier to measure."

CHAPTER
TEN

THE SCIENCE SHIP Utopia informed them that the person in the capsule was named Seth, as in Media Presence Seth-is-on-the-Edge. Like they were supposed to know who that was. He was on Utopia to document its trip to study a red dwarf, but the ship had been diverted to diplomatic duty and sent to Arkhide instead. The scientists of the Utopia would appreciate it if the people of Arkhide could keep the negotiations brief, so they could get back to their real jobs.

The people of Arkhide were not sympathetic.

Katla knew she would be assigned to babysit this Seth. The fact that they did not have the month they'd counted on to prepare had sunk in, and everyone in the assembly's ad-hoc diplomatic crew was scrambling. Plus, absolutely no one else wanted anything to do with the cause of the damage to Macadere's beachfront, to its oceanic ecosystem.

To its people's psyches.

Viram flew Katla and Haydee in the assembly's bigger hopper, which somehow already contained everything that had been packed into Katla's little hopper, including the rocking chairs. They soon shot past the hauler drones with their awkward capsule cargo. She hoped the sphere was upright, for this Seth's sake. She'd taken a trip via hauler bots once—she'd begged for the chance to ride with the cargo to Landing Island—and it was a rocky ride over land, much less water. And way too slow.

The hopper banked just before reaching the island. Viram tapped the comm headsets on. "Change in plans. Short stop on Glovis first. Picking up another passenger."

The human-form passenger waited directly beside the landing pad. Katla's step-sib Arcan wasn't affected by the wash of the propellers or the roar of the approaching craft.

One of the few synthetic humans who had chosen to "rebirth" themselves upon arriving at Arkhide, Arcan had lived only as long as Katla herself. She couldn't match their absolute thirst for learning, though. She'd been glad to finish the last of her six community rotations, while Arcan was on their twelfth.

Viram landed perfectly and dropped the entry ramp. Arcan was on in a flash, and in another flash they were airborne.

"Arcan!" Haydee grinned at them. "It's been so long!"

"You look well," Arcan said, stowing their duffel neatly under the seat and settling in. "And you, too, Katla. Saw you on the newsfeed."

Katla rolled her eyes. "What did they call me this time?"

"Let's see." Arcan tapped their thin, silvered chin. Their joints, invisible under their tunic and slacks, were usually burnished gold, but the joints on their fingers were currently very bright. They'd redone their hair into a sort of silvered buzz cut. She'd liked the bowl cut better. "Ah. 'Arkhide's diplomatic corps.' Which means we have more than one now. That's you?" They looked at Haydee.

"Roped into it," she said. "I thought there would be more time for practice, and learning about treaties. Wasn't it supposed to be months before the Co-op got here?"

"We didn't count on them sending a science vessel to do a diplomatic vessel's job," Arcan said.

Katla frowned. "I'm not sure what authority they have. Can they even negotiate?"

"Unclear," Arcan said. "Looks like the hope is the science vessel can get the treaty signed fast, and then the Co-op won't have to haul a bunch of diplomats all the way out here."

"Good luck with that," Haydee said. "Their treaty is toilet paper. If the star-watchers can't negotiate, we'll just be sitting there, staring at each other."

"We'll know more when we know more," Katla said, without really thinking it through. Everybody laughed, including her. "Anyway, Arcan, are you a super-doctor now?"

"Pretty much," Arcan said. "Surgical rotation complete—I did a liver transplant!"

"Really? That sounds terrifying."

Haydee nodded. "And who donated the liver?"

"We grew it. We had the time; we caught it early. The young person's cancer was progressive but not rapid. I was going to assist, but by the time everything was ready, I'd passed all my practicals, so Doc Breatheed had me do lead."

"Were you nervous?"

"Was I. And there was one moment when it just seemed like there was too much blood. But Doc suctioned it away, and I could see that my sutures were good." Arcan smiled, a silver gleam. "It was so fun. I'm so glad I added the surgical to my other rotations."

"And now we have a doctor to send up to the platform," Viram chimed in.

This was great news. "Really? You're clear to go?"

Arcan's smile grew even wider. "I am clear to go."

"It's going to be like old-home week up there," Haydee said. "Your mom, Arcan, you, me. All's we need is Olve."

At Olve's name the hopper went quiet—as quiet as a hopper in flight can go. Olve was serving as Arkhide's underwater preservation lead. With the splashdown and ensuing chaos, his job just got a whole lot harder. No way would he be joining them up-platform.

"Anyway," Arcan said after a moment. "I'm lead on the human quarantine. Another team is going to manage the capsule. So I need your help."

Katla groaned. "Can we start tomorrow? And can I have something for muscle pain?"

Arcan went into immediate doctor mode. "What are your symptoms? How acute? How long?"

"Oh, I don't know," Katla said. "Maybe since I had to hit the booster on the hopper, and crash-land, and then rush off to Landing Island."

"Very funny," Arcan said. "I get it. Muscle tightness and general malaise."

"Who are you calling general malaise?" Katla puffed her chest and pretended to be affronted.

"Prepare for landing," Viram said.

CHAPTER
ELEVEN

LANDING ISLAND WAS a flat swath of grasses and pressed stone, too small for even a village but long enough for roll-down craft and wide enough for touch-down craft. The Central Processing Facility sat at the edge, near a short, wide pier. No boats were moored, but Katla could see a couple solar-sails coming in past Sankofa, the closest island. Probably with fresh food. She hoped.

Or more doctors. This Seth was going straight into quarantine, in the west wing of the facility. Haydee and Katla would stay in the south wing. The capsule would stay on the farthest small landing pad, under a quarantine tent.

They should keep this Seth in the tent with it, Aimee Five had said. Less mess.

More work for everyone else, Sofia responded. Just put him in a clean room, and seal the doors. For as long as necessary.

Katla figured that meant until he was safely loaded into a shuttle for transport off the planet. But both shuttles were currently up at the platform, unloading cargo. It would be days, at least, before they returned. If this Seth did prove clear of poisons—at least to life on Arkhide—it was up to her what to do with him.

Katla and Haydee barely had time to get all the pieces of the hazmat suit on before they heard the clamor of six drones buzzing at slightly different frequencies coming in. Viram had taken off directly after unloading, and Arcan had gone to power up and prepare a quarantine room, leaving the two of them as welcoming committee. Probably for the best, if this Seth was a typical Co-op.

The drones waited for another bot to lay out a big tarp below them before setting the capsule on the ground. Katla winced at the force of its landing. The capsule's gray-white shell was streaked with green algae, its bottom level speckled with sand. The two window-portholes were intact, but water must have gotten in, because they were fogged.

Katla and Haydee stomped around to where the entrance was, facing away from the building. Whoever piloted the drones had done a good job; it wasn't twenty steps to the correct door into quarantine. They waited.

And waited.

Katla looked at Haydee, whose face looked like it was in 3 parts through the odd tripartite window of the suit's helmet. Haydee shrugged. Did this Seth need an invitation?

He wasn't responding on any channel. What if he was injured?

Katla called to ask Arcan to send a floating stretcher. She stepped up to the door. She knocked on it with her gloved knuckles, three times.

She heard an answering knock. Three times.

She looked back at Haydee. How stupid was this? Why didn't this Seth use his comms array?

Forget it. She waved at Haydee to step back, and stepped to

the side of the door. Then she punched the button on the side of the door that read, emergency egress.

The door hissed, and then the whole thing popped forward, a hand's width away from where it was. Then it dropped. It hit the ground at vertical, giving Haydee another moment to back up even farther. Then it fell flat, shaking the ground under them.

Good thing the tarp was big.

The first thing out of the capsule was a camera drone. And the second. And the third. They whirled around the capsule, whirled around Haydee, did not seem to notice Katla, and arrayed themselves facing the capsule's opening.

Seth appeared. A tall human, brown skin, eyes, hair probably. Right now, the hair was straw-bright yellow on the shaved sides, green neon for the long tresses flowing down the center and onto his upper back. He was in a Co-op tan atmosuit, with the helmet off, obviously. He'd brushed his hair, and the glitter along his temples also looked fresh. He waved to the cameras in the royal way.

"Welcome to Arkhide!" He pronounced it ark-high-day.

"It's ar-keed," Katla said, hoping she wasn't in the picture.

"Oh! I didn't see you. Could you step back a bit? You're in the shot." He ducked back into the capsule.

Katla stepped forward. She looked inside the capsule. It had benches instead of separate seats. She didn't see any blood, or vomit. She did see a duffel bag being zipped closed.

Seth stood up. "Better to have the bag, anyway. Looks like I planned this." He turned around and saw her. He waved his hand in a shoo-ing motion.

Katla swallowed her indignation and went to stand with Haydee.

Seth appeared at the door again, his duffel slung around a shoulder, his other hand doing that inane sideways wave. "Welcome to Ark-heed!" he said.

At least he was a fast learner.

He jumped to the side of the fallen door, and landed gracefully. He pulled out a tablet and started poking at it. The drones started to wander in a pattern, cameras on, she assumed. Katla watched them go, bemused.

"Hey!" Haydee was not bemused. "You, Seth! You're under quarantine. Pack up your toys and follow me."

Seth looked a question at Katla, as if to say, is she serious? It was as if no one had ever forced him to do anything in his life. Katla did not roll her eyes. Instead, she swung her hands toward the building in the sign for "this way."

Seth's huff came from his chest, lifted his shoulders, and sent his eyebrows arching. It also got him moving—either that or Haydee's scowling presence striding towards him. She passed, and he followed, not too close.

As he started moving, actually taking normal steps, she could see he was hurt. Something about his hip, or knee, on the left. She ordered the float stretcher to convert to chair, and caught up to them. She caught Seth's attention, and waved at the chair. Want it?

He nodded, and the chair buzzed into range. As he sat, gracefully, relief washed over his face. "Might need an aspirin," he said. "You know, if you have that sort of thing."

Of course, there was one in his escape pod. There was always an emergency kit. How did he not know that? She shook her head as she pushed to guide the chair into the building.

Down a warm cream hall, toward the only room that had lights on. Haydee stepped to the side, and Katla pushed the chair across the threshold of a small dormitory-style room. Single bed, galley kitchen with what looked like a dozen quick-make dinners stacked on the counter. Small bathroom to the side. Small outside window, where she could see a drone camera peeking in.

Haydee pressed a button on the door panel, and the force field came on, trapping Seth on the other side. Another button turned the hall's decontamination shower on over the two of them. Seth watched the shower with interest.

Feeling somewhat safer, Katla unlatched her helmet and took it off. She was sure her hair did not look its best.

"The diplomat herself!" Seth said. "I am honored."

"Right," Katla said. "And why are you here?"

"Oh, that's a mistake. Just a little one." Seth crossed one leg over the other, settling into the chair. Katla told the chair to sit down, hard.

"Woah! Sassy piece of furniture you got there. Anyway, there's this big debate up on Utopia. How does your safety-net thing work? It blocks so many transmission. We almost missed you altogether! But I saw it, a tiny wobble of nothingness where something should be. They told me I wasn't 'interpreting the readings correctly.' Well. I was right about that, too." He crossed his arms and nodded, once, in agreement with himself.

"Anyway," Katla prodded. Haydee, still off to the side, rolled her eyes. She hadn't taken her helmet off. Probably the best idea —wouldn't want both of them infected if there was anything bad lingering. Katla told herself she trusted the decontam unit.

"Anyway," Seth continued, unperturbed. "I said the net was porous for objects. Candy said—she's the chief scientist, and a very cranky person—she said if it blocked signals it would block objects too. So I went out to see.

"I wasn't planning to drop by, so to speak. I was just going to send a drone. But the gravity caught me. Forgot these flying bubbles are so underpowered. Anyway, have you seen my drone? I could use some wide shots."

Haydee threw up her hands. She turned and walked down the hall, back to the dressing room.

"Your drone is dust," Katla said. "You are wrong about the net. It also stops meteors and weaponry."

"But not people," Seth said, tapping his chin in a parody of thoughtfulness. "Kind of a flaw, in terms of protection, isn't it?"

Katla growled softly but kept her expression calm. "We weren't expecting an invasion."

Seth perked up. "Is that what I am. A one-man invasion? Won't my family be proud. They believe I don't have a martial bone in my body. How relieved they will be that I can be just as dangerous as them."

Katla was done. "Great. So, over there is water and some prepared meals. Bathroom's where you see it. All the water is drinkable. Stay hydrated. Oh, and there is a scanner in the drawer beside the bed, there, see it? Run that down whatever parts of you hurt, and it will send the data to our doctors. They or we will be back with help, once we know what's wrong." She turned to go.

"Wait! You're just going to leave me here? Don't I even get net access, or something? You do have a CommNet, don't you?"

Katla put her fake smile in place before she turned back. "Surely you can use your tablet and the connection to Utopia?"

"Actually, no." Seth finally looked abashed, sort of. Mostly pouty. "They've disconnected me. They're kind of mad."

Katla set her hands on her hips rather than throw them up in disgust. "I'm not surprised. Seeing as you started our negotiations with what in Cooperative space would be a declaration of war."

"It was a mistake!"

Katla turned and walked away, ears closed to him.

CHAPTER
TWELVE

SETH'S INJURIES WERE MINOR, a spray of big bruises and maybe one sprain but probably not. By the time Arcan got there with analgesics and a splint for the knee, the Cooperative buffoon was dead asleep.

"I pushed them through the door," Arcan said. "So he'll find them when he wakes up. Wasn't sure if you'd told him about the pass-through panel yet."

Katla and Haydee had chosen to stay in one of the family suites: four tiny bedrooms and a big washroom on one side, with a living area and a full kitchen with a dinner table on the other. It looked like every hotel they'd ever been in, with a stronger scent of antiseptic. Even the furniture was freshly extruded tan and orange.

Arcan settled on one of the comfy chairs and Haydee dropped onto her back on an extremely orange sofa. Katla went in search of snacks. The same ready-meals were piled up on their more-capacious counter. At least there was more than water in the cooler.

"Miso noodles or crunch sticks?"

"Crunch sticks," Haydee said. "I need to expend some energy."

"Red juice or blue? They're not labeled."

"Bring both. We'll do a taste test."

Haydee made space for Katla on the sofa. "Can you handle this Seth on your own tomorrow?" she said through a mouthful of crunchies.

"Why? Where are you going?"

"I need to catch up. That very efficient Assembly assistant just sent me a year's worth of reading about treaties."

"All the Assembly assistants are very efficient. My mom's just sent me a new, thousand-page High Galactic grammar." Katla sighed. If only she had someone to practice with.

Haydee sat up. "Hey, I bet our Seth speaks High G. Lay your fresh grammar on him."

"He's not our Seth. He's the Co-op's man."

"Oh, right. Why would he help us."

Katla frowned. Why not? "If we promise him freedom. Limited freedom, yes. Where can he go on this island?" She looked at Arcan. "Are you listening, Arcan? What do you think?"

Arcan's gaze came back to her. "He's clean so far. Just the usual bugs and viruses, nothing a good wanding and a couple of shots wouldn't take care of. But Katla, what do you know of him? Why is a person like him even on a research vessel?"

"Takes all kinds," Haydee said. "The blue is better."

"Is not," Katla said. "That's not even a natural color for juice." She called up a screen and input "Media Presence Seth is on the Edge."

Haydee laughed. "You capitalized Media Presence."

"Wouldn't you?" Katla was distracted from that debate by the hundreds of video posts keyworded with that name.

Arcan leaned in. "Share the screen a little bigger, would you,

Katla?" She did, and pushed it toward the far wall so they all could see.

This Seth had been traveling the stars for at least the past year, now with a mining group, now with a ship of emigrants. And now with these scientists. Almost every week, he posted a short vid or audio clip illustrating their days.

They watched a few. Seth would open with a walk-on, introducing the topic, then he usually disappeared from the images. He showed how astronomers knew how to color new space images, how garbage was handled on a military transport, how hull-repairers modify their suits to make them easier to move in. Another series, Travels with Seth, were more like travelogues in the old-century style.

Haydee pointed at one of those. "That's what he wants to make here. A tourist brochure."

Katla shrugged and drank more of the green juice. "Pretty clear he's not a spy. Everything about him is on the surface."

"Maybe not," Arcan said. "People like him make the best spies."

THE RAINS STARTED OVERNIGHT, thick, sharp, and thunderous.

Katla loved it.

Tucked cozy warm inside a building overdesigned for safety, she felt the rumbles in her bones. Flashes of light cracked the near-black dark outside her window in the tiny bedroom, throwing brief images on the wall beside her. She tried to make a picture from the reddish afterimages in her vision. Fired-up mountains, dancing.

The weather watchers predicted two whole days of this, the only variety being winds that would be mildly raging or fully raging. There was a reason no shuttle landings were planned for this week.

And no reason to have to rush to decide what to do with Seth.

As if she had conjured him up, his image flashed from the screen on her wristcom, which she'd left on the table beside her.

He was throwing himself at the force-field door, banging his head against it every time. His hair was wild, his eyes wilder. He slammed against the field, again and again. He was hurting himself.

Katla picked up the wristcom, waving the image a little bigger. She turned the external comm on in Seth's room.

"Seth. It's Katla. What's wrong?"

He whipped his head around, looking for the speaker. "Get me out of here!"

"Are you ill? Is it withdrawal?"

He shook his head, frustrated. He started banging at the force field again.

"Stop! You'll hurt yourself. I'll be right there."

By the time she had yesterday's tunic and leggings on, he had sunk to a tiny ball against the wall, as close as possible to the doorway. Heading out of her room, she nearly collided with Arcan. They caught her by the upper arms and swung her gently toward the living room.

"I was just going to get you," she said. "What is it?"

"Can't tell from the ambient readings." Arcan waved at hand past their eyes as if shooing a bee away from them. "Racing heart, shallow breathing, sweat response. It could be many things." They waved her toward the outer hall. "Go and I'll catch up. I need to pick up my medkit."

As soon as her feet hit the main hall between the building's wings, Katla remembered her feet were bare. The beautiful stone flooring, its colors popping with each sizzle of lightning, was freezing. Luckily, the wings were both floored in recycled rubber, a little warmer, a little more forgiving. She ran past the prep and service rooms. Seth's was the first dormitory room in the wing; the longest walk from the door they'd entered in this afternoon but the shortest from the main hall.

She put a hand out to the wall beside the door to stop herself. He had not moved. Katla crouched down, and then sat cross-legged, in front of the doorway. All the lights in his room were on full. She could barely see the lightning through his window.

"Seth. Can you hear me?"

"Get me out of here," he might have muttered.

"What's wrong?"

"What's wrong," he whispered. He lifted his forehead off his knees. "What's wrong!" he shouted at the room. He rocked to the side, unwrapping his arms from around his legs. He crawled on hands and knees toward the opening. Toward her.

His face—the part not shrouded by a tail of bright hair—was rigid. The eye she could see was glazed. He could not keep his shoulders from shaking.

Katla didn't know how to help. She shouldn't touch him, but how would she know what was wrong? He was broadcasting his panic so strongly she was starting to panic, too.

"Seth! Talk to me. Let me help you. Did you eat something wrong? Are you missing your medicine?"

A flash of lightning close enough to strobe through the window of even a brightly lit room raked Seth's back. He winced. At the mighty—and long—rumble of thunder that followed, he squeezed his eye tight. He held his hands so tight the nails must be digging into his palms.

He was afraid of storms.

Katla let out a breath of relief. This, she could deal with.

She flicked her wrist, and the comm sent up a screen. She calmed her voice, trying to shade it into superfriendly. "Hey, Seth. Take a look." She waited for him to look up.

He took a shaky breath. It seemed to take a gargantuan effort for him to lift his head up. But he looked at her.

She waved toward the screen. "This is us, here, see? Landing Island. Next door is Samata, where I used to live. Maybe we can go visit there while we're here.

"Okay. Here's what's happening outside. There's a big storm, yeah. See how we're right at the edge of it? It's going to pass all the way across us, east to west. It might stall over us for a day."

"Why?" His voice barely above a whisper.

"Oh, you know. Heat dome. Which means it will stay warm here, which is good. Sometimes when the wind blows so strong here it can chill you good. So, watch." She set the map to show the hours and pushed the image predicting the storm through each hour of the next day.

"A whole day of this?" he whined. Katla winced, but had to count it as an improvement.

"Two at the most. But then, whoosh. It's gone. And then we can go outside."

Oops. She hoped Arcan could clear Seth in time for that promise to come true.

Seth leaned his shoulder against the wall by the doorway, tucking his legs to the side. Katla tried pushing her screen through the force field, so he could manipulate it, but it started to dissolve. She pulled it back.

"And here? Where we are?"

"Inside here, you mean? It is solid-solid. Triple-thick windows, double-thick walls. It's withstood two typhoons that I know of. Probably more. We had to come and smooth out the landing strip again after one storm, but the building was perfectly intact."

That piqued his interest. He tilted his head, frowning slightly. "Why? I mean, super, but isn't that an unnecessary cost?"

Ha. "Not here on Arkhide," she said. "We build to last.

Especially this kind of building, that isn't used but a couple days a month. When we need it, it's got to be here." She didn't say that new building lately had grown even more solid and safety conscious. Once Arkhideans knew they were on their own.

Suddenly, he jerked back from the doorway, eyes going wild again.

"What. Is. That?"

Katla turned to see what he was seeing. Arcan.

Of course.

It was the middle of the night. She didn't have the energy to deal with two phobias.

Katla reached up and pulled Arcan by the hand behind her and to the side. She motioned for them to sit against the wall, out of Seth's range of vision. She steeled her voice to remain calm and light.

"Oh, that's just one of our helper bots." She squeezed Arcan's hand, hoping they understood the signal for I'm sorry please don't say anything. Distracted, she reached for something to keep Seth focused on the conversation and not the wondrous storm outside. "So, you don't have thunderstorms on your home world?"

Argh. She would have hit her forehead with her hand, except Arcan kept hold of it.'

"On Zichi? Not like this."

Katla swallowed, hard. "You are from the Cooperative home world?" She glanced at Arcan. Who was this Seth?

Seth waved at the window. "My home is opposite yours. One massive continent. And our water is a lot tamer." He pushed his tail of hair out of his face and smoothed it toward the nape of his neck. "Why didn't you terraform?"

Katla's hackles rose. "Why didn't you?"

"Zichi is old and settled for millennia. You all are recent immigrants, I understand. You could have had it done before you started moving in."

Bossy piece of Co-op trash. Katla was about to give him a sharp piece of her mind when another thunder quaked. He shivered, and she remembered why she was here.

"Most of us left places that wanted us to be reformed into their image of correctness. It seemed wrong to do it to a whole planet. Besides, we're just stewards of the land here. Lots of life lived here already. Anyway, how are you feeling now?"

"I could really use a double sake bomb right now."

Arcan snorted softly. They rummaged around the bag and pulled out a strip of tablets. They tore two from the strip, still safely sealed and held them out to Katla. "Benzo."

"I've got a benzodiazepine. Are you allergic to those?"

"Yes! No, I mean, not allergic. I usually take two."

"Perfect. Look to your right. Your other right. See the box in the wall? That's a pass-through. I'm putting the pills in there now."

Seth was so tall he didn't need to get off the floor to open the square door. He pushed the carousel-style platter inside the wall around, and took the pill pack. He apparently did not need water to swallow them down.

"Fifteen minutes, usually." He looked at her. "Will you stay?"

"Okay, but we have to switch to High Galactic. I need to practice."

"Seriously?"

He sighed. A massive thunderclap shouting out only made him blink.

"Greetings and hopes for the health of all your family," he said, complete with the proper hand gesture. "How did you fare on your journey to our beloved city?"

CHAPTER
THIRTEEN

THE STORM still whistled its monstrous tune at mid-day, when Katla managed to drag herself out of her cozy warm bed. The bitter cocoa scent of fresh coffee lured her out of her room and into the kitchen. A clear box of savory pastries sat on the counter next to the pot of elixir. Real food! A delivery drone must have made it through despite the bluster outside.

Haydee sat reading her tablet at the plain white rectangle of a dining table, her cup half-filled and looking cold. "Top you off?" Katla said.

Haydee gestured a no. Katla sat down the table a ways so as not to bother her, but Haydee looked up and set her tablet down anyway.

"I never thought I'd say it, but you are no longer the planetary champion of sleeping in. Our most-favored guest has not yet stirred." Haydee, of course, was a morning person, perky and bright. Katla always volunteered for the late shifts, savoring the dark and the quiet.

"Nice," Katla said, meaning Haydee's use of High Galactic. She didn't match it; too early for that. "But he's been doping.

Took a benzo in the middle of the night." At Haydee's raised eyebrow, she went on. "Scared of storms. Plus being locked in."

Haydee nodded grudgingly. Katla took the first bit of a pastry that turned out to be hickory protein and sage. It mixed perfectly with the lingering coffee aftertaste. Unexpected bliss.

She flicked her wristcom, pulling up a screen to catch up on her messages.

"Don't do that," Haydee said. "Enjoy your breakfast. I'll fill you in." She waited for Katla to wipe the screen down. She held up four long fingers, their tips freshly painted black. "Because of the storm, no one is coming to look at the capsule for another day. The bots have wrapped the whole thing—tent and all—in some magically impermeable wrapper. Don't ask." She pushed her baby finger down.

"Two. Because of the storm, the cargo for the shuttle will be late. It includes a complete medical facility, apparently plug and play, and nobody wants to take chances with that." The next finger curled into her palm.

"Three. Because of the storm—see a pattern?—we are having trouble getting a connection for our guest to speak to his shipmates. Actually, Aimee Five thinks it is not because of the storm. She thinks the Utopia has sent home for instructions and is waiting for a reply."

"Makes sense to me," Katla said around a mouthful of pastry.

"Yeah, but Aimee says we should force them to start negotiations now. Scare the pants off them, she says."

"Do they even wear pants? Seth has a kind of skirt thing, all wrinkly from the suit."

"How do you know that?"

"Told you. Night terrors."

"Could have been his jammies. But then," she tapped her chin with her one remaining extended finger. "He probably didn't pack an overnight bag. Anyway," she pointed the finger at Katla.

"Four. You will find a message from your mother—the one up in orbit. It will contain an impossible treasure hunt of a list of things for us to find and bring up with us."

Katla groaned. Mama Claire was an artist, and a chef, and a knitter. And she wouldn't trust anyone but family to obtain her always-critical materials. "How long is this list? Did you see it?"

"I did not. But your other mom said to warn you, so it must not be good. But," Haydee threw her arms wide. "Thanks to me, you already have one thing. She wants a rocking chair. Says facilities built for synths do not meet the needs of human spines."

Ugh. Outside, a flash of lightning mighty enough to strobe all the way into the kitchen was closely followed by a stomping giant of a thunderclap.

"You said it," Katla said to the storm.

HAYDEE HAD MISSED one important message, from Arcan.

Seth could be released from quarantine.

Arcan came into the kitchen from the outside hallway door, a miniwagon piled with waxy boxes of food floating in their wake.

"Have you weighed in yet? Only thirty minutes to go." They knee-checked the miniwagon into a lower cupboard and started unpacking the big box of cold stuff first. "Peach lassi. Somebody knows you're here, Katla."

Katla knew a backhanded request for assistance when she heard it. She mock-groaned herself up and out of the surprisingly comfortable straight-backed chair and took her now-empty saucer of coffee to the pot. More later. She grabbed the dry foods from the other end of the miniwagon and started filling an upper cabinet.

"Enough for two?" Haydee said. "And weighed in on what?"

"Plenty for all. What to do with our honored guest, of course."

Haydee swiped at her tablet "Wait. we get to vote on whether to shoot him back into space without a capsule?"

Arcan smiled at the tofu block he was setting in the chiller. "I voted to let Katla decide."

What? Katla, bent over the miniwagon, stood up so fast that she cracked her head on the cupboard door. She reeled. "How is that an option?" Of course she knew how: somebody had added it to the options list. Anybody could.

Arcan reached into the pocket of their tunic, a pretty blue with the symbol for medicine stitched on the right shoulder blade, and pulled out a med scanner.

"Put your hand down," they told Katla. "And stand still. They waved the scanner past what was sure to become a mighty bruise near Katla's temple. "You'll be fine."

Fine. Katla set the rice on the shelf hard. Her balance must be a little off. She went to the coffee pot for a refill, flicking her wristcom on as she stepped. Sure enough, there was an active thread in the gigantic conversation channel titled "Cooperative First Contact" about what to do with Seth now.

Agreement was above ninety percent to get him off the island as soon as possible. Only three percent wanted to kill him. Pretty good considering the Cooperative would kill a good forty percent of their population—all the synthetic humans—on sight.

One debate was if the diplomatic team—Arcan, Haydee, and her—should travel with him to the other landing island. Almost exactly opposite their position on the planet, South Landing Island was experiencing less-severe weather, but it would take them up to two days to get there. Katla voted against that idea.

"What do you think of the idea to take our honored guest back to Macadere and make him help clean up?" Haydee tapped a spot on her tablet, probably voting for that. She's had a list of tourist spots to hit in the capital city and all they had ended up seeing was a communications station.

Katla shook her head slightly, scanning for that thread "He should stay here. Away from people. You didn't see how he reacted to Arcan last night."

"Rude," Arcan said.

"Ignorant. And terrified. He was terrified of everything last night."

"Not you," Katla said, grinning at her. "What were you wearing?"

"Yesterday's clothes that I left in a mess on the floor. And cranky face."

"Bet you were using your soothing voice."

"She was, indeed," Arcan said. They lifted the last of the boxes—more pastries!—from the miniwagon. "It was quite effective."

Katla couldn't spare them a thought. She'd found the thread Arcan was talking about. Mom Sofia had started it, so it must for be some political reason. But a lot of people were agreeing with her, and were convincing others to change their votes. Some argued that Katla was on the scene and would have to make decisions quickly; she couldn't wait or wade through long threads of deliberation. Many said it was traumatizing to think of anything to do with the Cooperative; they didn't want to focus on it yet knew they had a responsibility to weigh in.

The saddest messages were from the synths. Instead of their usual screens-long analyses and bullet-pointed arguments and tricky what-if scenarios, many were leaving one- and two-word replies. Mostly to the can't-focus messages: *I agree. Yes. Please.*

Please protect us.

Katla didn't want the weight of all this responsibility. But she knew she could handle it, with Haydee, and Arcan, and Mama Claire, and Mom Sofia. And, she was sure, Aimee Five and her mighty assistants. She wouldn't have to make the hardest decisions on her own.

She was in the best position. She had the skills. She had the support. She would have a direct line to the Assembly and all its experts.

It was up to her. She had to do it.

Katla tapped into the thread and added her vote. And her comment.

I agree.

CHAPTER
FOURTEEN

KATLA WAITED for the room sensors to tell her Seth was up.

And then waited twenty minutes more.

She should have waited longer. When she arrived at his door, he was still in the tiny bathroom. He had not made his bed, or opened any of the food packs, or even made coffee or tea. She settled down on the floor outside the door and opened a channel.

"Seth, Katla. I'm here at your door. When you're ready."

In the next ten minutes, Katla worked her screens, managing to scare up mama Claire's special yarn in two of the three shades she wanted, and sent a message to their friend Celina to see if she had the third. Everybody said mom Sofia was the picky one, but that was because they never had to live with mama Claire.

When Seth finally slid open the door and stepped out of the bathroom, he was perfect. His forest-green skirt—or maybe it was culottes?—was neatly pressed, his hair tousled and sassy, and his sparkles on. He'd swapped his shirt for an Arkhidean tunic in a complementary shade of orangey-red. With the green-and-yellow hairstyle, he outshone the room, the building, and everyone else. Easy to see why he was a Media Presence.

He sketched a short, single-leg out bow, complete with fluttery hand. Very formal greeting. Katla scrambled to her feet, closing her screens, feeling rumpled and drab.

But in control.

Until he opened his mouth. "Your choice in foodstuffs is subpar, Diplomat Katla. Is there anything else on offer?"

She crossed her arms. "I was going to invite you to have savory pastries in our suite, but perhaps those, too, would not meet with your approval."

His eyebrows rose, the sparkles at the corners of his eyes also rising. "I am to be freed?"

"You are cleared from quarantine. You are not a danger to Arkhide. We're ninety-six percent sure we're not a danger to you."

"Excellent odds." He crossed the room in two long strides. "Lead on, madame diplomat. And might I also be freed from the torture—" he stretched out the word into four syllables—"of High Galactic?"

Katla's mouth quirked before she could stop it. It was going to tough to remain a fierce and formidable planetary negotiator in the face of this colorful scarecrow. "Yes. For now." She cut the door's forcefield, and waved a hand through the doorway to show it was off.

Seth flicked his wrist. Four of his tiny drones lifted from the duffel beside the bed. They formed a loose halo above and behind his head. He rolled his shoulders back, straightening his already good posture, and strode through the door.

Katla waved down the hall to show him where they were going, but he signaled that she should go ahead of him. "Do you need the drones?" she said. "We're just walking down the hall."

"Every part of first contact is critical," Seth said loftily. "Who knows what the people back home will find interesting."

Katla lifted her wristcom and sent a voice message to Arcan

and Haydee that they were about to be recorded and was that okay. Arcan assented immediately. Katla could hear Haydee's screech from the central hall. Then her okay came through.

Neither was in the main room when they arrived. Katla sighed, relieved. Arcan could be so considerate. Seth took a step inside and stopped. His drones roamed the living area, focusing on the sofa for some reason.

"Tell them to stay out of the bedrooms," Katla said, gesturing at the tiny hall to the sleeping areas. "Kitchen is this way. Coffee? Tea?"

"Coffee," he said. The drones gathered back, and they all proceeded into the kitchen. Katla showed Seth how the coffeemaker worked, making a pot for four. She opened the cupboards, and the cooler, describing all the foodstuffs available. She almost closed the cooler door on a drone. They were so nosy.

Seth wisely chose a savory pastry. Katla put two on a plate, and one on another plate for herself. She handed the plates to Seth and waved toward the table. He set them in the Cooperative way, opposite each other on the long edges close to one of the short edges of the table.

As Katla was preparing the tray with the coffee fixings, Haydee slid into the kitchen. Fresh-brushed hair, sky-blue tunic over unwrinkled trousers, she grabbed a bottle of lassi from the cooler. Katla set the tray to the side of her place, and started serving. Haydee settled at the table in Arkhidean position, on the short edge between them. Seth leaned slightly away from her, but, she suspected, not enough to be noticeable in the drone's field of view.

"I'm Haydee. The other negotiator. Katla says you're aces at High Galactic."

Seth took the saucer Katla offered him, swirled the coffee around the edge, sniffing gently. "Ambrosia," he said, and took a sip. "But it's not really coffee, is it?"

"We call it coffee," Katla said. "You call it a kind of tea—matcha?"

He nodded, and turned to face Haydee. "Greetings, negotiatrix Haydee," he started in High Galactic. "Yes, High Galactic was actually one of my mother tongues."

"Seriously?" Haydee set her bottle down. "I didn't think that was possible."

"It is with the old families," Seth said. "Which brings up a point I wished to make last night but forgot in my ... distraction." He savored another sip of coffee. "You don't need to practice Hi-G. We won't be using it in the negotiations."

Haydee looked at Katla, who shrugged. It was news to her, too.

"I mean, you'll need it for reading the contracts, of course," Seth said. "But for talking we can use plain Galactic. In which you're both fluent, I see."

"Why not?" Katla said. She'd spent hours practicing and relearning grammars. She called up the Cooperative message to be sure. "It says here all negotiations in High Galactic."

"Sure, they usually are. But it's really the chief negotiator's choice."

"And the chief negotiator is always on the Co-op side," Haydee said. "Right?"

"In this case, yes. What is this amazing pastry called? I've never had anything like it."

"Breakfast," Katla said, impatient. "Explain what you mean."

Seth did something to his wristcom. "Turned the drones sound off."

Haydee glared at the closest drone. "You mean it was on?"

Katla winced. "Sorry. I didn't know that. I would have asked about that, too."

Seth held up a hand to block the drone from seeing his mouth. "This is the thing," he said. "I am the chief negotiator. If I hadn't been on the Utopia, it could not have been seconded to this mission."

Katla frowned. She held up her hand to block the drone's view. "You're that special? You're a Media Personality."

"Media Presence," Seth said. "I am also." He paused. "The quiet child of the Regent. You know, the Cooperative's current head of state."

CHAPTER
FIFTEEN

HAYDEE JUMPED UP, knocking her chair back to the floor. Katla stemmed her impulse to do the same. She gripped the edge of the tabletop so hard the fingers sank a tiny bit into the semi-soft material.

Haydee looked at the drone, hovering. Recording. She picked up her chair and settled back into it. She glared at Seth.

"You could have said something."

A quiet child was one sent to foster in another family, usually for safety but also if there was some other trouble in the family. It was a Cooperative thing, but had been adopted by many of its satellite worlds.

"I couldn't," Seth said, his mouth still behind his hand. "It's need-to-know. I wasn't raised in the Central District. I'm the spare's spare. Hardly anyone knows what I really look like. I was hoping it would stay that way, forever"

"But you couldn't resist the limelight," Haydee sneered. "No low-key lifestyle for you."

Seth dropped his hand and picked up the half a pastry

remaining on his plate. "You'd be surprised how lonely being a spacefaring Media Presence can be. It does have its entertaining moments though. You would not believe all the words and phrases people use to describe my mother."

Katla let go her grip, and touched her wristcom.

Seth stretched across the table, almost grabbing her hand. "Don't tell anyone!"

She gave him a cold stare until he drew his hand away. "I'm Arkhide's representative," she said. "I'm not going to keep secrets from my people."

"Put it on main-channel," Haydee said. She seemed to enjoy Seth's look of horror.

"I'm not doing that, either," Katla said. "Honestly, you two. I'm sending a message just to my mom and Aimee Five. With a label: Eyes Only." She grinned at Haydee. "I've always wanted to use that one."

Haydee rolled her eyes.

———

LUCKILY, the heat dome did not materialize. Everybody needed to go outside and take a deep breath.

The howling wind had dropped to a mild whistle, and the rains were tapering as Katla, Haydee, and Seth walked out the main door of the facility. By the time they reached the close landing pad, five minutes away, skies were clear. Seth wanted to see his capsule, a thirty-minute walk. They had plenty of day left, though Katla wished she'd remembered her polarizing shades. The far landing pad was directly west of them, and the white-orange blaze of the setting sun right at eye level.

Her mother and Aimee Five had both written back to say they would discuss and get back to her. They agreed to keep the information need-to-know, at least until Seth got off the planet. From some points of view, holding a member of the First Family without their leave could be considered an act of war. Even if he did do it to himself.

Haydee headed to the supply buildings to see what manner of vehicles were available. Katla and Seth took off for Seth's capsule. They walked along the shuttle's strip, in the pounded-down sourgrass, fragrant in the moist air. The sturdy grasses would pop up again overnight, prettier but harder to walk on. Katla hadn't worn shoes—way too much mud—but Seth had dainty spacer feet, so they'd scared up hard-soled boots for him. Their khaki brown did not match the greens of his outfit, he noted sadly.

He was missing a lot. The cool watery grass roughed up her toes and the pads of her feet, while the black mud smoothed them out again. At least he could smell the grass, the loam, the weird tang of the runway composite. Some people used sourgrass as a garnish, but Katla preferred seaweed, when she could get it.

Seth's drones fanned out, some low, some going high to get the terrain view. On a rise, Katla pointed to the south, at the purpling peak was the island of Samata's volcano. Seth sent a drone to take a wide shot. He was careful to match her shorter stride until they came within sight of his capsule. He didn't seem to notice when he left her lagging behind.

As Haydee had reported, the capsule was wrapped in wide swaths of khaki. Bands of the waxed cloth were wrapped across and across again until the sphere—even with its bumps and projections—was completely covered. Seth didn't stop until he'd reached the capsule, until he had his hands on it.

"Don't know why I care," he said when she caught up to him. "It's just a pod from a ship I've been traveling on."

"Did you have more stuff inside?"

"No. Just." He paused, running a hand along the edge of one

of the wrappings. "Wanted to see something familiar. I guess." He rested his forehead on the wrappings. "This is all a bit much."

Katla turned and leaned back against the capsule. Her wristcom pinged, and she took a look. Two nice sail craft with solar engines and a bunch of smaller boats suitable for fishing, Haydee reported. Any one of them could get a couple of people over to Samata.

Katla looked across the pounded-down grasses to the hint of water in the distance. "I want to show you my home. One of them. It's on Samata, just next door. Will you go with me? Tomorrow."

Seth lifted his head, blinking hard. "I would love to."

First things first. On the way back, with the sun warm on their backs instead of burning stripes in their eyes, she brought it up.

"Synthetic people. You know we have them here."

Seth jammed his hands into the front pockets of his tunic. "I heard. You keep them on their own islands?"

"Of course not. They live wherever they want," she said, a little too hotly. She shook her shoulders slightly to settle down. Seth wasn't the only one with triggers when it came to synths.

Katla looked out at the runway whose materials synths had designed. They would be taking a watercraft with an engine whose capacity had been multiplied threefold by a synth engineer. When she was a little girl, she wanted to be a synth, so clever, so competent. Sometimes, she still did.

She started again. "Last night, you had a lot going on. When my friend Arcan, a synthetic human, came to bring you the benzo, you reacted harshly."

Seth stopped and closed his eyes. The crickets were starting to sing their evening song. After a long moment, he opened them and looked at her. "I don't remember. Probably the benzo."

"That's logical," she said. "What I need to know is how you will react today."

He shivered. "Can't it stay away from us?"

Katla forced herself to observe how the nearly horizontal rays of the sun touched the grass like a drop of watercolor. He didn't know any better, she told herself. Maybe he can learn.

"Arcan is staying with us. Me and Haydee. I was going to invite you to bunk with us, too. But if it will be a problem, you are welcome to stay in your own wing. There are no synths there."

Seth bent to pick up a long blade of the grass, one that had bent too far and broken. "You want me to stay away from it."

"What I want is everyone to live in harmony. I understand that is not the Cooperative way." Katla winced. Not quite diplomatic, that.

Seth squeezed the blade of grass up, between his thumbs, and blew a breath through them. The whistle went low, then high. Katla was tempted to scoop up a broken blade of her own, but she wanted to make this point, not show she was the better whistler.

"In fact," she said, "You're wearing Arcan's boots."

Seth came to a dead stop. He stared at his feet.

"Do your feet feel poisoned?" she said.

He looked at her and half-laughed. A good start? She pushed on.

"I think you would feel better with more people around. Those quarantine rooms are quite sterile." She had to chuckle at herself. "That actually is their purpose, yeah."

Seth tilted his head, considering her. His drones drew closer, all but one forming an arc around him. Katla bit her lip.

Something decided, he nodded once. "How about this? You get me net access—not to your systems, just to the outside—and I'll play nice with your synth. There's just one, right?"

She looked out, toward the sun, so its bright light would stop her from rolling her eyes. "There are twenty-some thousand. But only one currently in the building with us."

He looked around, scanning the horizon. Looking for synthetic human patrols? "No problem, then."

He didn't sound as confident as he probably thought he did.

CHAPTER
SIXTEEN

AFTER ALL THAT, Arcan didn't show for supper, even though they had made the fish casserole that was sitting in the warmer, ready.

Neither did Haydee. She'd taken one of the skimmers out for a test run and twisted her ankle dragging it back up the beach. Arcan was practicing medicine on it, which apparently included playing one of those intricate puzzle games they loved to devise. The pair of them would be up all night, apparently in the med center.

After a quiet supper, Katla and Seth so deep in their thoughts that conversation remained at the "this tastes nice" level, they went to the quarantine wing to fetch his gear and bring it to the suite.

Back in the last remaining open bedroom in the suite, Seth dropped the duffel onto the bed and immediately started setting up a kind of physical editing suite for video. The screens weren't as good as hers.

Once he had his rig set up, and Katla had gotten his link to the

Utopia's long-distance band cleared through the protective nets and Utopia's comms chief, he settled behind his screens, put fat sound-muffs over his ears, and started working with single-minded focus.

Katla took that as her signal to finish off her mom's shopping list. Celina did have the right yarn, and was sending it to the shuttle-prep station directly.

The assembly had agreed to fast-track the shuttle's return. The station would not be quite ready for humans—it needed the shuttles for final outside work—but getting Seth off-planet was the priority. Weather permitting, the shuttle would arrive tonight and be ready to leave tomorrow night. The shuttle's pilots liked to have at least two days between flights, but they agreed with the priority and so would send extra crew to work through the safety protocols as quickly as possible.

If all went well, Katla would be off-planet tomorrow. Going to fight with the Cooperative.

Everything suddenly seemed way too real.

"Might be a good thing, meeting this Seth ahead of the negotiations," Mom Sofia had written. "Try to find out everything about him, especially his weaknesses and pain points."

Katla hated thinking like that. When she was little, fighting with Olve about some slight or some unfair sharing of cookies, Sofia would tease her. "You always want the solution to be win-win. It so rarely is, peanut."

Rare didn't mean never. Why not now?

WHEN MORNING CAME, Seth was again the last one up. Katla was in the kitchen on her second coffee and third text exchange on Aimee Five's admin channel when she heard him in the washroom. Haydee was on the couch in the living room reading, Arcan in their usual chair doing whatever they were doing.

Seth stomped to the entry to the living room, and froze. His color today was magenta, with grays as complement. Katla considered telling him to change into something that might withstand an ash-swirl, but decided she'd give him a raincoat instead. The magenta matched the high color on his cheekbones.

After a moment, Seth came one step into the room, his attention fixed on Arcan. Arcan remained still, facing the back window, apparently in thought but probably reading some medical text.

Seth cleared his throat. "Arcan, is it? Pleased to meet you." His voice was steady, but he didn't come closer. He bowed slightly instead of grasping hands or forearms. Katla stood up, to be ready, for what? She wasn't sure.

Arcan turned their head, slowly, to face him. Seth tried not to react; the flinch was slight but easy to read. "Seth," Arcan said, voice flat.

Katla raced to Seth's side. "Well, that's great. Seth, why don't you come into the kitchen with me? We have a porridge that you can dress however you like." She reached for his forearm and gently tugged. He didn't move. "And coffee," she said, a thread of desperation already creeping into her voice.

"One more thing," Seth said. Katla's heart sank. Seth cleared his throat again.

"I wanted to say thank you." His voice choked off. He swallowed. "For the loan of the boots. Very generous."

"Accepted," Arcan said, in a slightly warmer tone than before.

"Great!" Katla said. "Porridge, this way." Seth let himself be led into the kitchen. Katla cast a glance back at Haydee. Her friend arched her perfect eyebrows.

GETTING Seth into the skimmer was another unexpected problem. He balked at the shoreline, and claimed he didn't know how to board a boat already in the water.

Katla groaned as she pulled the stern back to the edge of the sand. "Your planet is mostly water, too. And you're afraid of it?"

Seth lumbered onto the craft, clumsy for once. His boots hit the deck like an explosion. Katla flinched. The hull wasn't so thick as all that.

"We avoid it," he said. "It's dangerous."

"So is land," Katla said, pushing the boat off again. She waded with it until the warm water was knee height, then hopped in. Haydee had left the sheets out, so it took only a minute to get mainsail and jib up and secured. Light wind, regular, not too gusty. Only a little chop. Clear, beautiful, semitropical day, nothing like the day before.

"Trip takes about an hour. You'll want to watch for this part, the boom. It swings back and forth with the wind. I'll try to remember to tell you when it's about to swing."

Seth nodded, and almost lost his balance. His forehead was damp.

"Not feeling so great," he said. They weren't even to the deeper water. Katla had forgotten that some people got seasick.

But Haydee hadn't. The emergency kit had ginger chews, and wristbands with buttons that somehow worked. She gave both to Seth. His sickness must have been mild, because he was sitting up and launching his drones only minutes later.

Katla was glad Seth was busy with his cameras. It gave her time to be herself, on the water, thinking free. Of course, all her thoughts swirled around him. Find his weaknesses, her mom had said. So far, he had nothing but weaknesses. Thunderstorms. Open water. Synths.

But he could overcome them all, too. Would she have done as

well, faced with fear after fear after fear? Unearned confidence can only take you so far, she'd thought, but here Seth was, planting a stake for the Cooperative into their recalcitrant world.

CHAPTER
SEVENTEEN

ON A FLAT MAP, Samata Island looked like a crescent pastry. In person, the land was far more steep, rising quickly to jagged black and bright-green mountains ranged along the edge of its long arc. Its central volcano, once its highest peak, now had a cratered top. All that earth and ash had been shot into the air and onto their little town during the last eruption.

No one had been hurt. Their multiple warning systems were top-notch, and the last human left the island with days to spare. The last synths, who had gone building to building with heat sensors to make sure everyone was clear, were off with eighteen hours to spare.

Katla had been eight, and it had been a grand adventure. Usually they had to move islands because of earthquakes—a little wobbling now, her moms had said, that could lead to a lot of wobbling later. This was the first time gas and smoke and fire sent them on their way.

She'd liked living on Samata, studying hard and then running free the rest of the day. Before she found out she'd never be like the other kids. Before the disaster of Wala changed everyone's vision of the future.

The beach had been rocky before, thanks to an eruption sometime in the past. Now, boulders that looked like black coral also dotted the span—and surely lurked under the waves. Luckily, the water was relatively calm and clear today, and whoever had been here last had marked a good path through the rocks with nightglow yellow paint. Katla headed in close, keeping an eye on the rocks above and below the waterline. The wind stayed steady all the way in. She dropped anchor.

Seth's drones roamed high above them. He was hunkered down to avoid the boom, poking at a screen projected from his wristcom.

"You might want to take a look for yourself," Katla said. "It's beautiful."

"In a minute," Seth said, jamming a finger at the screen. "I can't get the swoop right. Wide low on the water, and then up a little over us, then big and wide. Don't look at the camera!" he said as Katla turned to watch the swoop. "Do that thing where you're reaching for the rope that goes into the water."

"The anchor line?"

"Yeah. Good."

Katla sat on the gunwale, leaning over, one hand on the line —completely unsailorlike—and waited for her director to call "Cut." The water below them teemed with shallowfish, darting here and there, trying to kiss the hull. Eruptions on land often led to an explosion of the number of plankton and tiny fish, eager to munch on the new minerals and deposits exposed. They drew shallowfish and their friends—and perhaps bigger friends, too. This shore was too shallow to see any of the big swimmers, though. Perhaps undersea life migrated like life on land did—only toward the volcano, not away. She liked that idea.

"Got it," Seth said. He dropped the screen and looked up. "No dock?"

"Yes, it *is* rugged and beautiful," Katla said, hoisting a small supply pack onto her back. "See those lumpy rocks? That's from the volcano twenty-five years ago. When I lived here, we would play on the smoother boulders, beyond, see? And we'd have to almost swim to get out to an anchor here. The island has gained a new swath of land thanks to the eruption.

"And yes," she continued. "You have to take two steps in the water. Or try to jump from the front of the boat."

Of course, he was going to try that. Katla finished tying off the sails while he was judging the distance. She scuttled back to the rudder, to try to keep the boat somewhat steady after his jump kicked it backwards. His jump was graceful, and successful.

He looked at his wrist, and then turned around to face her, hands on his hips. "I have to do it again. The big pole was in my shot."

Katla slid into the water, only knee-high and warm from the sun, and stomped up to meet him. "We'll do it on the way home," she said, knowing they would not. She checked the sky. Clear and crisp, just as the predictors said. "Do you want a tour or do you want to wander?"

"Wait," he said. A drone zoomed down at them. Katla stepped behind Seth. Let that little cannon ball hit him first. He nodded, ready.

"So. This was a town of about six thousand folks when we found out the volcano was waking up. The town actually started there." She pointed to a single row of smoothed boulders, about two meters away. "When I lived here, that was the last of about a two-meter-wide collection of smaller boulders. All the rest are now under the new ash. The new sand."

Katla navigated the sharp, unpredictable stone-coral and stepped onto the new, black, glistening beach. Her thick-soled sandals sank only the smallest bit. "The wind has swept the lightest ash away here. We'll see it up farther."

They crossed the expanse of beach to the first houses. Even with the winds, at least a half-meter of ash and rock sat on the angled roofs. The gray matter had pushed its way inside, drifting to the sills of the windows. Most homes here were one-story, with an attic space. They looked like charcoal-topped mushrooms.

A drone zipped inside one. "Why didn't you come back?" Seth said.

Katla didn't answer right away. She led them to the left, counting the houses until they reached where her road should be. Sixteen houses up, she found it.

Her house had almost none of the walls showing. Just a hint of its bright coral pink. It felt weird to stand at the same level as the attic. And it didn't smell right—no cinnamon, no vanilla, no cocoa butter. Just a faint touch of charcoal and freshly turned dirt.

She squatted in front of the peak of the roof. "This was our house. Four bedrooms, two main rooms, kitchen." She swept away some ash from under the peak, exposing a hand-sized ornament made of yarn. "My mom knitted a bell, here, because she had one back home. On Wala. But we didn't need a real one here. I had my wristcom to call me home."

She heard the drone coming up behind her, and blinked back the tear before it fell.

Seth crouched down next to her, reaching for the bell. "I'm surprised your mom didn't take this with her. Did you have to flee?"

"Not at all. We had days to pack. She must not have remembered it. Or maybe she couldn't reach it. We're a pretty short family."

"And no one came back?"

Katla stood, clapping the ash from her hands. "Not worth it. Yet." She brushed at the roof, exposing one of the wrecked tiles.

"We use solar, mainly, for power, see? And that was all buried or wrecked. Also, volcanoes that erupt might go off again soon, and nobody wanted to be here for that. But this new ground will prove very fertile. We'll probably be back in another couple decades."

Seth still had a hand on the homemade bell. "Take it with?"

At the thought, Katla's heart skipped. The tears burst out. So much had happened here. So much good. She missed it.

Just as quickly, the tears subsided. She kept her face turned from the camera. Seth hadn't moved it.

"Good idea," she said.

Seth unlatched the ring holding the ornament to the roof, and shook it hard. After the ash poured out, the colors returned. It had been a rainbow of colors; only the brights of the dyes remained. He lifted it so the camera could get a clear shot, then moved toward her. He unzipped the small pocket on her pack and tucked the ornament in.

Katla slid one of the backpack's straps down, and swung the pack to her front. She touched the small pocket, but opened the larger one. She took out a thin canteen, turned, and held it out to Seth. He took a gulp, wiped the mouthpiece with his sleeve, and handed it back to her. The water tasted extra fresh after an hour on the ocean and a stroll through the ash.

"How are you feeling?" she said, tucking the canteen away. "Need a breathing mask? I've got a couple. No gases anymore, but the ash can bother people, too."

"I'm fine. We have sandstorms at home, so I'm used to it."

"I thought your world was one big continent."

"Right, but that makes the inside—well, most of it, really—a desert. We all live in the fertile ring, only going in a few hundred clicks from the shoreline."

Katla looked back, at the bay. "And still, you don't make use of the seas?"

"Our seas aren't as safe as yours."

Katla shook her head and started walking up the street. "Ours are off-limits, too, except for the shallows and the shipping and travel lanes."

They slowly made their way across to the main street, and through the town. It was just as steep as Katla remembered. She pointed out the bakery, the yarn works, one of the open-air schoolrooms. Good thing it had rained last night; the ash was mostly solid under their feet.

Most of the buildings were only half submerged, but at the upper plateau where the big community rooms were, the ash had collected more. All she could see of the biggest dining hall was the round window under the eaves.

"We gathered here to eat and discuss stuff and play music and games." Katla put her palm on the wall. beside the window, miraculously still intact. "Touch." The building was made to retain the cool of the night, but now it retained heat. "Dig down only a little bit here, and you'll find pockets of warmth. Still."

"You all ate together?" Seth sounded shocked.

"Mostly. People could always eat at home, of course. It started when our humans first arrived here, almost sixty years ago. Everybody had a lot to do, setting up towns and comms systems and farming and all. It was more efficient to all eat together. And more friendly. And I guess we've just kept doing it."

"What about safety?" he said.

Katla swiped at the drone in her face. "What about it?"

"You haven't said anything about police, or courts, or jails."

"Oh. We don't have much problems like that, so far."

He looked shocked.

Katla searched for a way to explain. "So, we're a chosen community, right? Nobody came here who didn't want to come. We don't have the crime I see on your entertainment shows. Everybody here had to agree to certain ground rules to gain passage." She frowned. "Well, except the little ones. Maybe we'll have a problem later?"

"Wait," Seth said. "Nobody ever breaks the rules? Not at all?"

"Oh, sure they do. People are going to disagree, right? Mostly we just handle it by debating on the comms streams, and the wrong-doer agrees to some restitution. The worst thing would be to send someone outside all communities." She looked around. "I guess we could send someone here. But I've never heard of it being done."

"How idyllic," Seth said, but it didn't sound like a compliment.

"Anyway," Katla said, wiping her hands together to free them of ash again. "This is what I wanted to show you." She slowly swept her arm in a circle from the dining hall. "The hospital. The backup generators. Battery storage. The comms network building."

Seth and his drone followed her lead, looking across a flat stretch of ashy dirt. "I don't see anything but baby green plants."

"Exactly! All those buildings and instruments are portable. We took them with us when we left for the new town. Minimal waste. And that's why nobody's coming back here soon."

Seth raised an eyebrow. "The whole hospital?"

Katla nodded. She walked to a smooth patch of sand near where the hospital used to be. "Like this," she said, squatting down. With a finger, she drew stacked squares and complementary rounds. "Each room, almost, is a separate component. They are built in these easily attached units and come to us one by one as we need them. For instance, we didn't need a separate obstetrics facility on this island, because most of the pregnant people stayed on our home planet for the first few years. I was born in the central city, and I was one of only five born on this whole planet that year. The rest of the people here who are my age now immigrated to Arkhide."

"Must have been lonely for you." Seth's magenta cuffs were all dusty.

Katla shrugged. "Not really," she said, but it sounded like a question. "There were plenty of people around. And I did have one friend my age, luckily."

She stood and swept her arm toward the bay. "So beautiful. It was wonderful living here. We sailed, and begged cookies from the bakers, and snuck into places we weren't supposed to be. Oh." She looked up the hill. "There's one more place I want to show you, but it's a bit of a hike."

"Lead on," Seth said. "If I can't make it, my drones certainly can."

CHAPTER
EIGHTEEN

SETH DID MAKE it all the way up to the jutting natural perch high above the town, but at the cost of his fine clothing. Ashy dust coated him crown to boot. It sparkled in his ponytail hair. It covered the many small rips that Katla heard forming as they scrambled up the tiny winding path. She probably looked the same.

But it was worth it.

Plant life had rushed back to this area, drawn by the generous amounts of rain and sun here. And not as much ash: The sooty specks had filled the space here only to about knee height. And the building, a castle that looked like it came from an earlier century, was completely intact. Dark clinging vines with tiny red seed-bulbs had claimed the first meter of visible wall; bright green moss had claimed the second-floor windowsills

Seth sent his drones scurrying. "Who ever put a stone keep up here? Even to the parapets."

Katla squinted at the building. It had always been gray, and really, didn't look that much changed. "Parapets?"

"Those up and down parts along the roof." He shrugged. "I

was wild for castles with I was small. Some of the terminology seems to have stuck." He patted the strong wooden doors. "Think we can get in?" he said, voice as eager as she'd ever heard it.

"Got a shovel?" His face fell. "Wait," Katla said. "I thought of something."

She led them around to the back of the building. The emergency exit stairs, metal with a generous coating of ash, looked as sturdy as ever. She and Olve had snuck into the building when they were littles using these stairs.

"There's an overhang over the second-floor entrance, there," she said. "Might not be as tough to get that door open."

Katla's legs didn't want to cooperate. They had had enough of ash already. Seth put a hand on her shoulder, and she stopped on the second step.

"I'll take the lead on this one," he said. "But first, wipe my face clean. Cleaner."

He was going to make a production of it. Katla decided she didn't mind. The castle deserved the effort. She took a startlingly clean cloth from Seth and brushed lightly at his face. He had to lean down for her to reach his forehead. The sparkle powder by his eyes emerged, as intact as the castle. She smiled away the comparison.

Intent on his drones and his wrist, Seth didn't notice except to say thanks. He stepped on each stair with a sort of sideways kick, moving a good swath of ash from the tread. Katla gratefully stepped in his footprints all the way up.

Seth used the same kick-sweep move to dislodge the small piles of ash from the doorway. The solid wooden door was unlocked, but it took the two of them to drag it open. Seth walked through the door, a drone just behind his shoulder. Katla waited for them to clear, and then came in herself. A sense of outlaw, of transgression, shivered down her spine.

The balcony—stretching down three of the four sides of the square open space below—looked the same as ever. Still no railing; it didn't have to conform to human safety codes because humans weren't supposed to be in here. The wall hangings were gone, leaving the beautiful stonework exposed. Almost no ash had touched the interior. The tall outer windows, looking out to the bay, had shattered and let a little in, but it would have been only blowback ash. The shutters on the windows downstairs had held.

Seth, drone partner in tow, strode down the balcony toward the huge windows. They gazed out at the beautiful view.

Katla joined them. "You can easily see the new parts of the island," she said. "Both ends of the crescent are far longer, but skinny. Also, the path of the main flow, from our left to the right. Down the deepest valley. Or it was the deepest valley."

Seth shook his head. "Such power."

"This was a mild one. A lot of ash and rock and steam, but not enough to carry so far it affected the atmosphere. And hardly any poisonous gas. We have a couple that we know will belch up sulfur as acid. When that happens, everything living nearby suffers."

"Terrifying," he said.

Katla frowned. "Essential. Without the blows and the flows, we wouldn't have such marvelous cropland. Plants in the ocean wouldn't bloom enough to feed everybody." She shrugged. "It's a small price to pay. So long as everybody gets aways safe."

"If you say so." Seth's drone flew up to where the broken window would have been, and through it. It made a wide sweep of the view.

The angle of the town reminded Katla of the slope of Mt. Awala. She called up her data feed from the monitors on that slope. The dome had arched a centimeter. Might be something, probably not. Still, she packaged a moment of data and sent it to

Macadere Island's lead volcanologist, in case they were still off-island at the twin eruptions.

Seth turned back to the inside view. "This building seems safe enough. Not portable, like your hospital. What's the story here?"

Katla smiled, remembering. "It was a side project. For a while, people were wild to try all manner of building, from domes to houseboats to stilt houses—as if lava flows were only monsoons. A group here wanted to see if they could build in a supra-old-fashioned way: stonework without mortar, arches with keystones, all that." She led Seth around the corner to the wide stone stairs down to the main room.

"It took the longest time to find all the stones. Finally, friends of the builders started sending barges piled with stones from their own islands. News and images about the building of it ruled the social nets for months. Every little bit was worth talking about." She stepped onto the main floor. "And once it was built, everyone came to see it. Once I saw a couple hundred people in here, having a debate."

"Your first tourist attraction," Seth said. He took the last step too short, and stumbled. "But its proportions seem off."

"Well, yeah. It's not built for humans."

That stopped him. "What?"

"Yeah. We called it the synth clubhouse, back when we were littles. They built it to see if they could, not to serve a purpose. But once it was up, and obviously sturdy, they gave it a purpose. They called it The Aerie. I was so keen to see inside.

"But humans weren't allowed in. The synths wanted a space totally for themselves, here in this majority-human community. So we snuck in. Stupid kids. We got in plenty of trouble after." At the look on Seth's face, Katla snapped out of reverie.

"Why would robots even care about construction techniques?" he said.

Ignorance. Katla looked for the camera, and faced it squarely.

"Maybe they don't," she bit out. "But synthetic humans certainly do. Why wouldn't they? They live here, too."

Seth just moved on.

The light pouring in from the bay windows made it easy to see where the furnishings had been removed. The castle was bare. Only dust danced on the smooth wide stones of the floor.

Seth pointed his cameras at details over the main door and along the risers of the stairs. Katla showed him where the elevator was, but it had no power so they couldn't see if it still worked. She went back to the bay windows as he finished shooting. He spent more camera time here than anywhere else on the island. And they hadn't seen the best part

When he joined her at the windows, she asked, "Want to see the roof? Best view of Landing Island. I would come here to watch the shuttles land over on the island."

But the higher they went on the outside stairs, the deeper in ash they got. The roof was covered, not even the tallest benches visible. Mini ash dunes in very slow motion. They stayed on the stairs, which had an obstructed view of the other island, and Seth sent his drones up to get the better view. Unexpectedly but deeply disappointed, Katla didn't wait for him, but stepped on their old footsteps down to the ground to wait.

She' d spoken so casually about change. But sometimes, it would be nice if some things could stay the same.

CHAPTER
NINETEEN

THE SHUTTLE LANDED while they were sleeping. A massive, long, thunder in the night, but Katla, Haydee, and even Seth slept right through it.

Arcan had done it. "It's a new protective force field," they said when Katla stumbled out to breakfast and saw the ship. "Not only did it shield the building from potential crash debris—which will never be necessary, touch ash—but it dampened the sound. More than expected. Not even our morning bird Haydee woke up."

Haydee again sat on the sofa staring at her screens, but as Katla moved to the kitchen she got up and followed. "Hard to believe, I know. Anyway, want the rundown?"

"Coffee first. Any pastries?"

"Two, stale. From yesterday."

Good enough. Katla grabbed them and a mug of still-hot coffee and plopped herself at the table. Haydee slid into the seat catercorner. "Good news," she said. "Claire says the base is minimally ready for humans. We're go for launch anytime." She pinched a corner from one of the pastries and popped it in her mouth. "Interesting news," she said around the pastry. "Your mother Sofia is also coming with us."

"What?" Katla choked on her own pinch of pastry. That wasn't in the plan. "But she can't even talk with them. She's fully enhanced." Beyond enhanced, probably.

"She's not staying, apparently. There's a non-Cooperative cargo hauler just docked, and she's bringing them something or receiving something, I don't know. Intentionally cryptic about it, if you ask me."

Sounded like her mom: Wheels within wheels. "So, she's carrying something supersecret, going to drop it off for shipping, and then coming back?"

Haydee shrugged. "So her assistant says. The assistant might even be coming. Her synth assistant. I couldn't get clear on that either."

"Politics," Katla said. "That's it?"

"All your deliveries for your mom Claire are here except one box of yarn. Scheduled to arrive with the fresh food, last thing before we leave."

Good news. "And when is our departure?"

"That's the bad news," Haydee frowned, looking at the half a pastry remaining. Katla waved her assent. Haydee pinched another piece. "We have a window. Everyone has to be stowed in four hours."

"Four hours! The cargo's not even all in yet."

"We need to go in before the last of the cargo does, remember? But." Here Haydee paused for effect. "If the cargo is more than a few minutes late, or some other thing that makes us not a go at the right time, a storm front will encroach too far into the flight path. And then we sit there until the storm lets us go. Maybe five minutes, maybe half a day."

"Who decided that?"

"Your mom." Haydee gave Katla a look. "She is a force of nature."

Katla sipped her coffee for a moment, looking at it from Sofia's point of view. "She thinks we'll dawdle—no, she really uses that word—because there's no set flight time. So she's set one. Basic operating procedure." The orange-flavored protein in the pastry overwhelmed her tongue, but the coffee made the flavor perfect.

Steps sounded in the hall. Seth, today in a deep blue with gold accessories, nearly bounced toward the coffee pot. Haydee leaned back to get a better view of the tunic. Something on it was pulsing, lighter gold then darker.

"How many more outfits do you have?" she said.

Seth turned. "Like it? I can make the golds change in four patterns." He demonstrated. The last pattern—a strobing effect—made both women reel. "Or I can turn it down."

"Or off," Haydee said.

Seth harumphed, but the tunic did go quiet. He rummaged in the cooler and pulled out the last of the lassi. He poured it neatly into a glass before he brought it to the table.

"To answer your question, this is my last full look. I need to do some laundry."

"No time," Katla said. "We're leaving in three hours. Maybe two."

Seth jumped up from the seat he had just settled down in, panic in his eyes. He downed the lassi in one gulp while moving toward the sink. Then he was out the door.

Haydee looked at her, and winked. "Basic operating procedure."

"Guilty."

KATLA NEXT WOKE in a strangely sterile bed under a soft white knitted blanket in a large room with three other beds and many, many instruments arrayed around walls painted a peaceful blue.

Hospital.

"Welcome back!" Haydee bounced into her vision. As Katla started to sit up, Haydee jammed another pillow between her and the headboard to help. Luckily, since her head started to spin, already dizzy trying to make sense of this. And throbbing.

Dehydration.

"Drink up," Haydee said, handing her a drink-bulb of orange-flavored electrolytes. "What do you remember?"

Katla sucked the drink dry, not even tasting the sweetness, and reached out for another. Haydee took the first and slapped another gently into Katla's palm. "We were boarding, strapping in. Seth and I were arguing about who would get the window seat." Was the throbbing easing already?

She closed her eyes, to remember better. "I felt squished, crowded by all the stuff packed behind us." Trying to fit Seth's capsule into their payload, the shuttle techs had come up with a plan that involved taking down the bulkhead that divided the hold from the seating area—and taking out most of the seats. The change kept the pod intact but meant that only one row of people could make the trip this time. Not only that, but everyone had to wear spacesuits for the whole trip, so the techs wouldn't have to figure out how to keep the gigantic hold filled and flowing with breathable air.

The capsule, still wrapped in its protective tent of material, was last in. First in was the equally bulky but squared-off medical facility. If Katla reached a hand over her head, she could touch it. If she reached down into the aisle—she'd taken the aisle seat, avoiding the argument altogether—she could touch the wrapped cables that would connect the medbay to other parts of the station.

"Then what?" Haydee waved a third drink in front of her, but Katla was still on the second.

"Liftoff. Wow! I thought we'd pushed our limits rocketing the hopper to Macadere, but this was so much more. I felt squished, but in a different way. Very fun."

"Yes," Haydee said. "You were cheering up a storm, and your smile almost stretched to the sides of your face, thanks to the force. Shoulda took a picture. Then what?"

"Then." Katla frowned. "Nothing." What had happened? Her heart stuttered. She grabbed Haydee's arm. "Is Mom all right? Did we crash?"

"We didn't do anything, Kay. It was all you." Haydee sat on the edge of Katla's bed, holding her friend's hand. "Before we knew what was going on, your mom called it in as an emergency. You scared the whole planet! But then Arcan recognized it, and right away knew what to do." She looked guilty, and then said, "Arcan's with your moms right now. But nobody's hurt!"

Katla shook her head, confused, and then regretted it. "But what did I do?" she whined.

"You're allergic—or something—to no-G. As soon as the thrusters cut off, you started convulsing. Your eyes got so red! You were looking at me so desperate and I didn't know what to do, because you were in the suit. And so was I, and so was everyone!

"But Arcan recognized it. They programmed your suit to knock you out. It lasted a little longer than we thought, but here you are. Safe and sound, pretty much. And your eyes will get better. I think."

Katla lifted her arm and let it drop, the sleeve of her tunic following close, to try to isolate the feeling of the gravity in the room. "I float in water just fine. And fly in hoppers, and all."

"It's a fluke. A genetic flukey thing." Haydee squeezed her hand. "No big deal. But listen to this: As soon as everybody knew you were going to be okay, the med chat boards lit up. All these theories, all these arguments about it. Was it something to do with your allergy to implants? Something about being born on Arkhide? You are one tasty medical puzzle tonight, Katla Sofiasdotter."

"Great," she said. Another crap way she was special. "Well, at least Seth's gone. His capsule was first-off, and if I'm in our shiny new medbay, he must be long gone."

"Well," Haydee said, drawing the word out.

"What?"

"Seth said you promised him a tour of the new base. I didn't know!" Haydee held up her hands. "And then your mom—Claire —thought it might be a good idea, so the Co-op flunkies can know what to expect when they come here. So he's in your room, as the guest, and we're bunking together."

"Supra. But didn't my mom—Sofia—say that we didn't have enough food to keep him here?" She looked pleadingly at Haydee.

"You know you don't want me to talk to him." She looked up, toward where the entry door usually was. Katla considered turning her head to see, but her neck vetoed the idea.

"Get ready for the drones," Haydee said.

CHAPTER
TWENTY

KATLA WAS NOT ready for the drones. She sank down on the pillows and lifted the soft blanket over her head. The warm but whisper thin weave washed its mild lavender scent over her.

Her hip was suddenly cool where Haydee had been. "Where have you been?" she heard her friend say. She flicked part of the blanket down so one eye could see out.

Seth had not found the laundry. His blue tunic had not fared well being shoved into the spacesuit for hours. His hands raked the long part of his hair. "She's asleep again already?"

"Almost," Haydee said. "We're not supposed to tire her out, remember?"

"Not my fault! I asked the ship's computer where the medbay was, and it sent me up and down long hallways to an empty spot where the original one must have been. I had to come all the way back, just to find out the real one was practically next door."

"I told you where it was." Haydee crossed her arms and locked into her stiff, straight I-mean-it posture.

"But so much was going on!" He lowered his voice. "Is something up with Katla's moms?"

Katla pulled the blanket down to her waist. Her tunic was just as wrinkled. "What about my moms?"

Haydee reached to put a hand in front of Seth's face, but he dodged it, and frowned at her. Something had changed between them. He caught Katla's gaze, and his face softened.

"Your moms, Katla. Are they having trouble? I mean, relationship-wise."

"No?"

Haydee sighed, her shoulders sloping. "Weirdest thing, Kay. Claire met us after we had our suits off. You were still in the shuttle. We just left you sleeping until the medbay was ready. Anyway, Claire comes up to Sofia and gives her this big hug."

"They always do that. 'Hug upon meeting,' they call it."

"But then," Seth said. "They let go. And the way they looked at each other, like, I don't know. The air in the room dropped to freezing."

"That's a metaphor," Haydee said. "The temperature on the station is stable. No worries."

"And we couldn't go anywhere," Seth said. "We weren't sure where to go on the ship, right? What parts were safe and ready for us. So we just stood there, and they just stood there, glaring at each other."

"Talking in their heads, I guess," Haydee said. "It was excruciating."

Another thing for Katla to mediate, once she got out of the medbay.

"Luckily," Haydee said. "Sofia's already gone."

"What?"

"Yeah. She must have done whatever she needed to do with to that rogue hauler—"

"Independent shipping agent," Seth interrupted.

Haydee hadn't stopped. "And then quick caught the shuttle going down."

"Interesting that you have trade agreements with tricksy non-Cooperatives before you'll deal with us." Seth's brow raised, very telegenic.

"The emergency shuttle?" Katla frowned. That didn't sound good, either.

"Now it's our shuttle that's the emergency one. Claire had a new list of critical items, and didn't want to wait for the big one to recycle and launch." Haydee shrugged. "Seemed kinda wasteful. Our shuttle can carry so much more cargo."

Katla couldn't solve any of these puzzles while lying here in bed. She tried to push them to the back of her mind. "And your shuttle, Seth? It can take you to the Utopia?"

Haydee cut in. "Utopia doesn't want him."

"Yet," Seth ground out. "They are coming in to dock with us. Your base can make a good tunnel to ours, so I'm to wait until I can float over." He laid his hand over hers on the bed. "I'm glad you are improving. You scared us. I asked my captain about it, and he'd heard of it, too. Had a fancy name for it. Said it was really rare."

Whatever. Katla drew her hand away. "And the negotiations? When do they start?"

"Two days, maybe three," he said. "Depends on when you feel well enough to give me and my cameras a tour."

She sighed. She did not feel like getting out of this bed anytime soon. And if her eyes really were red, ugh.

"You can do it, Haydee," she said. "You've actually traveled on this ship, right?"

Haydee pushed Seth out of Katla's view. "We'll do it together, later. Now, we're going to help unpack the kitchen supplies."

Seth smacked his lips. "Good plan. Find those protein pastries, and figure out if they taste the same in space."

EVERYBODY WAS CLEAN AND PRESSED, eyes back to normal, the next morning when Seth fired up his drones. They started at the far end of the hallway of the base living quarters, where a window to the outside showed much of the rest of the base. Katla was to narrate, while Haydee, onscreen, performed any demonstrations.

"So, background," Katla started.

"Keep it short," Seth said, staring at his floating screen, which showed four camera views. Two drones hovered by Haydee, and two near Katla—one on each side of her head. She cleared her throat.

"We planned to build this base in stages. First stage was as a dock and storage, so we could tether mining craft and deliver supplies up and down-planet. Looking through this window you can see the oval of the dock, with a half-built miner-hauler. Building that hauler was the second stage, but we had to put that project on hold when the Cooperative called.

"The dock is attached, there, to the usual caterpillar-style main base. That's mostly warehouse space with a few modules that the crews live in. Two piers for visiting ships, and two for cargo ships. The mirrored wings are solar collectors, of course. That was it, until a month ago."

Seth frowned at the view. "But where do the people go?"

"In the crew areas. I told you. These first stages, all crew were synthetic humans. They were most eager to come up, and it was the quickest way. It wasn't until we got to stage five, after the giant main ring was built so it could provide gravity, that humans were going to come up.

"But here you all were, suddenly, on your way. Wanting to meet on the base. And we wanted to meet you here, too." Katla paused, and waited for a drone-eye to look her way. "We needed a human-worthy base right now, faster than actually possible. So here it is." She swept her hand toward the long stretch of hallway. The camera tracked her motion.

"Welcome to module Aurora, formerly passenger transport Aurora. Years ago, after the last of our people arrived here, we refurbished Aurora to serve as cargo transport. But we didn't take out the plumbing, so to speak. It's your typical transport. It has planting rooms, that we've had to re-start, kitchen facilities we had to reconnect, rooms for passengers, and the big meeting hall we needed for negotiations. Air, food, waste, safety, walkability. The only things we needed new were a medical facility—we'd scavenged that out right away to use on-planet—and fodder for the 3-D printers. And, ideally, gravity."

She stopped. "Short enough?"

Seth nodded. "We'll trim it." He waved at Haydee to start walking down the hall. Two drones tracked her, while a third zipped to the other end of the hall, stopping to catch a glimpse of one of the bunkrooms through an open door. They'd agreed to focus on what Claire and her team had changed about the transport, since everybody apparently rode in transports all the time in Co-op space and knew all about them. Everybody who watched Seth's vids, that is.

At the new permanent airlock, which connected the common-area level of the Aurora to the main base's innermost pier, Haydee went into action again. She demonstrated how, after the Utopia locked onto the same pier, farther down, her people could float comfortably and without rebreathers to the new airlock. Once in, the gravity took hold, and they could easily shed their safety equipment in the newly built entryway cupboards.

"From here," Katla went on, walking behind the drones that trailed Haydee down the hall, "the module looks mostly like the ship it was. We've redecorated the biggest meeting room for the negotiations. We cut doorways into the two adjacent rooms, so each team has a quiet place to gather. This is the Cooperative side."

Haydee waited for the door to slide open, and stepped through. The furnishings and decor did not hide the fact that this was once a small café, complete with a service counter, but everything was clean and comfortable and painted in the golden rod and bright yellow of the Cooperative. For a moment, Katla thought she smelled coffee, but it was surely an illusion. Or a craving.

Haydee waited for the signal, and then turned and walked through the door into the meeting room, a drone at her shoulder and another a meter behind her. She paced the three steps to reach the near end of the medium-sized dark oval of the table and set her hands on the high back of one of the gray padded chairs.

Katla's mama Claire had done all this, from safety to comfort, in a matter of days. At last night's supper, the first time Katla had seen Claire, her thick braids as long and jingling as ever, she'd marveled at how much she had accomplished. Claire waved the feat away with the flick of a hand. Not worth mentioning.

She wasn't really with them anyway, but deep in her internal feeds. Sure, she was busy, but she could maybe spend a little time with her Chief Negotiator.

"We want everyone to feel at ease, as much as they can," Katla said. "So we painted this wall opposite your negotiators in Cooperative colors, like the ready room. But if you turn, you'll see that the wall we will be facing is the sunny ocean blue of Arkhide. But best of all is down at the foot of the table. Floor to ceiling, a window on our world."

Haydee walked toward the glass and looked out. A drone angled out to catch her reflection in the window. Synth techs had double-glazed the three layers of glass, and double force-fielded the opening. It was worth it.

Seth waved at Katla to join Haydee. She took the side away

from the camera. Haydee was so tall and vibrant, surely no one would see Katla in her shadow.

Arkhide was so blue. And green, and white, and only a little brown-black. She could see it spin! Katla felt a pull, at her heart, as if the planet held her in its orbit, even up here.

A buzz near her ear gave notice that she had her own drone. She looked at it and winked, ruining the shot.

"Quit it," Seth hissed from the other side of the room. But the drone moved off, to sweep across the table and back into the Co-op's ready room. Katla tried to etch the image of Arkhide against the gray-black of space into her memory, and then turned back toward Seth.

"What else do you need?"

"What about the greenrooms?" His focus on his screens did not waver.

"Still a work in progress. Your capsule bumped the greens that were supposed to come up with us for planting. No peas for you."

"Hate peas anyway." A message crossed the top of his screen, typed out in red letters. Katla drew closer, but her skills in reading reverse-blur were limited.

But Seth saw her try. "Utopia wants me back. I'm to be standing at the hatch as soon as they dock." He shook his head. "Way too dangerous. No way my security would allow that."

"You have security?"

"Not here, no. I wasn't supposed to ever get off the ship. Ha, ha. But they did drill safety into me, so I know what they'd say."

"What about the thing with the capsule?"

"Anomaly," he said, wiping his screen back into his wristcom. "We're done, Haydee. Gotta go."

Haydee hadn't moved from the window. Her hands were up, almost touching the glass. Trying so hard not to. "I'm not leaving this spot."

CHAPTER
TWENTY-ONE

THE INITIAL MEETING was set for morning, Arkhide time; afternoon, Cooperative time. Two negotiators for Arkhide, Katla Sofiasdotter and Haydee Cooper; two from the Cooperative, Captain Elaine Manning and Special Envoy Sandreth diCimino. ("That's me," Seth had said as he was finally leaving for the Utopia. "Don't act surprised when you see me.") The meeting would be live-streamed to various channels on Arkhide and available later to media outlets in the Cooperative Realm.

Fifteen minutes before the meeting, the tension in the blue ready room crackled. Once a dressing room for stage performers, the space had too many mirrors and not enough chill. The blue on the walls was nice, but clashed with the odd brown of the sofas and knee-cracking end tables. There should be soothing music, but nobody could agree on what kind. Arcan sat quiet on the nearest sofa while Mama Claire picked at Katla's outfit.

Katla swallowed the last of her protein drink without tasting it. Her tastebuds also apparently disliked outer space. But her nose was on overdrive—the gel Claire had used to smooth her wayward hair gave Katla the impression she had turned into a pine tree. "It's calming," Claire said.

It wasn't.

Katla ran through the lists of must-haves, nice-to-haves, give-aways, and never-giveaways over and over in her mind. She could not forget a thing, or the planet would never get it, never have it, never be able to keep it.

She batted their hands away from her formal tunic and leggings. Her shoes couldn't be helped: Everyone wore practical, magnetic soft-soles that could grip floors and walls if necessary. But at least they were the Arkhide blue of her tunic and not the dull brown of her tights. Real officials wore black under their tunics, which was pretty much the only argument Katla had found for becoming an official.

Claire wore turquoise and black, Arcan a deeper shade of blue. Even Haydee was in blue, the palest shade that perfectly matched her eyes. She got the good posting, waiting at the Coop-eratives' airlock to greet them and show them the way to their ready room. That meant she could walk off her nervousness pacing back and forth along the pier while she waited.

In the Arkhideans' ready room, no one seemed their best. Claire, tight-lipped and looking unusually severe, forgot to kiss Katla good morning. Arcan must have reminded her, because she came bustling over a minute later, bracelets and braid ties jangling, to give her a peck on the cheek.

"Sorry, sweetie," she said. "No hugging. Don't want to muss your drape. Did you get the changes the assembly agreed on last night?"

"Yes, mama, and we both memorized them. Who are you listening to now?" she asked as her mama's eyes went glassy.

Claire's gaze snapped to hers. "The alarm. The Coop airlock has opened."

Haydee came racing in. "They shouted a message that no one

should be in the hall when they arrived, so." She shrugged. "I think there's more of them than we expected. I saw four shadows."

"We'll find out soon enough," Claire said grimly. She clasped Haydee's arms in formal salute. Arcan did the same.

Claire clasped Katla. She could feel her mama's tension through her palms. Claire finished the salute, but then set her hands on Katla's shoulders, pushing her back slightly for one final up-and-down inspection. She let go, and reached behind her neck to undo the clasp on her pendant, a stylized version of the seal of the Greater Assembly. A gift from Sofia. She reclasped the pendant around Katla's neck. The pendant fell near her collar-bone. Near her heart.

Claire stepped back. "Perfect. I'm so proud of you, Katla."

Katla swelled inside, hope and pride and determination. When Arcan's turn came, they slid something into her pocket.

"Real paper?" she said.

"Just a prayer. A meditation. If you need to take a moment during the talks. If you need to make up a reason to."

Katla stepped in front of the closed door and waited for the small light that would be activated by the opening of the Co-op's door to blink on.

They took their time.

She could feel Haydee's breath on her neck. "What do you think Kay," she whispered. "Should we synth it up? I'll do Arcan; you're better at Veerill."

"What?" Katla turned, her face full of shock. Who knew how the captain would react to that. If Seth was any example, she might flee and scuttle the talks.

"Kidding! You should see your face. Bet you're more relaxed now, huh?"

"If by relaxed you mean adrenaline spike, then yes." She turned back to the door.

"Worth it," Haydee said. Katla had to grin.

The light blinked on.

Katla squared her hips and rolled her shoulders back. She waved at the door panel, and the door slid open. She took a step through and waited.

The captain, a severe-looking person with tassels on her dust-colored stiff coat, was first in, followed by Seth—or rather Sandreth.

Katla tried not to gape. This Sandreth had dark hair that fell straight from a center part to sweep his shoulders. His irises were brown, his outfit was stiff khaki. There was no glitter, no bounce, and no smile. He looked thicker, somehow. She couldn't take her gaze off him.

His face betrayed no recognition of her.

"Pspsps," Haydee whispered, still in the ready room. Wake up. Katla came back to life, and performed the formal Cooperative bow. The captain's bow was shallower, less polite—or maybe less practiced? She matched the captain's two steps to the table and stood behind her own chair.

Now she could see the other people, four tall humans in gray jackets, armed with long gray weapons, arraying themselves along the blue wall behind the table. Startled, she turned back to her door. But the force field was already up and opaqued, to avoid the chance the Co-ops might catch a glimpse of any synthetic humans.

Haydee stood just inside the room, looking as stunned as Katla felt. The Co-ops had promised not to bring weapons.

Already they had broken a promise.

Not only that. Firearms were forbidden on the base. They were standing in tiny cans in the middle of a giant vacuum! Not to mention completely unnecessary and, really, unhelpful in peaceful negotiations.

Katla gripped the back of her chair. Should she call the

meeting off? She glanced at the far corner where she knew one of the live cameras was positioned. What would her mother do?

She'd tough it out.

Katla realized that Haydee still hadn't moved. Her friend's face was granite. What horrible memories was this stirring up?

Wala.

"Pspsps," Katla said to her as softly, as gently, as she could.

Haydee blinked. She turned her gaze from the martial lineup and toward Katla. Her face did not relax. She stepped, stiffly, up to her seat. She took in a breath, slow, to speak the greeting.

"Welcome to Arkhide," Haydee said in crisp High Galactic. She executed a flawless Cooperative bow, even to taking the full two seconds to reach the full depth. Arms at the perfect angle.

Body smooth as a synth.

The room seemed to shudder.

Katla caught a movement at the corner of her eye. Seth must have seen it, too, because he was moving that way. But he was blocked by the captain, who had pulled out her chair to sit.

The human standing on the far left had raised their weapon.

As Haydee rose, slowly, perfectly—even to her hands being entwined right hand first—the human made the gun roar.

Haydee collapsed backwards. Dark blood flew from her chest onto the chair. Onto the table. Onto the floor.

Onto Katla.

Katla dropped to her knees. She had to stop that rush of blood. She pressed her hands against her friend's chest. The hole didn't feel so big. It might be okay. But it would be bigger on exit. And Katla only had two hands, and they were busy.

Haydee's breaths were fast and shallow. Her hand closest to Katla spasmed. The other hand was bloody. She opened her eyes, seeking Katla. Finding her. Holding her.

"Stay with us," Katla whispered.

"What in the hell?" blared Seth's voice, higher pitched but still recognizable.

"Synths are neutralized on sight," a masculine voice said, wavering. Then, "It isn't synth?"

Katla might have heard Seth say no, but louder was the shoosh as the door behind her opened. Mama Claire was there, with actual compression packs. She slipped one under Haydee's back and slapped another over Haydee's chest. Katla pulled her hands away before the pack could trap her. She grabbed Haydee's hand. Her friend's eyes, so blue, so bright, had closed.

Claire lifted Haydee by the armpits and pulled her through the door and out of the meeting room. As her hand slipped away, Katla grimaced. She needed to be there, helping.

But Arcan was there, in the ready room. They were a real doctor, and they had a full medbay. Haydee would be okay.

But the blood. So dark. So thick.

So much.

As Katla pushed to her feet, she saw how much was on her. Wet and sticky, from her knees to her ankles. On her chest.

On her face.

The captain had not seated herself. They all just stood there.

Murderers.

Katla held her bloodied hands out, toward them.

"Get. Out."

CHAPTER
TWENTY-TWO

ARCAN WAS ALREADY in the medical suite, pulling the surgical bed frame out, gathering tools, unzipping the inflatable tent that would make the space around the bed sterile. When Katla arrived with the float-stretcher carrying Haydee, Arcan was priming the printer.

"We don't have enough blood," they said. "I can't reach her family. They must have been watching. Why don't they call back?"

Haydee's family were purists, and avoided enhancements. It didn't look like Haydee could avoid it and live. "They have to call," Arcan repeated, almost a chant. "Call, call, call."

"It's not enhancement if it saves her life. That's," Katla searched for the word, but her dictionary seemed covered in blood. "Repair?"

The stretcher pulled itself onto the frame and settled down. "The bed says immediate surgery," Arcan said, slicing Haydee's tunic with a knife so sharp it didn't make a sound. "Gotta get the fabric out of the wound, first thing. And I can stabilize her. But we need her family's permission to do more."

"Just save her." Katla tried to stay out of the way of the throbbing pressure pack. Tried not to see all the blood still seeping through. Tried not to notice the absence of breath.

A boxy synth bright medical-orange and about half the height of Arcan trundled up, towing a miniwagon with three big oxygen canisters. They started setting up at Haydee's head, forming the cannula that would feed her breath.

Arcan set a gloved hand over hers. "You have to let her go, for now. I'll take care of her. You go wash up and be ready for when she wakes up."

"Can you do this, on your own?"

"I have Arvee, here." Arcan waved at the boxy synth, now feeding material into the printer. "And I have the head of the surgeon's guild on the line." They pointed at an octopus-like tool that looked like it had cameras attached. "She says we have the right tools and can do this surgery."

Katla heard the hesitancy in Arcan's voice. "But?"

"But it would be better if we had time to grow a real heart, not just print one."

Her throat went dry. "Haydee needs a new heart?"

Mama Claire ran in, breathing heavily. "Got a sec?" she asked Arcan.

Arcan took a small step away from Haydee. "One second."

Claire called up a screen showing Haydee's mom and pushed it to face them. Amity Cooper usually stood tall and straight, but now was bent into herself, arms squeezing tight around her middle. Her eyes, so like Haydee's were wet and edged with red.

"Tell me, doctor."

"One shot, precise in its destruction," Arcan said. "The heart, but only the heart. The projectile missed her spine, even her ribs. Just a sliver of lung. But she needs a heart."

Amity Cooper squeezed her eyes shut. "Bruce collapsed when it happened. We were in the dining hall."

Claire pushed the screen away from Arcan. "No parent should have to see that," she said. Arcan looked at the printer, hidden within an opaque white box. It was making noises like it was printing.

"It's not our way, Claire." She hiccupped a sob. "We have to let her go."

Katla reeled. How could she say that? Haydee was right here.

"We should show Haydee to her," she whispered to Arcan.

They shook their head. "That would only strengthen her argument. And no, not you either. You're soaked in her daughter's blood."

She'd forgotten. No drape to the cloth now, the tunic was stiff and yet sticky. Bloody. Katla resisted the impulse to rip her tunic right off this instant.

Claire laced her fingers and cupped the back of her neck with them. "What would Bruce say, Amity? Would he be so eager to give up on his only daughter?"

"It's not like that! And you know it. And Bruce would agree. Only nature, never enhancement."

"It's not enhancement! It's therapy. Not improving, restoring."

"A new heart?" Amity's voice could cut obsidian. "An artificial heart. It won't be stronger than her own was? Won't last longer? Won't give her an advantage over her nonenhanced peers?" She said that last with a sneer.

Katla seethed. Haydee was right here, and they could help her. And somebody else said no?

"We have to wake her up," she said. "Ask her. She'd said yes."

Arcan waved a hand past Haydee's mouth. "She's barely breathing enough for life. Certainly not for consciousness."

They looked at Katla. "What we need is blood. We only have the all-type replacement liquid, and probably not enough of that. Go find out who matches her type among the humans here."

"You know that already! It's just me and mama." Katla felt the desperation in her throat, her voice, her heart.

Arcan shook their head. "Right. Forgive me. She's a good match; you less so."

Haydee's mother was upsetting Haydee's doctor. This had to stop. Katla steeled herself to let go of Haydee. She was going to explain things to Amity.

The tone of her own mother's voice stopped her cold. "Amity, please. Consider the question from Haydee's point of view. She has not formally joined your … community. Is this decision— your decision—truly what she would wish?"

"Don't play that game with me. Haydee is one of us. She thinks as we do. Exactly as we do."

"Katla," Arcan reached for her arm, clasped it. Their cool hand, usually so good at soothing, did nothing for her. "Amity's position is clear."

No.

Katla started squeezing Haydee's arm to the rhythm of her friend's favorite song. It was faster but in the same tempo as the heart-replacing beat of the compression pack. "Haydee, Haydee, wake up. Wake up! Tell us yes. Tell us to go ahead."

"Katla—" Arcan started.

"No!" She glared at them. "Haydee needs to decide. It's her —" she choked off. The breath she took in tasted of ozone and metal. Air for Haydee. "It's her choice. Her life. Hers."

Katla moved her hand up. She started squeezing Haydee's shoulder, staring at the so-still face. "Just a moment. Just a word. Tell us, tell us. Tell us yes." It was the lyric to the song, she realized with a sob.

"Amity—" Claire started.

"Stop it! Stop hounding me." Both mothers were crying, sobbing. "I loved my daughter. She was my life. And now she's gone."

Haydee stirred. She grimaced in pain. But her eyes did not open. Arcan reached for Katla. To push her away? Katla batted their hand away, glaring. She had to do this. She had to try.

"Just for a sec, Hay-Hay. We need to hear you say yes."

"Katla! That won't be definitive. She won't know what she's saying yes to."

"Will so." Was Haydee's breath deeper? Katla kept up the rhythm. "Recording on. "Hey, Hay-Hay. You got hurt, bad. We can fix you up good. But you have to say yes. Say yes to let us fix you. Can you say yes?"

Haydee's chest shuddered. Her eyes fluttered. She couldn't seem to get them open.

Claire wiped at her eyes. "Your directive is clear. I will inform the medical staff."

"Just the word, Hay-Hay. That's all we need. One word. Just yes. Yes."

Katla kept the beat going as she played the song in her head. On the second verse, she started to hum the tune softly. Maybe Haydee was singing it, too, in her own head.

If it must be, Katla hoped, let this be the last thing she hears. A song she loves.

Katla kept humming. Third verse.

Last chorus.

"Yes," sighed Haydee.

CHAPTER
TWENTY-THREE

YES.

"Permission recorded and logged," said Arcan. "Preparing for surgery."

Katla would never let go of her friend again. She leaned close to Haydee's ear. "Arcan's got you, Hay-Hay. You are going to feel so much better."

"Preparing for surgery," Arcan repeated, sterner. "Nonsterile people out."

Katla shot him a look. Never.

"Out. So Arvee can inflate the surgical theater." Arcan waved toward the washroom. "Clean up and get some rest. You're swaying on your feet. And you smell bad."

They were right. Not about the smelling bad, but the rest. But Katla didn't want to leave Haydee with nothing. She lifted the pendant over her head.

"If I wrap this up, can it stay with her?"

Arcan paused. "Give it to Arvee. Yes, we'll bring it back. We'll put it around her wrist. Now, go!"

In the washroom, Katla walked fully clothed into a shower

stall and opened the spigot. Cold water pounded her face, slapped her arms, and she was glad of it. Wake up! This must be a dream. A nightmare.

As the water warmed up, Katla started to thaw. First tears, dripping, rolling, gushing. Shaking. Sobs that ripped out from deep inside.

Suddenly, she could not stand her clothes. She pulled them off and let them fall. She stepped out of her shoes. She finally looked down.

The water was still running into the drain red.

But she was clean.

She was so done.

Wearing soft post-op pants and top, Katla dragged herself toward the bed she had taken up only a few days ago. The surgery tent was up, and people were moving and talking inside. Calmly, no panic. The so many lights inside made the tent glow like a vanilla meditation candle.

She wasn't sure she could get up on the bed, it was so high and she was so tired. She pulled the mattress pad onto the floor, tucked herself under the blanket, and slept.

Sometime after, she felt a warm hand push her to her side.

Mama Claire, snuggling in with a sigh. Hugging her close.

When Katla woke, her wristcom said it had only been a few hours, only just afternoon. Mama Claire was gone, but her scent lingered on the blanket. The surgical tent was still up, still glowing. Arcan was communicating with Arvee via one of the synth languages, which sounded to her like musical beeps, boops, and clicks. They must be really stressed, or need to work fast, or both.

She checked her messages. She didn't have Haydee to sing them out to her. Katla sent a plea to Moa, the goddess in the magma, for her friend's well-being. She hoped the goddess could hear her, so far from Arkhide.

Surgery expected to take twelve hours. Cargo shuttle already launched—in the thinnest of turnaround windows—bringing medical supplies and the food and plants that Seth's capsule had bumped from the previous flight. His capsule was finally back with the Utopia, and good riddance.

The Utopia was still here.

Someone—another synth, maybe that short skinny tube hovering at the entrance to the tent—had run her clothes through the cleaner and piled them neatly next to the bed. The beautiful tunic was a loss, but the leggings were soft again, if a lighter brown. The shoes, too, looked worn but wearable. She'd grab a sweater on the way to the plant room.

She needed to put her hands in some ground. Some earth.

She was done with space.

MORE THAN A DAY LATER, the captain of the Utopia sent a formal letter, almost apologizing for trying to murder a diplomat. Captain Manning asked if Seth could come aboard to give their non-apology in person. It was the minimum amount of time it would have taken to send a standard message to the Co-op's Central District and get an emergency message back.

Standing beside the new, triple-wrapped plants stacked against two walls of the plant room, Katla tried to picture a way the Cooperatives could have done less.

She couldn't.

She didn't join in the bombast on the "first contact" comms channel. Let other people sort it out. Instead, she replayed a new version of Haydee's song, as she now thought of it. Someone from Sankofa had already done an acoustic version of the tune, and it made her shiver every time it hit the third verse. *Say yes, say yes, say yes.* Katla intended to look for more work by that artist, but for now set the single song on repeat.

The plantings room was a sad sight. As big as the meeting room at home, the open space held rows and rows of rich soil, all barren. Without the grow lights going, and the misters, and a gardener's love, those plants had given up the ghost. Sad for them, but good for her. Enough work for a week. More than enough: She'd only managed to dig up and replant one short row yesterday.

She squinted at the floating screen that held the gardeners channel's consensus schematic of the new plantings. Big, dark ones on the lower racks, rising to little, lighter ones on the upper shelves and the walls. Tubers were coming later, for mini-field that filled the center.

S-P, the skinny-tube synth from the medbay, was hovering. Had offered to help.

"Find me some garden shears," Katla said. "Probably still in the warehouse room."

S-P gave the boop pattern for disappointment. They rolled about a meter away from Katla, and pointed at the cart. She'd forgotten that everything here had an ID chip.

"Sorry," she said. "I just need to be alone. Okay?"

The little synth booped agreement, somehow shading it sad. They brushed her hip as they passed on their way out the door. She'd make it up to them later.

She'd placed a half-dozen basil plants into the tray near the corner when consensus broke: Seth could come and formally apologize. But not to Haydee. To Katla.

Haydee—okay! so far—had been awake for just a few hours, and didn't want to see anyone yet. Not even Katla. Like S-P, Katla had done her version of booping softly to herself and turned away from the tent door.

Katla for sure wasn't ready to see Seth's shiny Cooperative-royal-family face, but that was a problem for tomorrow. She went back to her young basil, which did not shoot at anyone. Its sweet, citrus scent reminded her of summer days and fresh tomatoes. Singing songs, then sleeping on the beach. The hot days were coming, back on Hackie Island. She couldn't wait to go home.

Her wristcom pinged, overriding her do-not-disturb setting.

Seth was on his way.

Of course.

CHAPTER
TWENTY-FOUR

THE CYLINDRICAL SYNTH opened the door and rolled in, Seth in their shadow. Little S-P had figured out a way to help her after all.

The Cooperative ass had returned to the flamboyant hair, but his clothes were quieter. Shades of the formal tan, but softer. No sparkles. Something about him reminded her of Haydee's father. A whiff of pine—cologne?

Katla looked at S-P and made the hand signal for "record." The light went on above its camera. On.

Seth came within an arm's distance, saw her flinch, and took a step back. Between the wrapped-up ferns and the loosened berry bushes, he performed the Cooperative's most-formal greeting.

Katla did not reciprocate. This was appropriate for an apology, but she wouldn't have done it anyway. Or so she told herself.

"On behalf of my ship, the Utopia, I wish to send our condolences on the injury of your comrade. What occurred was not intentional. We regret the events deeply."

Katla forgot about the camera. "The events! You shot my friend."

"I didn't!" Seth fisted his hands at his sides. "I told them you were real. I don't know why they didn't believe me."

"Real? What does that even mean?"

Seth slowly unclenched his hands. "Is she okay, really?"

Katla didn't even hear. "What was that gun-toting menace thinking? Why the weapons? You promised! We did everything you said." She saw she was overwhelming him, but she had held on too long to her anger and her frustration and her fear. She needed an outlet, and the time was now. "Now do you understand why nobody wants you here?"

"But I didn't do anything!"

"You didn't shoot my friend," Katla sneered. "But you didn't think anything of invading our airspace. Of landing without permission. Or even telling us ahead of time."

"That—that was a mistake!"

Katla plowed on. "Made while you were quote-unquote testing our defense systems. And why would a Cooperative goon want to test our defenses anyway?" S-P quickly rolled forward to take the shears from her hand. She realized she had been emphasizing her words by waving her arms—armed with the shears.

Seth hunched his shoulders, sheepish. No, probably just acting sheepish. "For science?" he said.

Not a chance.

"Sure, Sandreth diCimino," she said.

He grabbed her arm, shocking her. "Don't use that name! You'll get us into more trouble than you'd believe."

She peeled his hand off her arm. "Don't. Care." She turned her back on him. "Now get out."

Just as she heard him start to move, her wristcom pinged again. Ugh. Why even put it on Do Not Disturb? She read the message, and groaned.

"Wait," she said. "I have to wash my hands."

"Haydee wants to see you."

AS THE DOOR to the medbay slid open, Katla caught sight of Arcan's back stepping behind the consultation curtain, out of view. Arvee hunkered close to the ground next to Haydee's new bed in the recovery area, trying to look like they were a boxy bright-orange piece of furniture. Katla gave Arvee the sign for recording, and the small light went on.

Haydee was awake, wearing her mom's soft purple sweater and propped up on the colorful cushions Katla had brought from their room. She was glad Claire had worked so hard to make their space seem less like a hotel bunk and more like a home, with cushions and hand-knit blankets. Haydee needed to be surrounded by the colors, the textures, of home.

Her face was so pale, her bright eyes dull and circled by bruises. Her long blond hair lay in two flat braids tucked behind her ears. Exhausted, but alive. Thank Moa.

Her face did not look welcoming.

Seth came up to the foot of the tall recovery bed. Haydee's face was on the same level as his. He performed the same deep genuflection as he had in the greenroom.

"Our deepest condolences," he said. "And my apologies."

Haydee did not respond. She just stared at him. A minute went by.

"Haydee?" he said.

Tears flowed from the edges of her eyes. They tracked down the sides of her face in parallel waves. She did not respond.

"Please," he pleaded.

"He shot me! Me!" Haydee wrapped her arms around her middle. One of her hands was bandaged. "What did I ever do to you?"

"Okay, okay," Seth said, lifting his hands. But before he could do the pat-down motion that Katla knew would infuriate Haydee, she interrupted.

"It's not okay. How can you say that?"

Seth folded his hands as if in prayer. He looked at Katla, beside him. "I am not supposed to argue. I asked to come so you would believe us. I know it is a big ask."

He turned back to Haydee. "I brought something you will like. May I show it to you?" He reached into his pocket.

Both Haydee and Katla flinched.

He stopped a moment, and then slowly pulled a hand-sized device out of his pocket.

"Pink?" Haydee said, already curious.

"I painted it last night. Didn't want you to think it was a weapon."

The device shone a light that resolved into a flat screen with an image of Seth's pod on Landing Island. He bounded into the picture just as he had in life. "Welcome to Arkhide!" The picture changed to an aerial view of Macadere Island, the Assembly buildings bright in the middle ground. Seth's voice told his story of landing and rescue, by "two friendly natives who just happened to be diplomats, too. As if they were waiting for me!"

Typical Co-op blather. Katla wanted to roll her eyes but she didn't want to miss a frame of the vid.

Seth quickly took the viewer on a sweeping view of the beach side of Macadere City and then cut to a similar sweep across Landing Island, starting with the capsule beside the welcome facility. The camera lingered on the flowing grasses of the island and the view across the water the distant crags of her home island, Samata. Then the sailboat on the way to Samata, and the view from the Aerie. "So much water. So much sun," his narration pattered on.

He did not use the awkward swooping shot they had retaken in the bay. And strangely, he had trimmed out almost every sign of ash and destruction on the island. He ended with the Aerie, telling a story of how everyone worked together on its building while omitting the fact that "everyone" was synths.

The last shot was of the big windows on the second floor, Katla in shadow in front of the center one. "Arkhide will be a jewel in the Cooperative crown. Another vacation destination for travelers who love the fringes of civilization. Subscribe now and be the first to find out more about this watery wonderland."

Seth swiped the screen away. "It's only been up for a day, and it has my best numbers of all time. Even better than 'Seth drops the chandelier.' I thought nothing could top that one." He must have noticed their blank looks, because he went on. "People are hungry to know more about your planet. The Mystery of Arkhide, all that."

"Not our planet," Haydee said. "Our home."

"We don't need more people," added Katla.

"You do so." Seth stepped over to Arvee and turned, as if he intended to sit on the synth. The little box shivered but did not make a beep. Katla stepped up and pushed Seth to the side. His hip hit the bed, softly, but enough to wobble it. Haydee gasped, but quickly recovered. Seth took her arm. "Sorry."

She shook him off with a huff and waved toward the foot of the bed. She was propped so high, with her knees bent up, that the end of the bed was clear. Seth sat sidesaddle on the bed. He faced Haydee but kept his gaze on Katla, who had a hand on top of Arvee, trying to comfort them while pretending she was manipulating some kind of invisible control panel. She met his gaze and crossed her arms, leaning a hip against Haydee's bed without jolting it at all.

"It's like this," Seth said. "You want to pressure us to give you more than we want to give, right? So, you need allies. One great ally is public opinion."

"Until it turns on you," Katla said.

257

"Which is why you need a professional. I can help you make more messages like this one. You can sway the universe from people's wristcoms."

"Sure we can," Katla said. "We're not on your socials. We have no following. Who would listen to us?"

"Easy: You use my socials. No, seriously."

Haydee frowned. "Why ever would you offer that?"

Seth shrugged. "Fact is, I'm done with this gig. Did you see that wig they made me wear? No way in the galaxy somebody isn't going to recognize me under that thing. But," he brightened. "Seth isn't dead yet! What a way to go, helping my new friends reach their dreams."

"But aren't you on the opposing team?" Katla said.

But Haydee pursed her lips, thinking. "What about the vid we shot on here? You could say that Arkhideans are recycling geniuses. Or something."

Seth actually bounced, carefully. "That is what I'm saying!"

Katla did not want to be swayed. "Wait. What does this vid you made actually say? 'Come invade this backward, castle-making planet.' That's not going to help us."

Seth didn't just roll his eyes but the whole top of his ribcage. "I know that! But it's the first one, before, well, everything that's happened. And it was a good one, obviously. People are aware of you now. New planets are common enough, but planets you can just step on and stay alive are platinum-3 rare. So now the universe is paying attention." He spread his arms wide. "Now's your chance. What do you want to say to it?"

"Don't shoot," Haydee said.

"Nobody is dead! Seth put his hand on Haydee's ankle. You really are feeling better, right?" he said, softer.

"I'm not dead," she said. "What happened with the vid that showed the shooting? The livestream of the meeting."

Seth recoiled. "Nobody showed that. Good lord."

Haydee nodded. "I say we make a vid that shows the shooting. Shows how your Cooperative treats the backward people from this gorgeous land."

Nobody spoke for a moment. Seth shifted on the bed, and then shifted again.

"Well, that's one idea. But let's start with the recycled shuttle. I've already gone through the footage. Just needs a clear story."

"Katla can do that," Haydee said. "She knows how to tell a story." She leaned against the cushions. Her color was worse. They needed to finish this conversation.

Katla motioned to Seth. He slid back to stand on the floor. "Really really," he said, reaching for Haydee's hand, above the covers. But he pulled back just before touching her. "You are going to be okay?"

Haydee turned her head on the pillow to look at him. "I guess. I'm breathing on my own, and I can feel my new heart beating." Her face sharpened, and her voice. "But I don't know how you can even stand talking to me, now I'm enhanced."

"You're not! Well, you are, technically," Seth amended. "But it was for medical purposes, not enhancement."

"Yes, but." Haydee glanced at Katla and away. "I'm going to get the enhancements, too."

"What?" Katla wasn't sure she heard correctly. "What about your people? They'll make an exception for you for the heart, I'm sure of it. It was an emergency. But if you enhance—"

That would be it.

"The rules are clear, Katla. I should be dead. I don't want my people to make an exception for me when they haven't made exceptions for every other person who's died before me. And after me. It's not fair to them."

Katla couldn't believe it. "So you're not going to let them make what you think is a bad decision by taking the decision away from them?"

"Isn't that what you did?"

"What?"

"It wasn't my hearing that went bad yesterday, Kay-Kay." Haydee said the name mockingly. Then she sighed, and slid deeper into the bed.

"I'm not ready to talk to you yet," she said. Maybe tomorrow."

CHAPTER
TWENTY-FIVE

HAYDEE WAS NOT ready to talk with Katla the next day, or the next. "Have patience," Mama Claire said. She was in the medbay with Haydee multiple times a day, chatting and enjoying the two rocking chairs that had come from downplanet. Leaving Katla even more on her own.

Her loneliness was good news for the greenrooms, though. All the new plants were now tucked into their beds, with the grow lights and the misters on. Katla breathed deep the fresh, loamy air, and wished they'd brought a third rocking chair, to put in here. Instead, she sat on the wide edge of one of the floor beds, filled with fresh-turned dirt and hidden seeds, and kept up with the planetary chat threads.

There wasn't that much new to chew over. It took days for the Cooperative diplomats in Central District to say that, with regrets, they could not agree to allow Haydee to watch the proceedings remotely and to speak to Katla through an earpiece. Katla, in turn, would not agree to negotiate when it was two against one. So it was another whole day before it was agreed that the Co-op would reduce its negotiating team to one person.

Seth. Sandreth.

Which one was the mask, Katla wondered as she stepped through her ready room into the long meeting room and began the formal greeting. He was Sandreth today, razor-straight hair and severe expression. He matched her greeting, and they stepped to the single chairs on opposite sides of the shiny black table. Arkhide, seen through the great windows at the far end of the room, looked bluer and more beautiful than ever. More precious.

The synths had figured out how to clear the gore from the recycled-tire flooring, and taken away the spattered chair. But they'd left the spray of blood on the goldenrod wall behind Katla. Let it be in every camera's wide shot forever more.

In a startling (to some) break with tradition, each negotiator already had two stacks of plain paper in front of them: One the Co-op's offer, the other the offer from Arkhide. To speed the proceedings and get the science vessel Utopia on its way, Arkhide had declared, it would hand-deliver copies of its document ahead of time to the Cooperative, in the form of Captain Manning. (Captain Manning had made S-P drop the package on the floor and move back before picking it up.) That way, they wouldn't have to take the time to read the whole thing out loud in the first (second) opening meeting. Of course, tradition was that only the Cooperative's version of an agreement was read aloud; the assumption was that it would be accepted intact.

Not today.

"Thank you for the documents," Sandreth said. "The captain and scientists of the Utopia appreciate your gesture. But we have perused them, and find many irregularities."

He paused.

"Please," Katla said. "Continue." Interesting how simple the command tense was in High Galactic.

"Arkhide appears to be asking for special status. The Cooperative Realm, as you may know, treats all worlds equally, including our home world. We are a union of mutual support, mutually shared."

That was their motto, if not their reality. Katla rested one hand on the palm of the other on the table, a Cooperative gesture. Not reacting, not tense. "I understand how your realm operates. We are not asking to join the Cooperative. We seek merely an agreement for open trade and nonaggression."

Seth matched her position. His nails today were unpainted. "We are not the aggressors."

Katla let go her hands, and let that comment pass. She picked up part of the stack of papers in front of her and started going through each one.

"For the open doors to trade, here are examples from the Cooperative's agreements with the Stackfield system and with the trade station at Rosing Base." She turned the pages to face Seth, and pushed them across the table. "For our request for 'friendly neighbor' status, here are examples from the Cooperative's agreements with Sherman's Wheel, the Moonstar system, and the planet Wala."

"Beg pardon?" Seth, focused on catching the sliding pages, looked up. "Wala?"

Katla folded her hands again. Staying calm, staying cool. She continued, "For our request that the Cooperative pledge to take no aggressive actions against our world, through intent or through unintentional error, we cite the precedent of the planet Wala."

"What does this have to do with Wala?" Seth looked genuinely flustered. Did he not know what happened there? Or maybe he didn't know enough.

"The planet Wala," Katla started. Calm, cool. "Was the home planet to all the humans on Arkhide."

Seth hissed in a breath. He obviously had not been prepped

by his people. And not surprisingly, no Arkhidean he'd come in contact with had chosen to speak of it.

"On the day a Cooperative bomb destroyed our home world," Katla pressed on, now deadly calm. "Two thousand of us were in a transport at the nearby jump gate. We were looking through the windows, we were looking at the viewers. We were bidding a temporary farewell to our planet. Instead, we saw our homes dismantled—disintegrated—in a matter of seconds."

She paused. "By accident. Allegedly."

"You may think there were only six survivors of Wala, Special Envoy diCimino." It felt good to ice that name with a coating of disgust. "But you are wrong. You did not destroy the Walan peoples."

Seth sat back in his chair. He looked down at the table, at the papers under his hand. He looked over to the window showing the beautiful view of Arkhide. He looked back at the papers. He looked at Katla. He swallowed audibly.

"Ah, thank you for this information, madame ambassador. Would you agree to a short intermission? To give my colleagues time to read over these documents."

"We would prefer not to." Katla leaned a bit forward. "I remind you, it was the Cooperative—and the Utopia—who asked for all possible speed."

"Right." Seth looked off again, toward the window.

He didn't speak for a long minute. And another. Katla dropped her gaze to her stacks of paper. To her hands, again clasped in the Cooperative manner. She moved her hands to the center of her forearms, clasping in the manner of Arkhide.

Seth sighed and lifted his hand, as if to rake his fingers through the green hair-tail he was not sporting today. The first finger stopped at the top of his forehead. The hand came down, into his lap. He turned his gaze back to Katla.

"The trade agreement is possible. We understand the precedents. We are familiar with the wording. We are, of course, disappointed that you do not wish to embark on the track that leads to full membership in the Cooperative Realm. Perhaps, someday, you might reconsider."

Katla didn't need to have an earpiece in to know what Haydee—or Aimee Five—would have to say about that. She waited for him to continue.

"As for the, ah, nonaggression language," he finally came out with. "This is a case of breaking new ground."

"The Cooperative realm is unused to agreeing not to attack its allies?"

He tried not to wince. "I refer, of course, to the formal language. Perhaps we might agree to the first and table the second until I can consult with my colleagues in Central District."

Katla shrugged, a small tip of the shoulder, trying to appear unconcerned. Fantastic news! The trade-only treaty was the best outcome possible.

She couldn't believe it would be this easy. Sure, they had worded it carefully to be acceptable to both parties, using language the Cooperative itself used, well understood by their legal system. But to change nothing? Not even to haggle? She had to fight not to smile.

As for the "don't kill us" language, that was gravy. The point was made, in her opinion, just by airing it here at the table, via its live video feed to her people, and via recording for posterity to the Cooperative at large. Other Arkhideans—a great swath of other Arkhideans—disagreed with her and wanted a promise, iron-clad.

Well, they might still get that.

She nodded once. "We agree, the trade treaty is acceptable as written." She took the pages that were the treaty and put them to her left. That left a single page in front of her. The nonaggression pledge. Four paragraphs of perfect High Galactic, its text clear as glass.

She tapped the page with an index finger. "We will wait upon you to continue discussing the second matter."

He nodded, at exactly the same depth. They pushed back their chairs and rose in the same rhythm.

They departed from their separate doors at the same moment. They left their papers where they were.

CHAPTER
TWENTY-SIX

WHEN KATLA WALKED out of the ready room, after a round of silent smiles (audio might still be recording) and a short wiggle dance with Arcan and little S-P, she saw Seth waiting for her.

He had come to the parlay alone, and was alone now, discounting the drone-bag hanging from his shoulder.

"That hair," she said, shaking her head.

He pulled the wig off, and the cap that pressed his own hair flat. "Not only that, it itches worse than sand fleas." He pushed the wig into the wide pocket of his bag with one hand while fluffing his skinny green mane with the other. "But yours looks nice."

Katla ducked, embarrassed. It wasn't her favorite style. Mama Claire had braided Katla's mess of dark curls into two plaits flat to her scalp, clipped together at her nape. Best they could do until more hair product arrived on the shuttle, she'd said.

"How is Haydee doing?" Seth said.

"Great. You know, for someone who got shot and then got a totally new heart." At his look of despair, Katla eased up. "She's responding so well, the doctors think she might not have to take the anti-rejection drugs forever. Just for a little while."

"No chance I could get to see her?"

Katla sat back on one hip. So that was how it was. "Dunno. Do you have any gifts or goodies to give her? A new vid clip?"

"Not yet. Actually," he looked at the gray wall to her side. "I was hoping to get another couple shots out the big picture window in there. The one I have is good, but the planet is pretty cloudy. Today it is so blue."

Katla never passed up a chance to linger by that window. "Let me check," she said anyway. She called up the livestream—turned off—and checked her ready room—still housing Arcan and S-P. "If we go through your door."

Through the window, the planet was a wash of gorgeous blues. Wisps of white and gray hid and then revealed the scatterings of archipelagos. Seth sent one drone to get the shot by zooming up and down the long table, and another to hover, still, at the top of the window. Katla stood at the right-side edge of the window, contemplating the tiny puff of ash from one of the continually smoking volcanoes. Pocketed in a swirl of dark blue water, it was slowly—over decades—forming its own island. Did it make a sound? Would the sounds it made be the same if heard underwater?

Seth came up beside her. "Could I move you into the picture? It's always good to have contrast." Katla stepped to the side, and again, until he nodded. She was one-third of the way down, which shouldn't cover the round ball that was the focus.

"Can we talk, or does that wreck the shot?" she said.

"Audio's off," he said. "Just picture. But don't turn your head! Keep looking out straight."

It was weird not to look at the person you were talking to. Katla squinted, and caught Seth's reflection, a sliver just on the edge of the window. It would have to do.

"Why did you go so easy on the trade agreement?"

"Are you complaining?"

She started to shake her head, but a quick inhale from Seth reminded her to stay still. The tiny whir of the drone behind her crept closer. It was a slow zoom-in. "Of course not. But the Co-op has made such noise about standard agreements and treating everyone the same. I expected word changes on every page, at the least."

Seth could shrug, since he was off-screen. "Arkhide is a special case. Specialer now. Is that a word? Turns out, the video of the shooting did get released, somehow. It wasn't shown on the news feeds—it was strongly suggested by the Regent's office that it not be shown—but it was chum in the water for the investigative reporters. There's a pack of them heading this way. Co-op wants to be done with you before they get here."

"Released. Somehow?"

Seth stepped closer to her. He leaned in to whisper. "Seems that the signal hit the raw news feeds before the diplomatic watchdogs knew to look for it. Our warning message didn't travel as fast as the news feed, for some reason."

She tilted her head a bit to look at him. His expression was as smooth as if he never held a thought in his head. But he was wheels within wheels.

"Why are you helping us?" she said. "Really."

"Really?" He straightened, and looked out at Arkhide. "Too many reasons to list. Getting back at an absent parent who expects me to jump when she says jump. Following orders to dig out from under the accusation of attempted murder of a diplomat by closing negotiations ASAP. Trying to be fair to one planet, at least, within our giant realm."

"We're not in your realm, actually," she said. "Our gate is outside Cooperative space."

"That's what you think," he said. "The Cooperative is like a gas. We spread to all spaces, all corners. We distribute ourselves evenly, everywhere, in time."

They contemplated Arkhide in silence for a moment. Then Seth pointed to a collection of islands near the middle. "Is that where I was?"

Katla tried to see which islands he meant. The day was so clear, the miniature world so sharp she could have believed it was just a stone's throw from the base. She sought out the pattern of reflections that would be the signal for a shuttle landing pad.

"No," she said. "See those shiny circles, there? That's the shuttle pad opposite the one we used. Our place is on the other side. But it will be back."

"It would be a great shot to close my next segment. Our next segment. Can we wait?"

They could.

CHAPTER
TWENTY-SEVEN

AFTER SHE SAID goodbye to Seth at the Utopia's docking tube, Katla went to her room to change into more comfortable clothes. Just walking into the room cheered her up. The bunkroom's walls were the same happy coral shade as home; Claire must have brought up their leftovers from the last house-painting. The wall-closet, dresser and bed were standard and dull, but the addition of a shaggy russet rug and pale pink knit bedcover made the room soft and crunchier.

Katla hung the diplomatic garb up carefully; it was her only non-bloodied set now and needed to stay perfect. Should she return the three thin bracelets Claire had loaned her? After the signing was done, she decided, and tucked them into the formal tunic's side pocket.

The door to her room slid open without warning. Claire rushed in, face flushed, hair wild, bangles jangling.

"Where have you been? I've been calling forever."

Katla looked at her wristcom. "Sorry. Forgot to turn it back on after the session."

"That's not acceptable, Katla." Claire stripped the tie off one of her untamed braids and it started to unravel more. She didn't seem to notice. "You have to be available when I need you."

"What's wrong?" She'd rarely seen her mama so frazzled. No claxons were sounding, so it wasn't a base emergency. Was she hurt? Was mom Sofia? "Mama, come and sit down. You're scaring me."

Claire paced a few steps toward Katla, and then turned and paced away. And then turned back. Sweat ringed the neck of her formal blue tunic. The red frizz of hair by her temples was soaked.

"You should be scared," she said, but in a weird, distracted way. Like they were words she was supposed to say, but she hadn't learned her lines well enough.

Next time Claire came close, Katla grabbed her hand. That stopped her. Her hand was clammy and cold.

"Mama. Are you sick?"

Claire pulled away, and went back to pacing. "We have to get this fixed!"

Katla was out of ideas. She dropped onto a seat on her bunk. "What do you want me to do?"

Claire pivoted toward her, and stopped. Her hands seemed to be washing each other.

"Right. You have to stall the negotiations."

"What? Why?"

"Only a couple days. Four, at the most." Claire wiped her hands on the hem of her tunic. "Yes. And after all, the Cooperative might not even respond by then. We'll be fine."

"Are you serious? We're trying to get rid of the Cooperatives, and you want me to slow down?" Katla's hands had started picking at her own braids. Claire's anxiety was contagious.

Katla let go of her hair and gripped the bulky knit comforter instead. Her fingers slid into the weave. She remembered Claire knitting this. One of her earliest attempts, it was forever trying to unravel and being patched up again.

Now Claire was sliding her many bracelets from one forearm to the other, and back again. The bangles' clinking and rustling, usually so musical and charming, brought only dissonance and chaos.

"Claire!" Katla tried to make her voice as stern as mom Sofia's could be. "Come sit down by me."

Her mama stopped, arrested. Her hands stilled. She did as ordered.

It must have been a good impression.

Katla leaned against her mama's side, quiet. Supportive. Waiting.

"This wasn't supposed to happen," Claire's voice started as a whisper. "I told her it would happen and she said no and it's happening and it's what I said would happen!" Shouting. "It must be done." Softe, decisive. "Right."

Claire stood up. She marched to the door. She turned around.

"Delay the agreement. Four days."

"But… why?"

Claire puffed up, an angry crane. "Orders. From the Assembly." She reached back and slapped the door panel. The door swooshed open.

"No back talk," she said.

———

AIMEE FIVE'S sub-assistant was very apologetic, but as the Speaker was currently helming the Assembly, she couldn't be spared to chat with Katla. Of course, the Speaker would return Katla's call at the earliest possible time.

Katla did not believe it. For one, she could see on the feed that the assembly was not in session. For another, the assistant's eyes were glazed, staring up and to the right. Accessing data.

"What about Allen Eleven? Is he free?" At this point, Katla just wanted to see a friendly face. Maybe Allen could talk her down as handily as he did his friend Aimee Five.

"Absolutely not." The assistant's gaze snapped back to the camera, and Katla. "My apologies, ambassador. It's been a busy day, and we've only started."

"What is it?"

"Mount Awala. We got a warning from the elders and all our systems confirm. Massive action deep and rising. Four-five days, probably a week, before it starts to blow. It will be big."

"Four days?" Katla said.

"Plenty of time, I know," the assistant said. "But Macadere is a big city, and full for autumn session. It's a lot of people to move fast. The Assembly's gone already, to the spring offices on Harborville. There are only a handful of us still here coordinating. Most of the coordination is off-site, as I'm sure you know."

Much of the coordination was on the internal nets, shared by everyone who had implants, which was nearly everyone. Every Arkhidean knew the departure drill, but there was always the unexpected. Katla found herself a little sad to be missing the excitement.

The Assembly and its support teams already had a campus in Harborville, the biggest synth city. Most of the non-Assembly residents would be going to one of two islands—but not too nearby. The closest was ready for an influx of tens of thousands of people; the one slightly farther away was not. The tents and other refugee supplies those folks would need were stored on a couple of the bigger skimmer-haulers. The haulers would offload their supplies and then start ferrying the people.

The last lines of the sing-song ditty they learned as littles about packing to go started to play in Katla's head. "There's only thing I need to bring, for sure, absolutely. And that's me."

"Sorry to take your time. For sure, Aimee Five, or Allen, or Sofia, shouldn't rush to call me. We're all safe and well up here."

The assistant looked perplexed for a second. Must be too much information flowing over the nets even for a synth. "Thanks. I've sent the messages. And thank you, ambassador, for your work today. Just to see that Cooperative's face while you dressed him down! Priceless."

Katla wiped closed the call and opened her Awala data. The magma chamber had swollen half a meter. Lots of little shakes. Some distortion of the cone. The elders were right: Time to go.

But none of that would be helped by delaying their treaty with the Cooperative. Katla had authority to sign the initial document. Aimee Five and the Assembly could approve it just as easily from Harborville as Macadere.

Could it be something on the Cooperative side? But why would Arkhide care about that?

She wasn't going to find the answer by kicking her heels in her room, as her mom Sofia put it. Katla headed toward the medbay.

CHAPTER
TWENTY-EIGHT

KATLA MADE a short stop at the mini kitchen; there weren't enough of them on base yet to need the giant main kitchen. She reheated a couple of the sweet pastries Haydee loved and a savory one for herself. She would hit the medbay bearing gifts.

Haydee was alone in the room, rocking in her chair next to the medbed, still wearing Claire's super warm purple sweater. Her platinum hair in tidy plaits. The tent was gone, and all the formerly beeping monitor machines sat quiet against the serene blue walls. Alone and quiet, Haydee set the tablet she had been looking at in her lap. She waited for Katla to come closer.

"I brought you two to choose from, fig and blueberry. Actually, they're both for you." Katla was talking fast. Nervous. Would Haydee be the sweet-faced person from before or the sharp-tongued person from after? "And Seth wants to come by. He's finishing the second vid clip, and wants to show us. You, I mean."

Haydee looked at the hand holding the berry pastry out, and then at Katla's face. "I can't believe you're just going to pretend nothing happened. Just go back to normal."

Katla's spirit sagged. She set both pastries and their napkins on a slightly used plate on the tiny folding table at Haydee's left side. The plate looked as if it might have already held a pastry or two. "What do you want me to do?"

Haydee waved at the other rocking chair, kitty-corner to the little table. "First, sit so I can look at you without straining. I'm not supposed to strain."

Katla slipped deep into the chair, setting it in motion. She held her own pastry between her hands, soaking in the warmth. Her sense of smell was so damped by being on-base that she could only remember the mix of flaked dough and spices she loved.

"I'm here," she said. "I'm listening."

"Promise you'll listen," Haydee said. "All the way through."

Haydee knew her. Katla shivered inside. This was going to be worse than the Don't Touch my Girlfriend talk when they were teenagers. And she still wasn't sure what was wrong here.

"Promise," she said.

Haydee set her toes on the ground, stilling her chair. She set her hands on the chair's arms, holding on but not gripping. She needed some nail polish, Katla noted on the to-do list in the back of her mind.

"I was pretty out of it after, you know," Haydee said. "I saw the gun, but it didn't connect that that was what had caused me so much pain." She paused.

Katla did not speak.

Haydee nodded. First test passed. "I saw you. You looked terrified. Next thing I knew, I was here," she scanned the room. "And you still looked terrified. But also determined." She paused.

Katla opened her mouth, and then clenched it closed. The urge to explain herself, explain everything, was almost overwhelming. Almost.

Haydee nodded. "I heard the voice of my mom—my mom!—

278

saying to let me go. I heard her talk about me in the past tense. Everything in my vision was red. Something kept pounding on my lungs. Breath being forced into me. It made sense, what mom said."

Katla briefly closed her eyes, the way Haydee's had been then.

"Then I heard you and Arcan, conspiring. Trying to find a way to weasel out of this, this." She picked up a hand and waved it once toward her chest. "This truth."

"I was confused. Why were you and mom disagreeing? I didn't know. Not until I woke up after."

Haydee leaned forward. She set her hand over Katla's on her armrest. "I knew you were in charge. I knew you were my friend. I knew you knew more about the situation than anyone could on-planet. I thought you had my best interests at heart. But you didn't."

Katla fought not to pull away. To stay still. To listen.

"You wanted me for yourself. To keep me with you, you discounted my beliefs, and my family's beliefs. Because you disagree with them."

Katla inhaled hard. That wasn't fair! She opened her mouth to speak.

Haydee held up a finger, stopping her. "You made that decision. Not me. Not my mom." She dropped the finger, and pulled her other hand away. "You stole that decision away from us. It was not yours to take."

"Now." Haydee shrugged, turning her palms up in her lap. "I have no people. Some will see me as a ghost. Others as a monster." Tears brimmed in her eyes. "No one will see me as Sankofan.

"What do I do now? Who am I? Who can I trust?" She looked at Katla. "You?" She said it in a tone that meant, never again.

Haydee reached for the plate with the pastries. She pushed

her chair to start rocking. She bit into the top pastry. She licked spilled berry off her finger.

Katla looked at her own pastry, squeezed out of shape between her hands. She could not imagine eating it. Her mouth had never been so dry.

She had never been so wrong.

"Mmm, blueberry," Haydee said. "My favorite. What's yours?"

Katla cleared her throat. "Savory. You know."

When she had finished the berry one, Haydee reached for the fig. Katla took a careful bite of hers. It tasted like ashfall, but at least she could swallow it down. How ever could she fix this?

She couldn't.

Haydee made short work of the second pastry. She washed it down with water from a covered cup on the table. "So, yeah. I'm mad at you. Furious. More feelings I don't even have names for. I don't want you to apologize, because I won't believe you. At least, not now. I just wanted you to hear. Hear how I feel."

Katla nodded. She wrapped her pastry back in the napkin and slipped it into her pocket. She wiped her hands on the seams of her tunic. She reached a hand out to Haydee, palm up.

Her friend reached for her, palm down.

They clasped forearms, in the Arkhidean way.

On release, Haydee burped, and chuckled. She patted her abdomen. "Digestive system's up and working, I guess." She put her hands behind her head, rocking the chair.

"So, this new vid of Seth's. Have you seen it?"

CHAPTER
TWENTY-NINE

SETH CAME BY SOON AFTER. Katla was still in the medbay with Haydee, quietly rocking and reading the online chats, commenting on some. Arvee had been by, checking in on Haydee and finding nothing amiss. They took the plate with a beep that sounded a lot like "Tsk."

The medbay's hall door swooshed. By the time she had looked up, he was posed, leaning hip and shoulder against the side of the door. He'd touched up his hair—neon bright—and added the eye sparkles. His ensemble, in rainbows of yellows and browns and purples, should have clashed. But they only did once in a while: Something was making his long coat-tunic swirl with colors, having a conversation with the rest of his outfit. Including the ugly-serviceable space boots, which he must have painted himself, cadmium blue.

"It's great to be back!" he said.

Katla, winded just by looking at him, couldn't rouse herself to speak. Haydee had no such problem.

"Intruder alert," she said mildly. "Don't you even ring the doorbell?"

"Your ship—pardon me, base station extension—let me in. She has good taste."

"You tip-toed." Katla had found her tongue.

"I heel-toed." He demonstrated the step as he walked toward them, holding one of his hands out in front of him, like a courtier in a Co-op history drama. He made only a whisper of sound, certainly nothing anyone could hear through a hall door.

He looked at each of them—really their rocking chairs—and then the bed beside them. "If I sit there, you'll have to crane your neck."

Haydee reached toward the center of the bed and pushed a button. The bed sank to knee height. Katla's knees.

Seth swept forward and sat down with a flourish. Way down —his knees came halfway to his chest. Unruffled, he stretched his long legs out straight, crossing them at the ankle.

"You look great, Haydee," he said. "Miraculous recovery."

A slight flush rose to Haydee's cheeks. She twisted her mouth slightly, as if she didn't believe him. As he pulled out the pink projector, her face cleared, curious and eager.

"Did our script work?" she said.

"Yes. Only a few nips and tucks, here and there. For narrative flow." He positioned the floating screen directly in front of Haydee and pressed play.

The clip opened with the pier door opening, and Haydee step-ping through. The camera followed her through the halls, past a bunkroom, the small kitchen, a gym. Katla's voice described the work that had been done to restore the ship to living space.

It was her voice, calm and low, but not her words. This voice knew the proper names for ornaments like the curtains in the living space, and the types of doors they were walking through. Seth's audience must truly know these vessels for that to be important.

Haydee walked past the couches in the Co-op's negotiations ready room. The shot included the bar in the corner, probably another familiar sight, proved by not-Katla's narration that pointed it out. Haydee paused in front of the door into the negotiation room, and then stepped in.

Now the words were entirely Katla's, describing the table, the meanings of its layout and the colors on each wall. This part of the clip was from before the blood, the wall still pristine. Finally, Haydee walked to the amazing windows. As she walked, her shape grew more shadowy; in front of the window, it was just a silhouette. The camera zoomed past her, until the view out the window was all it saw. This was the new material, showing a world made of infinite blues. He was right to reshoot this.

Not-Katla came back. "We are merely stewards of this marvelous land." The camera began to zoom out slowly. Haydee's silhouette came back into view. Except it wasn't Haydee. It was a shot from today, Katla, silhouetted in the same manner. As the view slid farther back, widening the shot, Seth's silhouette came into view. He was leaning in. Not-Katla, again: "Caring for Arkhide is our responsibility and our joy. We welcome you."

Seth wiped the screen away fast as a laser. "Pretty great, right?" sounded to her ears like "pregrayrye."

Katla blinked slowly. Even Haydee took a moment.

"Getting that new footage really made the ending pop," Seth said, just as fast.

"I didn't say half that stuff." Katla said. Not-Katla had told half-truths and shown expertise Katla did not have. In a way, it was like Katla herself was lying.

"Details only. I told you, a little editing."

Haydee growled her voice up to speech. "We do not welcome you."

"You kind of do, in a manner of speaking," Seth said, fast but soothing. "It's just a phrase! Certainly not a formal invitation."

Of course it was a formal invitation. "I sound like a travel advertisement," Katla said. "It's not even my words. You have to cut the line."

Seth cupped a hand around the back of his neck. "So, yeah, well. The clip might have already gone out."

Haydee tilted her head in that way she did before she ripped your heart out. In a manner of speaking.

"No, wait!" Seth said. "It's not what you think. I had to take advantage of the great swell of support and excitement about Arkhide. No, really. Truly."

He patted the air as if to calm them down. Both of them pushed back in their rockers, crossing their arms. Haydee scowled, but Katla was trying to fight back tears. Her heart hurt. She didn't want to be known as a liar. Welcome, the Cooperative was not. Absolutely not.

Seth rushed on. "There was a bit of the view of the planet in my last vid, shot from the Utopia, and it struck a chord in a bunch of viewers. One clipped it out and put it on merchandise: comm screens, T-shirts, you know the sort. But it was a little blurry, and remember? That day was cloudy."

He took a breath so fast he couldn't be interrupted. "I saw that, and thought we should use that to our advantage. Catch the wave. So I retook the shots here, on this more-beautiful day, and sent them up as soon as I got back to my edit deck. Those exploded! Billions of views, hundreds of thousands of down-loads. I needed to follow up on that fast. Keep the momentum."

He ran out of air, or steam, or whatever.

This was out of control. This had never been in their control. Seth was telling the Co-op's story, using their voices.

He lifted his hand, palm out. "I know what you're thinking. Seth is manipulating the story."

"No, actually," Katla said. "More like Seth is a lying liar."

"Traitor to Arkhide," Haydee added.

Seth winced. "But look beyond. You're pulling fantastic numbers! You have so many people who know of you and wish you well. And they're watching." He spread his arms wide.

"How could the Co-op possibly screw you over now?"

CHAPTER
THIRTY

AS IF WAITING for Seth's cue, claxons sounded throughout the base.

Katla fought the urge to cover her ears so she could call up her screens. "Ship! What is it?"

"Incoming ships. A small flotilla."

"Understood. Claxon off." She ran through the screen's commands that would get her to the views from outside the hull. Three—no four—little ships had popped out of the jump-tunnel, and were heading their way. Little now, but how big when they got here?

Katla looked at Seth. "You know them?"

"Can you blow it up bigger?" he said. "Fuzzy is okay. Wow, you have good cameras."

He nodded, confirming what it looked like he already knew. "The press. Members of the media."

"Confirmed," Ship said. "They are hailing us in an inappropriate manner. I will inform them of the correct manner to send a message. Stand by."

"This is just the vanguard," Seth said. "More will be coming."

Katla couldn't believe it. From no ships anywhere near them to a circus of strangers. "How many more?"

"Dunno. Some of the reporting teams work for multiple outlets, on multiple worlds. But lots of the big names want their own person there reporting. I told you; this is a big story."

Message alerts were blinking so often it was strobing the corner of Katla's screen. She wiped the screen away. "You did this."

"No." Seth actually looked serious. Nearly severe. "You did. You hid from us. You snubbed us. Of course, we're going to come look."

Katla wiped her forehead, suddenly sweaty. "Of course, we hid from you. We didn't want you around. What should we have done?"

Haydee had wrapped her arms around herself and was rocking shallow, back and forth, back and forth. Katla felt the same, with additional frustration and plain anger.

"Okay, listen," Seth said. "No one—no one—has been able to hide from us like you did. You have all the scientists on the Utopia aflutter trying to figure out how that works.

"Next. You have a beautiful, livable, unpolluted world. Resources desperately needed by many in our realm. Everyone who needs a decent place to live has Arkhide on their minds right now.

"Last. You are harboring an island's worth of fugitives. Every one of the synths on your planet fled from somewhere. Escaped from someone. How many? Twenty thousand? That's twenty thousand stories a reporter could tell."

More than that. And all with death sentences hanging over them, issued by the Cooperative Realm.

"To reporters, media presences, corporate spies—everybody—you are a tasty morsel," Seth concluded. "Which is why I had to get your story out first. "From now on, it will be buried in the chaff of the daily news cycles."

She had to get rid of all these people. Keep them off her planet. Get them out of the system. Now.

Katla pushed up to stand. She paced to the wall, still blue, still serene. She paced back to Seth, aswirl with color and energy and something that reminded her of burnt sugar.

Back and forth. Back and forth. This puzzle could be solved.

In her chair, Haydee shivered, and hugged herself tighter.

This puzzle must be solved.

"I can make you some magnets," Seth said. "Or stickers. Round, with just the planet, or rectangle, with the motto, too."

"The motto?" What was he talking about?

"Planet of Gold."

"That's not true. It doesn't even make sense."

"But it sings," Seth said. "So, a couple dozen of each?"

To get rid of them, she needed to make Arkhide less interesting. Less enticing. But she couldn't change the whole planet.

She wouldn't disappear the synths.

Dull, boring, like all the rest of the Cooperative.

She stopped. There was only one way to get rid of everyone. Get the treaty signed. Then they were just dull hangers-on to the mighty Co-op. Some other news would break, and the reporters would scoot off, leaving her people alone.

But Claire wanted her to wait. Told her to wait.

She would wait one day.

"Seth," she said, as if he'd just come in the door. "Let's do the signing ceremony first thing tomorrow."

"What signing ceremony?" He tilted his head and looked at her, like a goat that didn't believe you weren't going to come save her from the island in the middle of the floodwaters. "I'm still waiting on advice on the 'no shooting' plan."

Katla waved that away. "Can be a codicil. Main treaty can be signed, right? Initially, by you and me. Tomorrow."

"Why so fast? Aaaaaah," Seth said. "Reduce your newsworthiness and at the same time feed the media beast with one good story before they go."

"That would finish it, right?" Haydee said. "Right now."

Katla watched Seth thinking. "Will you do it?"

Seth grinned at her. "It's brilliant!"

Katla sincerely hoped so.

THEY COMPLETED the negotiations the way so many other negotiations end: Behind closed doors. In Katla and Seth's case, via a shared screenlink from their respective bunkrooms.

The Cooperative diplomats back home rejected whole paragraphs of the prepared language, but would agree to a statement that there would be no unannounced weapons testing nearby. Katla countered with okay, but delete the word unannounced. Seth took it on his own authority to call that a minor change, and he formally agreed to it.

By bedtime, they had an agreement they could print and sign in the morning.

Katla informed the Assembly and her team on-base that negotiations would start at the standard time. She let Seth filter all the reporters' queries for her, and invited eight of them to attend this "next negotiating session."

Only the two of them knew it would include the signing.

And Haydee.

CHAPTER
THIRTY-ONE

TEN MINUTES BEFORE THE MEETINGS' start time, the media was allowed onto base. Each of the eight had boarded the Utopia, which had security screening and a room to store their bags and boxes. No guns; everyone promised. When the reporters met her little cylindrical friend S-P at the airlock into the pier, they had only what they could carry. Most of them started rolling media then.

Katla watched their progress via the security drones floating ahead and behind the pack. Before they stepped into the Aurora wing of the base, the reporters pointed their cameras down the pier, trying to see what they could of the main base. One or the other of them pressed every door panel, in case a door would open and then they all could get the shot. Seth had warned her about that one. They didn't make as much small talk as he said they would, though, and they didn't dawdle or lag behind. She could see the wisdom in making them feel as if they were getting here at the last moment.

They followed S-P—freshly buffed and doing a fine job of bouncing along pretending to be a mindless drone, not a synth at all—straight to the center door of the meeting room, the one on the short side opposite the viewing window. Once they got inside, they all stuck to that end, so as not to wreck the planetscape background. Each had a chair they could use; four on each side. The reporter in a go-chair parked in the front, the others spaced themselves behind. Each wore glasses that carried cameras; each would get the feeds from the Arkhideans' cameras (six, today controlled by S-P) and anything they recorded from where they stood or hovered.

Katla checked that off the mental list she'd titled "Everything that has to happen, in this exact order."

Once the reporters were in, with their door closed. Katla pressed a button on her wristcom, not mute but send. She turned to Claire, who stood unnaturally still beside her. She'd avoided her mama yesterday after the weird thing in her bedroom. It hadn't been hard. Claire hadn't sought her out. Which was reasonable, really—as an expert in moving people and cities, Claire was probably busy helping with the Macadere migration. All the residents were off the island, as of this morning. Only the cleanup crews, all experienced synths, remained to dismantle as much infrastructure as possible for re-use in the new city.

"Forgot my lucky bracelet," she said. "The one you gave me. Be right back." She slipped out without waiting for an answer.

Seth stepped out of his room a moment later. They were the only ones in the hall. Katla told all the doors on the floor to lock for a count of fifty.

Again in his severe wig and bland outfit, Seth held two thin meter-long cylinders. He gave her one.

"Captain's here. She didn't recognize the cylinders. She thinks she's re-invited because you're warming to us." Really it was because the treaty needed two witnesses. The witnesses didn't need to be signatories, they just needed to be present, in person. Seth had checked that last night.

The witness for Arkhide rolled around the corner of the hall that led to medbay. Haydee wore her diplomatic attire, quickly pinned in by Katla this morning to hide the frightening amount of weight Haydee had lost. Luckily, it wasn't as obvious now, since she was settled into one of the medbay's go-chairs.

"No hover power?" Seth said, briefly grasping Haydee's forearm, outstretched in greeting. She shrugged.

"I like the wheels on the ground option. You two are about to rock our worlds, right?"

Katla smiled through the buzzing of her thoughts. If Haydee had the energy to tease them, she must be getting better.

"Like an earthquake," Katla said.

"A star system quake," Seth said.

"A galaxy quake!" Haydee said. She chuckled as she piloted her chair to the Arkhidean's door. She looked at Katla expectantly.

This was it. They were going to do this. It would work. It was their assignment, and their duty. No one would gainsay it. It was what everyone said they wanted.

Only maybe not so fast? That part sounded a sour note in Katla's happy march of thoughts. She shook the thought away. She positioned herself behind Haydee; she'd push the chair, to make sure it went directly to the meeting-room door and no one could waylay it.

Seth was at his door. He inclined his head to her; it was her lead.

And then he winked.

Katla couldn't help grinning as the hall doors clicked to unlocked. The two negotiators' doors slid open as one.

CHAPTER
THIRTY-TWO

KATLA AND HAYDEE made a straight line to the inner door, into the meeting room itself. Haydee, closer, palmed the entry panel. They were early—it would take Seth longer to get the captain in place—but with the door open, no one on her side could make a move against them.

Not with the media present.

Eight heads swiveled to look at her, their own eyes almost hidden under thick-framed glasses or face shields studded with tiny camera eyes. Bright lights attached to headbands or shoulders washed across Haydee, up to Katla, and then back to Haydee.

Good.

The door opposite opened. Seth led this time, with the captain following. Little S-P, moving quickly, had pulled a chair from beside the wall and pushed it to proper position at the Cooperative side of the table for the captain before she'd taken a full step in. They went back to patrolling in front of the reporters, keeping them in place, as the negotiators performed their formal greetings.

295

Seth began, as agreed. "Madam ambassador. It was good to speak with you last night." He performed a separate greeting angled to Katla's left, to Haydee. "Madame ambassador, it is wonderful to see you up and about again. Our best wishes for your continued speedy healing and full recovery."

They had agreed that Haydee would not say anything at this point, just tilt her head a fraction. Thank Moa. As Katla moved to sit in her chair, she glanced at her friend's face. Even eyes down, Haydee's expression was barely civil. But as she lifted her head, the disgust and disdain across her features seemed to drain away. A true diplomat.

"Let's start with a review of where we are," Katla said. "The treaty concerning trade and basic relations has been read once in our Assembly. We currently are in the comment period, where everyone on the planet can make their voice heard. In two days, the treaty will be read again, formally debated, and voted upon. Based on the tone of current discussions, the Assembly's leadership foresees no problems with its approval."

She stopped. Now it was Seth's turn.

"I have consulted with the Cooperative Diplomatic Corps, which suggested revised language in the addendum on weaponry. As we discussed last night, we wish to pare down the statement to one paragraph, adopting the agreed-upon language."

Captain Manning shot him a shocked look. Luckily, she was on his left, the side closest to the reporters, so they didn't see. Arkhide's cameras, though, would store that expression for posterity.

The way the lights, and the reporters' many eyes, swiveled from side to side was dizzying. Katla focused on the right side of Seth's flowing black wig. Was that the smallest wisp of bright green sneaking out?

"As we discussed last night, the pared-down language is not ideal," she said. "But it is acceptable."

The lights swiveled away. She relaxed a fraction.

Something in this room smelled like a savory pastry.

Seth nodded. "As we discussed last night, the Cooperative Realm finds the terms of the treaty as a whole acceptable."

The lights turned back to her. She looked away from them, toward Haydee. Her friend jiggled the tube, hidden behind the armrest of the go-chair. She had no idea how Seth had kept his hidden.

She was going to do this, for her people. Keep them safe, keep them secure.

Katla turned her gaze back to the Cooperatives. They sat framed against the wall of Arkhide blue. Small against that ocean.

"As Chief Diplomat to the Cooperative Realm for the greater world of Arkhide, I have the authority to sign this treaty in our name." This was High Galactic chest-puffing, but required, Seth had told her.

And it got the response he'd told her to expect. A collective gasp from the reporters, who were well-versed in the niceties of the realm's diplomacy. They would suspect what was coming next, and be primed to record it.

The lights turned to Seth. "As Special Envoy to Arkhide," he said, "I have the authority to sign this treaty in the name of the Cooperative Realm."

The media glare returned to Katla. "Then we are in agreement," she said.

This time the glare dimmed, but did not completely depart. Half the lights remained on her. The other half pivoted to Seth.

"We are in agreement," he said.

They half-bowed slowly to each other. Katla held her left hand out to Haydee, who placed the document tube in its palm.

At the sight of the cylinder, the press corps seemed to vibrate, but silently. Not interrupting the proceedings, but flavoring them with their contagious glee. They knew they had the story of the season. Or at least the cycle.

Seth simply handed his cylinder to himself, from one hand to the other. Captain Manning had leaned back in her chair, arms crossed, apparently willing to just watch the show.

They both opened the tubes and slid the thick and so-fancy paper that held the words of the treaty out. Katla scanned the words yet again. Seth had printed it on one of the science team's fancy machines; it did look like human calligraphy, until you came up close to see the letters were too perfectly identical. She pressed the paper to lie flat, and then turned it so the words faced Seth. She slid it partway across the table to him.

He had the longer reach, but also the longer arms. He lifted his copy past the new version, turned it to face her, and slid it over.

As Katla was pulling her old-fashioned pen out of her pocket, she heard the door slide open behind her. She got the cap off, and almost got the pen to the paper before Claire was at her side, grasping her arm. Holding her back

Her mama looked beautiful, every hair in place, all her beads and bangles singing. And panicked: the muscles at the corners of her mouth twitched. The pupils of her eyes were so wide they hid the hazel green.

Katla turned slowly to her mama, looking past her to the lights and the cameras, reminding her they were there. Claire swallowed.

"What are you doing?" she said under her breath. "There's an emergency," she said out loud. The reporters swiveled their beacons to her.

Katla looked at Seth. He'd signed his page. He raised an eyebrow. They'd talked about this. The green strand of hair was visible now.

She dropped her head the slightest bit. Dropped her hand to her side. Claire let go and stood back to let Katla rise from the chair.

As she stood up, Katla's arm also rose. Her hand swung toward the paper. She signed her name in full. When Seth signed this page, the treaty would be in force. The second signature, on his copy, was merely tradition.

She pushed her chair back from the table and pushed her paper forward to him. He swept it up, and pushed his toward her. She did not reach for it. She wasn't sure how far to push her mama.

Claire groaned.

Luckily, no one heard her.

Because the claxons were sounding again.

As one, all the reporters seemed to shrink down. They scrambled at their control panels. The noise must be like a knife to the head.

"Claxons off!" Katla said. "You mean there really was an emergency?"

"No!" Claire pressed her hands onto her forehead. "I don't know. Ship! Tell us."

"Unidentified vessel, coming in fast," Ship's calm voice said.

"Can you tell what type?" Seth said.

"Battle cruiser."

CHAPTER
THIRTY-THREE

ALL THE REPORTERS started to talk at once. Katla couldn't understand them, but Seth apparently could. He leaned down to speak with S-P. The little cylindrical synth sped toward the door to the hall.

"No further questions!" he said. He pointed to the now-open door behind them. "Follow Captain Manning back to Utopia. We'll get you back to your ships."

The captain was already out the door, practically running. Six reporters grabbed their gear and scurried to catch up with her.

The two remaining wanted to stay and report from the base. They were loud in their objections to being denied access. They went on and on.

Katla tuned them out. She walked to the window to look for this ship. But the window faced the planet; no help there. Her head spun, her thoughts all claxons that could not be turned off.

Why ever would the Cooperative send a warship instead of a diplomatic vessel? Were they one and the same?

How much danger were her people in?

She turned from the window, and took stock. Mama Claire

could organize anything but needed a first direction. Haydee could see the holes in a plan and work around them. S-P could keep Katla grounded. Arcan could patch them all up, including Ship's critical systems. Seth—

Was not on their team. Cooperative shill. He must have known the warship was on its way.

Now there were only two reporters, she could hear their questions. "Special Envoy DiCimino: Why are you staying?"

Katla looked at him. Why was he?

"My mission is here, on Arkhide Base." He didn't look the least panicked, except for relentlessly scratching his temple by the wig. "I'll stay here until the mission is completed." He glanced at Katla, then down at the single page in front of her place at the table. The page that needed a signature.

The other was gone.

Katla frantically scanned the area. Haydee lurched in her chair, recognizing the problem and doing the same search.

Seth caught Katla's gaze, and then looked at his chair. The paper tube lay almost out of sight on the seat.

Haydee saw it at the same time. She and Katla shared a glance of pure relief

The second reporter turned to the first. "You don't think they'll really shoot us, with a DiCimino on board?"

"Depends on who they are," the first said. They looked at Seth. "Who are they?"

Seth turned to Katla and shrugged. Katla looked at Claire and shrugged. Claire looked past her, at the window.

And gasped.

Katla turned back to the window. The cruiser had positioned itself directly in front of them. Not even a hundred meters away. She could see the seams on its beak of a prow.

She took a step back and held out a hand, as if to push it away.

It didn't budge.

The reporters rushed forward, cameras alight. Katla stepped out of their way, toward the table. She still wanted to see. Seth came up to join her. He stared at the cruiser, tilting his head to try to read the words stenciled on the side of the prow.

"Stingray," he said. "Not one of ours."

"What?" both she and Haydee said in unison.

"Water is fickle," he said. "It's unlucky to name a vessel after something that can turn on you as well as your enemy."

Before she could process that idea—water was life, wasn't it? —Katla heard Haydee calling to her in a whisper. And sobbing.

No, it was Mama Claire who was sobbing. She sat on the table, one foot still on the floor. Her eyes squeezed shut, tears rolling down the sides of her face. She held her forearms, pressing them into her belly. She was starting to deflate.

Katla had never seen Claire like this. No, one time—after the miscarriage. How could this be as bad as that?

Katla's mind fractured, kicking into a too-high gear she'd never experienced before. It was all too much. She was holding onto everything by her fingertips.

She looked at Haydee: Help me.

Haydee rolled toward Claire. Speaking softly, she reached for Claire's knee, and then her forearms. Claire's grip on her belly loosened. She said something, too softly.

Haydee, startled, looked at Katla.

Before she could say anything, Katlas wristcom chimed. Everyone turned to look at her, except mama Claire.

It was Mom Sofia's melody.

Whatever now? She glanced at Mama Claire, who would have recognized the tune. Claire, now holding tight to Haydee's forearms, focused only on her, did not seem to react to the sound, though the melody had now played through twice.

The message was a request to open screen and accept

incoming video. Katla took a deep breath, and waved open a screen above the table.

The screen sharpened into a view inside what must be the command room of the cruiser. Mom Sofia stood in the foreground, stern and lovely, her rows of twists neatly tucked over her shoulders and in front of her usual Arkhide blue tunic. Her tech whiz, Viram, in the background, moving among complicated looking panels. Probably flying the ship.

Wouldn't put it past him, Katla thought wildly.

"Cooperative lackeys, this is the cruiser Stingray, in service to the people of Arkhide. Please leave now and you will not be harmed."

CHAPTER
THIRTY-FOUR

SOFIA REPEATED the message and then waved the connection closed. In the meeting room, everyone needed to take a moment.

The reporters recovered first. They looked at each other. "We'll be going now," one said. From the window, past the table, to the open door to the hall, they gained speed.

Until the entire base lurched.

"Ship!" Katla said.

"Standard recovery pattern," Ship said calmly. "Temporary disruption caused by the Utopia dropping its airlock on departure. Utopia failed to release its secondary anchor. I am sending a team to correct the damage. Not a breach. No emergency."

"It's an emergency for us!" said the reporter who had fallen the hardest.

Katla had to talk to her mom. Now. She looked at Seth. "Handle them? Ship will lead you to the shuttle bay. Ship! Give Sandreth DiCimino access to shuttles in the closest bay."

"Understood," Ship said. "Sandreth DiCimino, do you need directions to shuttle bay Beta-3?"

Katla tuned that all out. She strained to remember how to place a private, shielded call. The memory would not come. She never needed such privacy.

Then she remembered: It was just the three of them now. No need for privacy.

"Arcan!" she called toward the meeting-room cameras she hoped were still transmitting. "We're clear. You can all come in now."

The side door opened. Arcan went immediately to Mama Claire, holding her shoulder as she cried. Arvee rolled up to the window and made the sound for amazement.

Katla wished she could be as easy about it. She went to the other side of the room, forcing the screen to pivot 180 degrees. Now its view would take in everyone except the boxy bot. She rested her hip on the side of the table across from everyone else and crossed her arms. "Open channel," she said.

The cruiser room hadn't changed. Sofia stood in her power position, weight back on one hip, one hand on that hip, one loose and ready to wave a finger at you. But her fierce expression softened when she looked toward Claire.

"Babe, who hurt you?" she said.

Claire tried to speak, but all that came out was a painful-sounding huff-huff. The breath she took in next seemed to shake her spine.

Sofia's face morphed back to stern general. "Katla, report. Why haven't the Co-op armada tried to contact me?"

That wasn't the question Katla had expected. It took her a moment to work through a reply. "Um, you didn't ask them to? You just told them to leave."

"Oh. Right. She looked off-screen. "What's your shuttle doing?"

"Taking Cooperatives to their ships. We were in a meeting."

"Why weren't they all in the Utopia? We gave them plenty of time."

Why was her mom being so dense? "Um, you didn't, really. You gave them no set time."

"Argh! Viram, why didn't you remind me?" Sofia turned to look at her security expert, who said something off-mic. "Those are reporters' vessels, the little ones?"

"Yes," Katla said. "They are here for the signing."

Sofia's head snapped back to the camera faster than her braids could keep up. "The what?"

"The signing. You know, the treaty, where we agree to trade and they agree to leave us alone. What we've been working toward all month." With a jolt, Katla realized it hadn't been a month. It felt like years. She wiped her brow. Telling her mom what her mom had assigned her to do was plain weird.

Sofia gazed past the camera, quiet. Maybe thinking? Taking advantage of the pause, Katla started to stand. She wanted to be at the side of the table where everybody else was.

Sofia was quicker. "Katla."

She sat down again.

"There's a treaty," Sofia said, voice flat. "With the Cooperatives."

Katla reached under the screen and grabbed the half-signed paper. "Here it is," she said, holding it in front of her.

"Blessed Moa," Sofia said. "Claire was right."

Katla heard the unspoken "about you" at the end. "Wait. You didn't think I could do it?"

"Not just me. Aimee Five, the whole upper leadership." Sofia shook her head. The tinkle of the clips on her braids did not transmit.

Katla tasted blood. She'd bitten the inside of her cheek. Her jaw spasmed.

They hadn't trusted her. Hadn't thought she could do it. They thought she was less-than. The poor, pitiful girl who couldn't get implants.

That's what they thought.

Even her mother.

She pressed her lips together. She unclenched her jaw. She released the treaty, watched it float to rest again on the table.

"Wrong." Her voice ice.

"Kay, you have to understand," Sofia said.

She understood. She understood all too well. Hadn't she been understanding it all since she was sixteen years old?

Every rotation, every assignment not earned, never earned, but a gift to the damaged girl. Because her mother held power. No, no, that wasn't the way of it, everyone said, protesting too much.

She understood indeed.

"I see," she said.

"No, please. Hear me." Sofia held up a hand—wait—and caught her breath.

"Getting that first message," she started. "Knowing the Co-op had found us, I can't describe it. A kind of primal panic, right down your spine, only on a community scale. Rippling, feeding itself. They were going to kill us! All the old terrors surfaced. The nightmares that once were real." She trailed off, gaze inward.

Viram stepped next to her. They rubbed Sofia's shoulder in comfort, amethyst eyes only for her. "Remembering all the running we had to do," they said. "The hiding. The fear—the terror. After they received that message, half the synths in Macadere froze and had to be coaxed back into motion."

Sofia nodded. "We took the blow, felt the feelings, and came back up determined. They were not going to take us. Never. We would make ourselves safe. We knew how. We would sell the patents to our tech. As many as we needed to buy this ship.

"But we had to have time. Katla, peanut, we didn't think anyone could get this treaty. Talking to the Co-ops was merely a stall until we could get our defenses in place. It wasn't meant to be you."

Claire snorted. "Ha! But so convenient that it was her, wasn't it, Sofia? A girl who could be left out of the loop."

Katla reeled. "Everybody knew about this plan?"

"Everyone in the Assembly. Every human in your family," Claire said. "I went along with it. I'm so, so sorry."

Claire reached again for Haydee's hand. "Sweetest. Your parents were in war mode when they had to make that decision about you. They'd just seen you shot! War had come, and the Co-ops would have them in their sights next. You know how they must've felt."

Haydee pulled her hand away. She backed away from the table. She rolled toward the hall door, and past it. She settled beside Katla.

"You lied to us," she said, glaring at Claire. "Inside and out."

Katla stared past the screen, through the big window, into the vast oceans of her world. "What did the elders say?"

Sofia answered. "What they always say: Keep it off planet."

Katla had heard enough. She would feel the feelings later. She would fix what she could, now, while her mind was in overdrive.

She looked back at where the camera was. "Will you listen to me now? Hear me?"

Sofia startled. "Of course. Peanut."

Katla bristled. Sofia was reaching for control, dominance, by infantilizing her own adult child.

Good luck with that.

"The treaty is signed," Katla said. "It includes only a small part of the non-aggression language. This turns out to be extremely fortunate. If they'd taken the original language, your actions today would have been a declaration of war."

She held up her hand, stalling Sofia's reply. "The smaller ships you see are reporters and media people from around the Cooperative. We have been feeding them a story about how peaceful Arkhide is. How it's no threat to anyone in Co-op space. We just finished allowing them to attend a meeting during which Arkhideans and Cooperatives peacefully agreed to a treaty that offers mutual benefit.

"And then you show up."

Katla shook her head slowly. "I understand that you all are in existential crisis. I get it. Which is why you delegated talking to the Cooperatives to us." She reached out to Haydee, who gripped her arm. "It was a smart decision. I suggest you continue to rely on us as we attempt to dig out from this PR disaster."

She glared at the screen. At Sofia. "Okay, mom?"

Silence. Sofia turned to look at Viram, and Katla knew she was on the inner nets with them, Claire, and whoever else. Talking secretly, silently.

Let them talk.

Katla slid off the table and knelt beside Haydee. "Oh, Haydee, I am so, so sorry."

Haydee grasped Katla's other arm. "Now you know how it feels."

"Monstrous. Unbearable." She looked away. "Unrecoverable."

"Maybe not unrecoverable," Haydee said. "So long as it's not repeated."

"Never," Katla said.

Haydee let go, and put a hand in her sweater pocket. She pulled out a very smooshed savory pastry.

"There was one here!" Katla said. "Thought I was imagining it. Wishing for it." She took it from her friend. "Want half?"

Communications silence stretched the length it took to eat half a pastry. Claire stirred, and on screen, Sofia turned back to the camera.

"We agree," Sofia said. "What do you suggest?"

Something pounded on the floor out in the hall. Seth grabbed the door jamb to slow himself, and swung into the room. He'd lost his wig and gained color in his cheeks. He must have run the whole way from the shuttle dock.

He grinned. "What'd I miss?"

CHAPTER
THIRTY-FIVE

"HOW DID you get back so fast?" Katla said. Seth couldn't have taken the reporters to two different ships and flown back in so little time.

"Just hopped 'em over to Utopia," he said. "Three-minute trip; two for docking. That's where their stuff was, anyway, their packing cases and all. Let the captain sort them out." He looked at the screen. "Isn't that your mom?"

"Who is this, Katla?" Sofia was back in commanding-presence mode.

"Madame president, this is Sandreth DiCimino, quiet child of the current regent of the Cooperative Realm. Seth, this is Sofia, recently retired as president of the humans of Arkhide and past speaker of the Greater Assembly of Arkhide."

Seth performed his regal salute, complete with hand gestures. Sofia did not reciprocate.

"What is he doing on base?"

"Until half an hour ago, he was negotiating in good faith with our diplomatic corps. Then he helped rescue two very popular reporters from imminent danger. And now…" She turned to him. "Why are you back?"

"Had to return the shuttle, didn't I?" He winked at her at her and Haydee out of the view of the camera. Then he grew serious. "I want to protect our treaty. I believe if both you and I are together, in the same place as the treaties, neither side will want to shoot. So far, it's working."

"We could hold you as a hostage," Sofia said.

"Mom!" Katla said at the same moment Claire said "Sofia!"

"Just saying," Sofia shrugged. "It's an option."

Katla rolled her shoulders back. "Okay. Here's the deal. The media has one story, but just had to live through the excitement—"

"Terror," Seth interrupted. "One of them hurled in the shuttle."

"Of a completely different story," Katla continued. "Which one will they lead with? We don't want them showing us as threatening or menacing—"

"The nice former president lady did threaten us," Seth said.

Katla did not rise to the bait. "We want them to continue to present Arkhide as not a threat—none at all—to Cooperative lives or interests. A place of peace and boring, monastic life. How do we explain the massive battle cruiser sitting right next to our base?"

"Move the cruiser," Haydee said.

"Say it was a mistake, and we're really sorry," Arcan said. "What? It could work. Sofia's been out of communications range for weeks. She doesn't even know about Haydee."

"What about Haydee?" Sofia glared at them, and then frowned. "Why is she in that chair?"

"We'll side-channel that," Katla said. "What about inviting the reporters back here? Introduce them to Sofia, explain about the great new products coming to them from our patents."

Claire nodded. "We could offer a formal dinner. Everybody together sharing a meal with one another. Very peaceful."

Haydee reached for the treaty on the table. She pushed it closer to Katla, text facing forward.

Sofia's snort carried fine over the transmission. "Conversation will have to be light."

"Could be good," Seth said. "We might also introduce the idea of safe synths." He looked at Arcan. "I can be seen talking with our friend, here, and walking away alive."

Haydee pushed a pen into Katla's hand while looking at Seth. "But can you convince everyone to come back, though?"

Claire tapped her lip. "And what food do we have to offer? Will they wait until we can get fresh fish and veg up here?"

"How long would that take?" Seth said "To bring the food, I mean. It will take no time to get the reporters back. At least their drones. But if we offer food, I'm pretty sure we'll get them in person."

Katla signed the second treaty. Haydee took the paper, rolled it, and set it into the tube she still held in a pocket of her chair. She tucked it back into the pocket.

"Sounds like a plan," Katla said. "Seth, would you take the lead on corralling the reporters?"

"On it," Seth said.

"And Claire, would you take the lead on the meal planning? Casual-formal, not formal-formal."

"Right," Claire said, already lost in the stream. "Clothes, too. Send me your sizes, please, Special Envoy DiCimino."

"Call me Seth," he said.

CHAPTER
THIRTY-SIX

IN THE MATTER of preparing a celebratory farewell dinner—emphasis on the farewell—everyone in and around Arkhide was the model of peaceful cooperation. The Stingray backed way off, nearly out of view in the penumbra of Arkhide. The Utopia loaned the use of its fastest shuttle to head down-planet and fetch the necessary ingredients. Katla and Haydee prepared the formal invitations and collected the RSVPs. Claire and Arcan prepared most of the food. Aimee Five politely declined her invitation but sent up the spicy coconut cookies her assistant was famous for. Seth prepared some weird dessert from his childhood on Zichi, which needed bowls and spoons that had to be printed at the last minute. The reporters brought camera drones, and their appetites. They had mighty appetites.

In the meeting room, the synths had dismantled the large table and replaced it with three tall, circular tables spaced so people could easily move from one to the next. They set a sideboard with a tabletop against the wall, to accommodate Seth's dessert and its accoutrements as well as hide Haydee's blood. In the rear corner was the drinks station. By the window the center space was open, with mini sofas perpendicular against the side walls, so people could stand or sit and enjoy the view. Which, now that the Stingray was moved, was as gorgeous as ever.

Arkhide was really showing her colors, Katla thought, watching her world while waiting for the guests to arrive. Sharp white at the poles, so many blues, the tiny blacks and greens of land, clouds thin and thick, and that one ribbon of gray.

The sweet smoke of the cooking pots, set into the center of each of the round tables, teased thread upon thread of memories from her. Birthdays, in swimsuits and sandals. Political galas, in full formal dress. Memorial services. Bonding ceremonies. House-warmings. All with food, shared and savored.

The islands that had welcomed the former residents of Macadere would be planning the new-home celebrations. Probably soon, even though everybody wouldn't be totally settled yet. It was better to have parties where folks could spill outside when it got too much. They'd have to do it right away to beat the ash.

"It's time," Sofia said from the doorway. They had not spoken yet of the Stingray and the rest of it. Katla knew Sofia would wait for her signal. She'd be waiting a while.

They lined up in the hallway outside. Katla first, then Sofia, with Haydee closest to the door. A short gantlet for their guests on the way to the food. Claire and Arcan had begged off joining the greeting line, saying they had to finish the food prep. There had been no food on the tables yet, just utensils and napkins.

They'd have to work fast. Everyone came in a clump. Captain Manning led the way, closely behind S-P. Cozying up to a synth! If only they knew.

Katla had decided greetings would be informal: a handshake if they wanted, a short bow if they preferred that. The Cooperative captain went for the handshake, but most of the reporters chose the no-touch option.

Seth was last, herding the last reporter, who was hastily

stowing some camera or other. Seth wore clothing in Arkhidean formal style, a long tunic with piping on the angled opening flap, skinny legged trousers, jewelry optional. But he'd made it his own, or Claire had. The tunic swirled with color—no staid solids for him. His hair was freshly poufed, not box braids like hers. And so many sparkles.

He gently pushed the reporter ahead of him and waited for them to finish greeting all three hosts. Then he somehow made himself taller, and then sank into what must be the full formal court genuflection. Katla could not even follow the humming-bird-like hand movements. Seth rose, regal, and then broke the mood with a sideways grin. Haydee was the first to laugh.

Katla nodded at him in approval. "I have never seen anything like that. You really do that in Central District?"

"A little-known fact of Cooperative etiquette is that one is allowed to freestyle the bit in the middle. At least, that's what my tutor told me."

He turned to Sofia and started to bow, but she waved him off. "Blessed Moa. Once is enough. Get in there and eat. Take Haydee with you." As they moved into the room, Sofia turned to Katla.

"A word."

"No, mom. Now is not the time." Katla had just known she'd do this, in the middle of everything.

"When, then? You must understand," Sofia whispered, insistent.

Katla understood plenty. "We'll see," she said.

In the meeting room, the lights were dimmed so the view of Arkhide popped. Fresh foods from sea and land sat in perfect display around each pot. Katla took a moment to appreciate the artistry. For a boring meeting room on a transport ship, it looked pretty festive.

Arcan had chosen to play the part of helpful robot waitstaff. Almost everyone crowded around them at the first table. They showed how the eating sticks worked together to lift a morsel. Then they lifted the piece over the flame at the center.

"Want it rare or medium or well-done?" they said. "You put it on the edge of the flame for rare. Deeper, for longer, until it's the way you like. Don't worry—everybody burns a few their first time." That drew a laugh, and started a conversation about the various disgusting meals people had eaten while on assignments.

Sofia had sequestered Captain Manning by the drinks table. Seth and Haydee were alone at the table closest to the window. Haydee's go-chair could lift, so she could be at the right height for even this table. Looking at Seth's face, Katla wondered if he'd be willing to share some of those sparkles with her friend.

"I've been waiting for this all day," Katla said as she reached the table. "What do you say, Haydee: fish or fruit?"

"Fish. That one." She pointed at a sturdy bit of white fish. Katla grabbed some eating sticks and snatched it up. She held it over the flame in the pot just long enough for the outside to brown and the inside to reach middling warm. Then she lifted it toward Haydee.

Haydee leaned in, allowing herself to be fed. "Perfect! Seth, do you like fish?"

Seth had been watching them with something like astonishment. "Sometimes."

"Try the white, then. It's so mild. Do you like it warm or well-done?"

"Cooked. Well cooked."

Haydee chose a piece of the same fish, but set it higher in the pot, to cook more slowly but thoroughly. Seth reached for a pair of sticks, but Haydee waved his hand away. "One at a time. And this one is for you."

"You feed each other?"

"Sure. It's nice to make something for someone else. You can tell how much a person pays attention to you by how close they come to cooking it like you like it. Katla, here, likes hers almost raw, but burnt on the outside."

"Singed."

"Like I said." Haydee pulled the piece out of the flame, and waved it about gently, blowing on it. "It is a fine line between freshly cooked and too hot to eat. Don't want to burn the guest." She reached the piece toward his mouth. "Open up. It smells so good, brine and blossom."

Seth paused, fisted his hands, and slowly opened his mouth. Haydee took no chances, quickly tossing it onto his tongue the way you would for a little kid. Seth's mouth closed, then his eyes closed, and his jaw moved slowly. "Mmmmm."

"Toldja." Haydee's satisfaction carried in her voice. "Katla. Same?"

"Yes. But singed."

Haydee rolled her eyes and picked up another piece. "That's what you say, but all your friends know better." She leaned toward Seth. "Watch this." In scant seconds, she'd waved the fish into the flame until it caught fire, snatched it out, waved it once to douse the flame, and headed it toward Katla's mouth. Katla took it in, closed her mouth and her eyes, and went still as her senses filled with the sweet-sour sauce, freshly caramelized.

"There," Haydee said, "That's her crunching through the outer crust." Katla hummed a sigh. "That's the soft inner goodness."

"Haydee, you are the best. And the worst," Katla said. Haydee laughed.

Seth dropped two pieces of fish into the fire, but finally got the hang of it with a firmer piece of fish. It was too burnt for either Katla or Haydee, so he had to eat it himself. They didn't tell him how absolutely rude that was; if they had, it would have meant one of them would have had to eat the ruined fish.

As people had their fill, they drifted over to the viewing

window. Seth claimed the sofa on the left in back, not coincidentally closest to the dessert board. He sat on the aisle end, with Haydee right next to the couch. Katla, on his other side, was glad for the barrier between her and the rest of the world.

One reporter broke protocol. "Special Envoy DiCimino, what's with the hair?"

"No questions, we agreed." Seth said, smiling. "But on background only, I did it in celebration of the treaty. Green is the color of life."

Captain Manning, listening in with interest, turned to look at Arkhide. "Looks like it's blue, here." She stepped closer to the window. "What's that gray?"

Haydee answered. "One of our many volcanoes. Ours is a young planet, with a rather thin crust. New islands are being made and remade every day."

"Isn't that a little…" Captain Manning reached for the word. "Dangerous?"

At the word, every reporter perked up.

Katla groaned inside.

"Arkhide is full of wonders," Seth said. "Every moment an adventure." He looked over his shoulder, at the sideboard. "How about those desserts? I hear the cookies are to die for."

Every reporter went for the sideboard. Seth leaned back, tossing his mane of hair.

"Thank you," Katla whispered. "It really isn't anything, but you know how reporters are."

Haydee leaned out of the way of an elbow holding a napkin full of cookies. "We all know, now."

"You know," said Seth, "I think we could make this work."

Both Katla and Haydee looked at him with horror.

"Don't say that!" Haydee said. "You'll jinx us."

Katla started counting out loud. "One. Two."

On three, the claxon sounded.

CHAPTER
THIRTY-SEVEN

"CLAXON OFF!" Sofia shouted. "You know you can turn that thing off, right? Just set it on strobe. Ship, what is it?"

"Unknown vessel. Destroyer class."

"Is a destroyer bigger than a cruiser?" Katla asked Seth. Both of her moms and Captain Manning had already called screens up, pounding instructions to their respective vessels.

"I believe so," he said. Louder, he said. "No worries, everyone. I think that's just my ride."

The captains stared at him. "A destroyer?" Captain Manning said.

"Yeah, it's overkill, I know. But it's happened before. You know moms." Seth spread his hands, trying to look sheepish.

"You're sure?" Claire said. "We can't defend against a destroyer."

"Hence the name," Haydee muttered.

Sofia swiped her screen larger, so everyone could see it. "Let's see what they say."

An official-looking person in Cooperative gray stood or sat in front of a goldenrod wall. "Greetings people of Arkhide. This is the destroyer Sirocco. We demand the return of our citizen, Sandreth DiCimino, also known as Media Presence Seth-is-on-the-edge."

Everyone looked at Seth. He shrugged, the picture of faux modesty.

The captains wiped their control screens away. Katla stood and waved her hand at the comms screen, so its camera would focus on her before she started talking.

"Greetings, Sirocco," she said. "This is Katla Sofiasdotter, chief diplomat for the world of Arkhide. He is here on the base. We'll send him right over."

"What?" Seth looked at her in hurt surprise.

"Excellent," the person on the Scirocco said. "We'll send a shuttle."

"We're done here, right?" Katla said. "Next is handing the treaties in a timely manner to our respective assemblies." She waved toward the back wall, in the direction of the jump-tunnel. "There's your ride."

"But I haven't had my cookies yet," he said. "And I wanted to visit Macadere Island. And convince Haydee to come to Central. You'll need an ambassador there now."

Haydee was about to respond when a reporter who was looking out the window shouted. "What the heck is that!"

Everybody turned to look. One-quarter of the visible planet was coated in light gray. As they watched, the cloud slowly grew, flowing via unseen currents.

Haydee rolled to the window. "Oh, that's just Macadere," she said, falling into lecture mode. "Mount Awala is erupting. We expect the ash it sends into the atmosphere will affect most of the planet for a few months to a year."

"How can you be so calm? This is an emergency." Captain Manning had her screens up again. "We can get the main shuttle down in two hours, and another about an hour after that. What do you need?"

"We're fine," Sofia said.

"Your planet is getting buried in ash! Full claxon alert," Captain Manning said.

"This happens all the time," Sofia said. "Well, not a stratovolcano like this one, but still. Everyone was evacuated from the island more than a week ago. We even had time to get most of our infrastructure moved" She looked toward the window. "She's actually a couple of days late."

The Cooperatives looked at her, and then out the window. One reporter spoke for all of them.

"This? Happens all the time?"

Katla suddenly realized what this meant. Of course, they would think that. She jumped to take advantage of it.

"Oh, yes," she said. "All the time. I've had to move five times already. Island to island. You learn not to take too much. All the physical things that are important have to fit in a single trunk. All the things that are really important aren't physical, of course."

This was not the Cooperatives' picture of a heavenly new planet. Katla played it up.

"After a blast like this, most of the planet goes dark for a whole season, sometimes a whole year. The sun is dim, so we have to ration energy. All the crops die. We have to stay inside more, until the poisonous gases dissipate. And then we have to wait a little longer, for the sulfuric acid spewed from the volcano to finish falling as rain. It's deadly, you know."

She shrugged. "Doesn't take too long. We usually learn a new skill. Last time, I learned High Galactic."

All but one of the reporters looked horrified. The odd one out looked morbidly fascinated. "What do you eat?" that one said.

Haydee took that question. "We store food. Everything, really. We always try to have three years' worth in storage. And the damage isn't uniform across all communities. Some islands can start planting again as early as the next season. That's why our population is so dispersed, so we can help one another through the dark years. That's why our motto: Together, we thrive."

Seth stepped toward the window. "The whole planet will look like that island you took me to?"

Katla followed him. The speed of the swirling gray was astonishing. "Only Macadere Island will look like that. Everywhere close will have to shovel out of piles of ash. Places far away will get a dusting. That's the ground. It takes longer to get the ash out of the clouds and air."

Seth shook his head, eyes round. "And then you'll be back on Macadere Island. In a hundred years."

"Absolutely."

"Waiting for the next one."

"Tomorrow is a gift," Katla said cheerily.

This was going to work.

CHAPTER
THIRTY-EIGHT

THE FIRST SHIP TO leave was the Utopia. "Red dwarves wait for no one," Captain Manning said. "Or so the chief scientist says."

The media vessels took off soon after, except for one. The reporter from the Daily Crisis wanted to do a documentary for his series, "Deadliest Volcano." Unfortunately for him, no one had died. No one was even injured.

Aimee Five declined his application, but did suggest to the gaggle of volcanologists near Macadere Island that it might be a good idea to consider doing a documentary of their own. Now that they could reach the greater Cooperative Realm, it behooved them to make their own messages for that audience.

Otherwise, the last thing most people in the galaxy would see about Arkhide was the blankets of headlines that came out over the next month. Beautiful New Planet Hides Deadly Secret. Volcanic Roulette in New Utopia. Fiery Chaos in Heavenly Abode. Where the Heat Goes to 11. Fried Green Planet.

Mom Sofia went back to the Stingray, to see if it could be partially repurposed as mining support, or even deep-space cargo hauling. Mama Claire went with her; she was trying to convince the assembly to keep the base as-is, safe for humans, and since that argument was all on the implant channels she could do it from anywhere. Now that the secrets were all told, everything was back to normal. For them.

Most of the bots and synths on base returned to the projects they had been doing pre-emergency. They did move their lodgings and recreation center into the shuttle/base, though. The gravity and big entertainment rooms were too much to pass up.

As for Special Envoy Sandreth diCimino, the battleship Sirocco sent an autoshuttle almost immediately to fetch him. Strangely, once on-base, the shuttle sprang a leak it somehow took more than a day to locate and another day to repair.

Seth mostly spent that time working in the second greenroom with Katla or walking the halls with Haydee, helping her gain her strength back. Eating leftovers. And cooking more of that strange but delicious dessert.

"It's like bananas," Haydee said, licking her spoon. "Only not." They all sat on the couch closest to the window in the meeting room. Everyone had agreed to leave the furniture as it was for the party, especially the sideboard.

"Flan is flan," Seth said sternly. "Nothing else like it." But Katla could see how pleased he was that they liked it.

Through the window, the round disc that was her world showed thick swaths of gray, as if it were tucked into a protective blanket. A really sooty blanket. It would be another week at least before any vessels could land, so here they would stay.

Unless Haydee chose to go.

"So," Seth started.

"No," Haydee said.

"Why not?" Katla said.

"Whose side are you on?" Haydee punched her gently on the shoulder.

"Yours, always. But you did so well at diplomacy up here."

"I lay in a bed most of the time we were here."

"You kept me on track. You helped me when I really needed it. And you kept the treaty safe."

Haydee pursed her lips. "Put it that way…"

"You know we need someone who will fight for us in Central District. The assembly even said so," Katla said. "And it's for sure not going to be me."

Seth perked up at that. "Why? You'd be great, too. Two is always better."

Haydee shook her head. "Kay has this mega-intense space sickness. She's on meds just to stay on-base."

"It's solid land or bust for me," Katla said. "Or even deeper. I'm thinking I'll try for a water rotation. See what my old friend Olve is really up to." She looked at Haydee. "Which would leave you all alone."

"Back at White Island. Where I'm doing important work." Haydee held out her bowl for Seth to scoop more flan into.

"Where Aimee and her team has it well in hand. Different Aimee," she said to Seth's puzzled glance. "So, until one of your other community members becomes fluent in High Galactic and loves diplomacy, looks like it has to be you, girl. What do you think?"

Haydee leaned back against one of Mama Claire's thick pillows. "I don't know. I know I don't want to see anyone on Arkhide. Not yet. I'm dead to some of them! How do I even get my mind about that? I've been thinking about this since I first woke up, afterward. Trying to find a way out of this.

"But if I go—if I leave—isn't that just running away from my problems? Or could I say it's 'running to,' heading toward something new. And important."

Both Katla and Seth held their tongues. It was Haydee's choice to make.

They watched the world gently turn. Now they could see the patch of reddish gray that was directly above the blast that was Mt. Awala. Not a swirl, like a hurricane; more like a wave, a water bubble popping and then flowing out in all directions.

Her world was amazing.

Haydee finished her second helping and did not ask for a third. She set the bowl in her lap with a sigh of satisfaction.

"Guess I'm gonna need some new clothes," she said.

"I am so on it," Seth said.

Haydee held up a fist for Katla to bump

Next morning, when the autoshuttle finally cleared its own flight precheck, there were two to board. Katla told Haydee to keep Claire's necklace—and take all the sweaters and cushions and rocking chairs the shuttle could carry. Seth went up to sit in the pilot's seat, saying he didn't trust autopilots.

Katla pushed her friend onto the ramp and into the shuttle. "Don't let them take your go-chair. I don't think we've patented all the workings yet."

"I'll put that on my to-do list," Haydee said. "Patents processes."

Katla leaned in for one last hug. "Safe travels," she said.

"Clear skies," her friend replied.

KATLA and her cylindrical friend S-P finished the last of the new planting in the two greenrooms. Someone else would have to manage the grains when/if that shipment finally came up. S-P had put in for a transfer to what they were calling the "gardening team." The debate on the comms channel was leaning in favor, especially after S-P suggested that anything grown on-base now, with no humans here, would be available to transport to Arkhide, where fresh produce was going to be rare for a while.

That left her synth-sib, Arcan. They wanted to go back to school—again. This time to perfect the techniques they had learned on the fly helping Haydee. Seemed to Katla they were plenty good enough already.

When the skies had cleared above his patch of water, Katla dialed in the channel to the deep-sea base. She'd guessed right: Olve was awake and could come to the comm.

"Hey, hero," he said.

"Hey, yourself. How is it going?"

"Not as bad as you'd expect. The language systems are growing so fast. Thanks for that tip about tenses; really helpful. And the elders say thanks for not harming the planet."

"The elders know me?"

"Duh. Hero."

"I'm glad. Relieved. Something. Everything. Anyway, how are you?"

He chuckled. "Okay, what do you want?"

"I want to come see you. I want to work on the language systems. Or just to see, if I can't stay."

"I'll work on it. Don't gush like that, I didn't say yes. Just, I'll work on it."

She knew Olve could do anything he put his mind to. "You're the best."

"I have to be," he said. "Did you hear my best friend is the Hero of Arkhide?"

"Stop saying that!"

"Can't stop me if it's true," he teased. "Now tell me, really. Do all Cooperatives have green hair?"

ALSO BY NICKY PENTTILA

Cosmic Weave

Cooperative Realm: Frankie's Journeys

Cargo Trouble

Frankie Takes a Holiday

Frankie Takes a Dive

Frankie Finds a Dot

Frankie Takes a Bow

Cargo & Chaos: Frankie books 1 & 2

Cooperative Realm: The Arkhide Chronicles

Hidden Planet

The Listeners

The Elders of Arkhide

Tales of Arkhide story collection

Historical Fiction

A Note of Scandal

An Untitled Lady

The Spanish Patriot

ABOUT THE AUTHOR

Nicky Penttila wrote her first story, a Mayan murder mystery, in seventh grade. But then came gymnastics, math team, and boyfriends. Later came husband, car payments, and a sleep-depriving work schedule at newspapers across the country. Then came a second career as a science writer. But the fiction kept trickling out, a story here, a novella there, and finally, a real live novel. And she hasn't stopped.

Find more great reads at nickypenttila.com